PINT OF NO RETURN

A SHAKE SHOP MYSTERY

DANA MENTINK

Published by Poisoned Pen Press, an imprint of Sourcebooks
P.O. Box 4410, Naperville, Illinois 60567-4410
(630) 961-3900
sourcebooks.com

Library of Congress Cataloging-in-Publication Data

Names: Mentink, Dana, author.
Title: Pint of no return / Dana Mentink.
Description: Naperville, Illinois : Poisoned Pen Press, [2021] | Series: A Shake shop mystery ; book 1
Identifiers: LCCN 2020048818 | (paperback) | (epub)
Classification: LCC PS3613.E496 P56 2021 | DDC 813/.6--dc23
LC record available at https://lccn.loc.gov/2020048818

Printed and bound in the United States of America.
SB 10 9 8 7 6 5 4 3 2 1

To my Grandpa, player of chess, solver of problems, teller of jokes, father of my hero.

Chapter One

IT WAS AN ABSOLUTE MONSTER.

Trinidad Jones rubbed at a sticky splotch on her apron and slid her offering across the pink, flecked Formica counter. The decadent milkshake glittered under the Shimmy and Shake Shop's fluorescent bulbs, from the glorious crown of brûléed marshmallow down to the candy-splattered ganache coating the outer rim and the frosted glass through which peeked the red and white striped milkshake itself. Her own reflection stared back at her, hair frizzed, round cheeks flushed. Something this decadent just had to be a crime. "What should I call it?"

Trinidad's freshly minted employees, twins Carlos and Diego Martin, were transfixed, eyes lit with the enthusiasm only fifteen-year-old boys with bottomless appetites could attain. They might have been staring at a newly landed spaceship for all the wonder in their long-lashed brown gazes. She still wasn't entirely sure which twin was which, but they were doing a bang-up job helping her ready the shop for its launch in a scant seven days' time.

Noodles, her faithful Labrador, cocked his graying head from his cushion near the front door and swiped a fleshy tongue over his lips, which she took as approval. He had already been consulted on a pup-friendly shake she'd dubbed the Chilly Dog, determining it to be more than passable. Noodles was an encouraging sort, which made Trinidad doubly glad she'd decided to adopt a senior citizen companion six months earlier instead of a younger pup. Besides, he had a wealth of skills she was still discovering.

Carlos whistled, running a hand through his spiky hair, sending it into further disarray. "It's like a Fourth of July Freakshake." He gripped the pink-coated paint roller he was holding as if it was a Roman spear. "Like, an eighth wonder of the world or something. You should put a sparkler on the top, you know, for the holiday. People would dig that."

Diego shook his head. "Bad move. Those things can burn at two thousand degrees Fahrenheit, depending on the fuel and oxidizer. Of course, temperature is not the same as thermal energy, which is going to relate to the mass, so..."

"Dude," Carlos said, punching his brother's arm. "You're such a dweeb. I mean, turn off your bloated brain and just admire it, wouldja?"

Diego ceased his impromptu physics lecture to join his brother in their mutual appreciation fest. He pulled a clunky video camera from his backpack, and his twin immediately grabbed a spoon and began speaking into it as if it was a microphone.

"This is Carlos Martin reporting live from the Shimmy and Shake Shop where an ice cream phenomenon is about to be revealed to the world," he pronounced in a booming baritone.

Trinidad laughed. "I didn't think people used video cameras anymore."

Carlos grinned. "They don't. We saw it at the flea market for two bucks along with a bunch of old history stuff and home videos no one will ever watch. We just thought it'd be fun to mess around with it since Diego wants to be a news reporter someday."

"And a physicist," his brother added.

"It's good to have goals," Trinidad said. "So, the shake gets a thumbs-up from the news crew, then? We'll skip the sparklers and call it the Fourth of July Freakshake. What do you think about adding a hunk of a red, white, and blue nutty brownie star in the marshmallow?"

Diego smirked at her. "Is adding brownies a bad thing, like… ever?"

All three of them considered.

"Point taken," Trinidad said. "I'll bake them when I get back from my errands and freeze them for the opening. I have to run to the storage unit and pick up a few final things. Go ahead and lock up the shop if I'm not back when you finish for today, okay?" She knew Carlos had afternoon football practice, and they'd chatted about doing some additional odd jobs around town in their effort to bankroll a used Plymouth while they were both studying up for their driving permits. She eyed the fresh coat of pink paint the boys had been applying to the walls. "Looks like you're almost done."

Diego pointed to the longest wall. "We calculated the volume of paint just right, considering we had to apply a third coat. Weird how your husband's name keeps showing through. Reminds me of a horror movie I watched, like he's rematerializing in town again since all his ex-wives are living here now…" Carlos broke off as his brother elbowed him in the ribs.

"Ex-husband," she said, "and that would be a good trick for him to rematerialize himself out of jail." She swallowed down a lick of something that was part shame, part anger, as she considered the spot where "Gabe's Hot Dogs" was once emblazoned in blocky letters. Moving to the tiny eastern Oregon town of Upper Sprocket, hometown of her cheating ex-husband Gabe Bigley and his two other ex-wives, was her most mortifying life decision to date. At age thirty-six, she should have been settled, married, and raising a family, not jumping into a highly risky entrepreneurial endeavor in her ex-husband's hometown, no less. Funny how pride took a back seat to survival. The faster her money ran out, the more palatable the notion of taking over the building Gabe had deeded her on his way to jail became.

Her grandfather, Papa Luis, used every derogatory word in his Cuban Spanish arsenal to convince her that Gabe "The Hooligan" Bigley should be obliterated from her mind and that moving back to Miami with him and her mother was the prudent choice. He was probably correct, but here she was in Sprocket anyway.

Now "Gabe's Hot Dogs," a store Gabe had never actually helped run, was being reborn as the Shimmy and Shake Shop, and it was going to be the most successful establishment in the entire Pacific Northwest if it killed her. Upon arrival in Sprocket, she knew the small town tucked in the mountainous corner of eastern Oregon would be the perfect home for her shop. A gorgeous alpine backdrop, sweeping acres of fields, a constant stream of tourists arriving to witness the wonder of Hells Canyon and participate in various festivals… It could not fail. Especially since it wasn't a paltry run-of-the-mill ice cream parlor. Shimmy's would specialize in extravagant, over-the-top shakes that would take Sprocket and the dessert-loving world by storm. Unless it had all been a massive mental misfire on her part. She swallowed a surge of terror.

Noodles shook himself, his collar jingling in what had to be a show of support. He gingerly pulled a tissue from the box on the counter and presented it to her, a throwback to his service dog training. "It's okay," she said, giving the dog a pat. "No tears right now." She realized both boys were staring at her.

"That's an awesome dog," Diego said.

She nodded her agreement.

"Um, sorry, Miss Jones," Carlos said. "Mom said we weren't supposed to mention anything about, I mean, you know, your ex or the other exes or…uh…" His face squinched in embarrassment.

"No worries. I know the situation is a bit unorthodox." And

delicious fodder for the local gossips. Somehow, she'd managed to be in town for six weeks and had not yet run into Juliette or Bonnie, Gabe's two other ex-wives, the ones she'd had no clue about until her life fell apart, but it was only a matter of time before their inevitable meeting; her own rented residence was only a short distance from Bonnie's property. She put Carlos out of his misery with a bright smile. "You didn't do anything wrong. It's a weird situation."

"Downright freaky," Carlos said, earning another elbow from his twin.

"Right. Well, I'll just go see to those errands." On the way to the door, Noodles stretched his stiff rear legs in the ultimate downward dog yoga pose and trotted after her.

"By the way, boys," Trinidad called over her shoulder. "I left two spoons on the counter. Someone has to taste test the Fourth of July Freakshake, right?" The door closed on the boys' enthusiastic whoops. She chuckled. There should be some perks to a job that only paid minimum wage and took up plenty of precious hours of summer vacation. If only she could pay them entirely in ice cream.

On the way to her car, she admired the whimsical pink and pearl gray striping on the front of her squat, one-story shop. The awning the three of them had painstakingly put up would keep off the summer sun, and some artfully arranged potted shrubs enclosed a makeshift patio with a half dozen small tables. Noodles had already staked out a location in the coolest corner as a designated napping area. She plodded down the block to spot where she'd parked the Pinto beneath the shade of a sprawling elm. What she wouldn't give to rest her aching feet. The doctor reminded her with ruthless regularity that losing thirty or so pounds would help her complaining metatarsals. Probably a nice vacation to Tahiti would do the same, but it was just as unlikely to happen. Her metatarsals would have to buck up and quit their bellyaching.

Trinidad regarded the shady main drag. Working from sunup to well past dark on a daily basis, she hadn't had nearly enough time to explore the charms of Upper Sprocket.

Somehow the quirky name suited the town settled firmly in the shadow of the mountains, with old trees lining the streets and people who still waved hello as they drove by. Five hours east of Portland, surrounded on three sides by the Wallowa Mountains, Sprocket was plopped at the edge of a sparkling green valley, with soaring peaks as a backdrop and air so clean it almost hurt to breathe it. The mountains were considered the "Swiss Alps of Oregon," and the nearest neighbor, Josef, hosted numerous events like the popular Alpenfest fall bash. Visitors had opportunities to take the Wallowa Lake Tramway to the top of Mount Howard—3,700 feet of eye-popping splendor. The multitude of outdoorsy activities and sheer loveliness brought plenty of visitors to the larger towns, and Sprocket, though more out of the way and shabbier than chic, pulled in its share of tourists too. Enough to keep Trinidad scooping ice cream in the warm weather months. Winter would be another challenge.

"One season at a time," she told herself. She passed a trailer and exchanged a friendly smile with the driver. The RV was one of many in town to enjoy the upcoming celebration. There would be plenty to do before the Fourth of July. Sprocket featured its very own lake, an annual apple festival, and even a third-generation popcorn stand that was a favorite of snackers far and wide. She'd also heard tell of hot springs in the area, though she'd not yet clapped eyes on them. It amazed her how much sunnier this little town was compared to her previous home in Portland with Gabe.

Her spirits edged up a notch. Sunshine, a fresh start, and a darling shop all her own. Rolling down the window, she let the air billow in, bringing with it the scent of dry grass and sunbaked road. On the way, she ticked off the items she needed to retrieve from her storage unit—something she hadn't yet had the time to tackle. There were three more plastic patio chairs she'd have the twins spray-paint a subtle shade of gray to offset the pink theme and her prized antique cookie cutter collection, passed down from her mother who had never so much as laid a finger on them.

Cruising away from the town's main street, she waved to the gas station owner who'd erected a card table on the sidewalk with a cooler on top and a scrawled sign that read BAIT WORMS, FIVE DOLLARS/PINT. As she drove along, she wondered exactly how many worms one got in a pint. The turn onto Little Bit Road took her to what passed for Sprocket's industrial center. It was comprised of an aged feed and grain store, a weedy property that used to be an air strip, and the Store Some More facility, a set of tidy white buildings with shiny metal corrugated doors. One lone tree in the lot next to the structure offered a paltry speck of shade and, nestled underneath, was a bird bath where a small brown wren was splashing with gusto. Parking the Pinto by the closest unit, she pulled out her key and unlatched the padlock that secured her space. The same young man who'd helped her sign the rental papers when she moved in was sweeping the walkway in front of the empty unit next to hers.

She waved. "Hi, Vince. Just back for a few supplies."

He nodded, hiking up the jeans that hung loose on his skinny frame. He was probably in his early twenties, by the look of him, a cell phone poking from his back pocket.

A woman with long blond hair stepped out of the office and pulled his attention. She held a bucket. "Call for you, Vince. Your mom needs you to deliver a half dozen pepperonis and two veggie combos."

Trinidad felt her pulse thump. Everything about the woman was long and lean, including the delicate gold earrings that gleamed against the backdrop of her hair. She appeared to do a double take as she spotted Trinidad. After a pause, she walked over. "I'm Juliette Carpenter. Formerly…"

"Juliette Bigley," Trinidad filled in. She'd known that Juliette owned the storage place, but she didn't imagine the woman was engaged in the day-to-day running of it. She'd only ever dealt with Vince. The hour had arrived. She could practically hear the bells tolling as she cleared her throat. "And it seems like you recognize me, too."

Juliette's face was seared into her memory even though she'd only spoken with her briefly at the trial where Gabe was found guilty of embezzling money from various companies as their accountant. It had been a tense conversation. After all, Gabe had still been married to Trinidad when he'd started the relationship with Juliette, and neither of them had suspected a thing. When Trinidad had discovered Gabe's cheating, and their divorce became official, it was followed quickly by Juliette's whirlwind marriage and divorce. Juliette had not even known of Trinidad and their defunct marriage until a few weeks after Gabe was arrested. He was an accomplished liar. The final shoe had dropped at the trial, when they had not only met each other but also learned of another wife, Bonnie, Gabe's first.

The turbulent storm of memories resurfaced as Trinidad stared at Juliette. She tried not to notice the generous five or ten years between their ages. *You're the older model. Gabe traded you in for one right off the assembly line.* How was it possible to feel old at the age of thirty-six? Trinidad cleared her throat.

"I rented one of your storage spaces. I'm…uh…opening a store in town."

"I heard. I meant to come by and reintroduce myself, but…"

But the whole situation was just *too* ridiculously awkward.

Juliette stared at the bucket, then continued. "I was, um, just filling the bird bath. It's been so dry this year. You wouldn't believe the animals that drink out of it: birds, deer, raccoons." Her stream of conversation dried up.

Trinidad was desperate to fill the silence. Noodles, perhaps picking up on her tension, nosed her thigh, leaving a wet circle on her jeans. "This is Noodles. He's very easygoing. His real name is Reginald, but the shelter workers named him Noodles since he has a thing for them. The noodles, I mean, not the shelter workers."

Noodles offered a hospitable tail wag. Juliette put down the bucket, crouched next to the old Lab and rubbed his ears. "Bet you would be a great watchdog. We could use one around here. More effective than the new padlocks I had installed, and way cuter, too."

The conversation sputtered again. Trinidad tried to think of something to say, but Juliette rose to her feet.

"Let's just clear the air here. This is strange, running into each other, but it shouldn't be. It's just...I thought you said during our talk at the trial that you didn't want anything to do with Sprocket."

Trinidad went cold with shame. "The truth is I had to swallow my pride and take what Gabe deeded me." She didn't add more humiliating details, that her stenographer work had all but dried up and she could no longer make the rent for the Portland apartment she'd shared with Gabe. "It was move to Gabe's hometown or return to my family home in Miami, and I really wanted to prove to myself that I could make it on my own." It was more than she'd meant to say.

Juliette's expression softened, and she surprised Trinidad by gently touching her shoulder. "Hey, I get it, believe me. Same reason I moved here last year. I figured Gabe owed me something, and he had signed over his storage unit business to me, the rat." She shrugged. "It was doing better than my hotel manager gig, so here I am. New life, fresh start, just like you."

Trinidad nodded. "And, besides, who wouldn't want to move to a charming town called Sprocket?"

Juliette blinked, then grinned, and the tension dissipated into the blaze of golden sunlight that edged over the rooftop. "Upper Sprocket."

"Is there a Lower Sprocket?"

After a moment, Juliette let loose a silver peal of laughter. "Not that I know of. One Sprocket is enough." She lifted a slender shoulder and tossed back her curtain of blond hair, which looked like it had not come from a bottle. Trinidad had always daydreamed about being a sleek blond, but her curly frizz of dark-brown hair, inherited from her Cuban father, would never be smooth, nor fair. She'd be content if it stayed brown for a while, though that was unlikely since she'd caught the glimmer of a silver strand in the bathroom mirror. Gray before forty? Another curveball.

"The ice cream place is a bold idea. Good for you."

Bold or boneheaded? The doubts crept in again. Sprocket's charms notwithstanding, would her wacky business idea fly in a town of less than three thousand people? A place where the locals specialized in raising goats and tending apple orchards, who rolled up the sidewalks promptly at six o'clock p.m.? But Sprocket was reinventing itself as a bona fide tourist stop for the hordes looking for their "alpine experience." They'd even constructed a railrider excursion, pedal-powered carts that tourists used to ride on old train tracks as they took in the countryside. Sprocket was aiming to get its share of the tourist dollars, and Trinidad meant to do the same.

"The funny thing is, I've never been much of a risk taker, but, after Gabe..." Trinidad trailed off. After Gabe, she'd felt snipped from her moorings, like she'd left her old self adrift in still water. The trouble was, she wasn't sure who the new Trinidad Jones was supposed to be. And why was she sharing her innermost thoughts, anyway?

"I understand. My life is sort of divided into B.G. and A.G., before and after Gabe." Juliette tipped her chin up, mouth in a hard line. "No one should have that much power over our lives, Trinidad." After a fortifying breath, she stuck out her palm. "Welcome to Sprocket. Hopefully this is the place where we will both find new beginnings."

Trinidad solemnly shook. "Here, here."

Juliette smiled. "I am glad to extend an official welcome. Come into the office for a minute. It's already too hot out here, and I want to get the rest of your contact info. Vince was supposed to do that, but sometimes his head is in the academic clouds." Juliette's cell phone rang, and she stepped away to answer it.

Trinidad gathered up her items and stowed them in the Pinto before she and Noodles made their way to the office. Juliette was still on the phone, standing with her back to her, tall and statuesque, like a dancer. Trinidad felt acutely aware of the extra pounds her doctor harped on as she noted Juliette's willowy frame. She considered sneaking away. It seemed entirely too painful to extend her visit with the woman who had been her replacement. However, she felt a strong connection to this other wife who had been a stranger only moments before. Of all the zillions of people on planet Earth, no one else could possibly understand how she felt better than Juliette and, perhaps, Bonnie, if she ever should happen to meet her.

Only eighteen months had elapsed since Gabe went to jail for embezzlement and assorted other frauds, but she was determined to make a way for herself in Sprocket, a life after Gabe. A.G., as Juliette put it.

After another hesitant step forward, her shoe crunched on something. Juliette whirled, phone at her ear, and took in Trinidad as she inspected her foot. "Sorry. I was throwing something away, and I didn't get time to clean up properly. Somebody's feeble attempt at a peace offering." Her eyes flashed with anger for a moment as she disconnected the call before summoning a smile. "The hours here are getting to me, and the storage unit business can be ugly. Can I get you some coffee?"

"No, thank you. Why ugly?" Trinidad scraped the sticky bit from her shoe. She realized after the fact that her question had probably been nosy, but Juliette did not seem to take offense. Trinidad, a natural introvert, realized she didn't have a whole lot of practice making chit-chat, a problem she'd have to remedy living in Upper Sprocket.

"We just auctioned off an unpaid storage unit Monday, and, now that everything's gone, I need to clean it out before it can be rented again." Juliette colored, a pink petal flush, not the blotchy scarlet Trinidad sported when embarrassed. The sin of comparison, her grandfather would have said. Juliette continued. "Between you and me, it's really a shame. The previous owner passed away suddenly. Edward Lupin, I don't suppose you met him, but he lived here in town and he was...well, he struggled some with reality, and he'd let the payments lapse. It was sad to see all his belongings auctioned off, but it's all legal, I'm afraid." She sighed. "I felt terrible about it."

Trinidad imagined her own tiny collection of possessions on display at an auction. It wouldn't fetch twenty bucks, she estimated. Aside from the ice cream equipment, it was not more than a few paltry trinkets, representing an unremarkable life. She raised her chin. *A new start, remember?*

"I startled someone skulking around the night before the auction," Juliette said. "Weird, huh? In this kind of town? I had to change the locks out. I put in a camera, too, but it's just one of those fake cameras; it doesn't actually work. Real ones are too rich for my blood."

"That would be too much for mine, too."

Juliette grimaced at a stack of invoices piled on the counter, all stamped with a blue "Store Some More" logo. Her brow under her neat bangs creased. "Too bad Gabe didn't own a quaint tea parlor or a posh hotel or something. I'm running a storage business, you're opening an ice cream place, and Bonnie got a piece of property and an old train car she's trying to turn into a bed-and-breakfast. We're quite the trio." Juliette gave her a sideways look. "Have you seen her yet?"

"Bonnie? No. Haven't had the time." The idea terrified her,

meeting the woman who had borne Gabe's only child. The only one they knew of, anyway.

Juliette observed her closely. "I know. I was reluctant to meet her, too, but we bumped into each other at Full of Beans. She recognized me from the trial. I didn't want to talk to her, honestly, but she kept inviting me over for dinner until I finally relented. Bonnie is the kind of person you just have to open up to. She will be your best friend before you know it."

Trinidad could not think of a response.

"I'll arrange a meeting when she gets back from visiting her sister in Canada. She's a real sweet lady, in her own odd way. And her daughter Felice is darling." She smiled at Trinidad and nodded her head thoughtfully. "We should all be friends. We have a weird bond, a sisterhood of exes or something."

Weird was an understatement. All three women with the same conniving ex-husband. What a sticky pot of glue that was. "I'll pop in when I can."

In truth, Trinidad quaked at the idea of meeting Bonnie. She experienced an odd blend of emotions at hearing that Juliette, Bonnie, and little Felice were close. Here she was again, on the outside looking in. Juliette, the beautiful blond, Bonnie, the loving mother…and then there was Trinidad. She tried to shake off the self-pity as Juliette handed her a clipboard.

"Anyway, go ahead and write down your particulars for me," she said. "I really hope we can be friends. I haven't found too many people in town—well, any really—to hang out with. Probably my fault, I come off as standoffish to some. I guess I'm not overtrusting after Gabe." There was a catch in her voice that shot right to Trinidad's heart.

"Me neither."

Juliette flashed her a wobbly smile. "Sometimes I feel like damaged goods, like I have to pay a price forever just because I believed the wrong man."

Trinidad's throat clogged. "But only if we let ourselves feel that way, right?"

"I guess so." Juliette sighed. "I think I'm going to be very glad I finally met you, Trinidad."

As much as she squirmed under the weight of their shared past, the offer of friendship sounded sweet and inviting to her. A new town, a new friend, a new adventure. A sisterhood of exes? Was that the blessing that would come out of her marriage disaster? "Ditto," she heard herself say, surprised to find she really meant it.

Juliette's phone rang again. Trinidad wiggled her fingers in a goodbye and walked out with Noodles. As the heavy door of the office closed, Juliette's voice rang shrill with anger, again with a catch that indicated she was near tears. "I've had enough. I won't let you treat me like this."

Just before it shut completely, Trinidad caught the last phrase.

"If you ever cross my path again, I'll kill you." The words were followed by the final bang of the door.

Chapter Two

TRINIDAD MADE A QUICK STOP back at the store to drop off the cookie cutters and patio chairs and three cans of spray paint. The boys had gone for the day to join a family picnic by the lake, which was just as well, since she was in a pensive mood after her encounter with Juliette. She began to scrub the kitchen, the stainless steel sink, the bins where the freshly churned ice cream would be kept, and every part of the giant shake machine. Thoughts tumbled through her head. Juliette's cell phone call bothered her. No, more the tone than what she'd said. There had been a glimmer of something wounded and wild in Juliette's voice that echoed in Trinidad's own soul.

Sometimes I feel like damaged goods, like I have to pay a price forever just because I believed the wrong man. Trinidad got it. Completely. There was solace in being understood, she thought. She hoped Juliette felt the same way.

In need of some comfort, she fixed herself a tiny shake for lunch with just one modest scoop of her homemade strawberry ice cream and supplied Noodles with a dog biscuit. The dog set about licking every square centimeter of the treat before eating it. They enjoyed their snack in the shady corner of the porch. It was quiet, save for the raucous squawk of a crow and the rumble of an occasional camper toting visitors along to Three Egg Lake.

Interrupting the quiet, a motorcycle roared past. The noise made Noodles go stiff-eared. The driver was Kevin Heartly, owner and proprietor of the Popcorn Palace. Seated behind him was a petite woman with a fringe of blond hair poking out from under her helmet. It had taken Trinidad a moment to recognize him. She had only seen him sporting a smile before, not the scowl he wore now. Kevin had inherited the popcorn business from his father, he'd told her when she first moved into her shop. It was a bit of an institution in eastern Oregon. Immediately after she'd plastered the SHIMMY AND SHAKE SHOP COMING SOON sign on the window, he'd come over to introduce himself, and she quickly picked up that his charming, boyish demeanor masked a shrewd mind for business. He must have a keen eye on the dollar signs to support himself in the popcorn biz throughout the long snowy months of winter when the store was closed, though he had mentioned his online business was thriving. She'd had the sense he was checking out her shop to see if she presented competition.

He must have decided ice cream wouldn't distract his popcorn lovers, because, right after that first meeting, he suggested a partnership, and they'd been splitting deliveries ever since. In fact, Trinidad had made a deal with him to pick up an order of hazelnuts from a nearby farm, which she suddenly remembered was due to be ready today.

Kevin parked the bike in a space in front of his corny palace and jammed the kickstand down. His passenger hopped off gracefully, removed her helmet, and gave him a cool kiss on the cheek. Trinidad hurried across the street to catch him. She wanted to collect his half of the payment before she retrieved the nuts, rather than add further debt to her already-smoking credit card.

The duo paused when they spotted her approach, and Trinidad introduced herself to Kevin's passenger.

"Tanya Grant," the woman said, extending a perfectly manicured hand. "Welcome to town. I'll stop by your shop when you open. Now, I've got to run. Bye, Kev."

Kevin watched her walk briskly up the street, a quizzical expression on his face. When he turned back to Trinidad, his genial, easygoing charm was absent. His mouth was bracketed by hard lines, brows knitted together.

"Did you need something?" His tone was polite, but far from warm.

She kept up the smile. "I got a call from Logan's this morning. I totally forgot until I saw you, but they said that our nuts should be ready today. I thought maybe one of us could pick them up."

"Great. I forgot about that, too. Appreciate it. It would be hard for me since my truck's in the shop." He jammed his hands into the pockets of his stylish jeans. A piece of caramel corn that had been stuck to his shirt fell to the ground.

Kevin eyed it, muttering, "Waste of good product."

She had no idea how to run with that conversational segue. "About the nut pick up..."

"Yeah. Thanks. Talk to you later." He pushed open his door, closing it firmly behind him.

"But..." Kevin was already gone. How rude. "Well, I guess I'm fronting the money after all," she grumbled to herself. A smacking sound drew her attention, and she looked to find Noodles snarfing up Kevin's cast-off popcorn.

"Is it a good idea to eat popcorn? I'm pretty sure you're supposed to be on a diet, too." Noodles seemed to regard her with cool formality, implying that an animal who ate Chilly Dogs was not concerned one whit about extra calories. They returned to her time-ravaged Pinto.

With the cooperation of her phone's GPS, Trinidad made the trip along rambling country roads to Logan's Nut Farm in under forty minutes. It almost gave her time to shake off the strange sense of unease that roiled in her gut. Was it meeting Juliette? Overhearing her angry phone call? Trinidad had certainly been angry enough with Gabe to wish him bodily harm, but never would she have contemplated killing him. Probably. Anger did funny things to human beings, and Juliette had been betrayed in the worst way. Did the person on the other end of the phone know that?

And then there was Kevin Heartly's foul mood that rivaled Juliette's. Perhaps it had been a lover's spat between him and the lovely Tanya who hadn't spared a backward glance as she'd strode away from Kevin.

Her own nosiness dismayed her. Why did it matter anyway? She had plenty of other problems to wrangle at the moment. She allowed the idyllic country lane to soothe her worries away as she parked at Logan's Nut Farm. Neat rows of well-tended trees backed a tiny wood-sided office. The shade looked cool and inviting as she wiped the sweat from her brow. A man rumbled into view driving a tractor that dragged a tire along behind to smooth the ground under the trees. When he saw her, he waved, cut the engine, and climbed off.

She guessed him to be in his mid-forties with buzzed salt and pepper hair and eyes the startling blue of summer skies. There was a hole in the sleeve of his rumpled T-shirt, the fabric so faded she could not make out the logo. He was trim and athletic in a way that made her try to suck in her muffin top. A cellophane-wrapped pack of cigarettes stuck out of his back pocket.

"Quinn Logan," he said, extending a hand. His fingers were warm and calloused.

"Trinidad Jones."

"I heard we had a newcomer in town. Going to have to change the population sign to add one more."

She laughed. "Maybe they should add me in pencil. If my

business fails, I'll need to pack up and pitch a tent somewhere else."

His gentle chuckle stirred something inside her. "Scuttlebutt is you're opening an ice cream shop. It'll be a huge hit; don't you worry. My brother will be your best customer." He beckoned her toward the office, Noodles following along, and he gestured to a tall, skinny man, likely a few years younger than himself, who was adding hazelnuts to a pile on the scale inside. "This is Doug."

Doug did not acknowledge his brother's comment or look up from his task.

"Say hi, Doug. Remember?"

Doug glanced up for a split second, waved, and then promptly returned his attention to his work.

"Nice to meet you both," Trinidad said. "I'll whip up a monster shake for you anytime."

"Doug only likes vanilla, but he'll eat it no matter what the temperature or season. We have been known to have a scoop for breakfast when the grocery supply is running low." He looked down at Noodles. "Who is this guy?"

She made the introductions, and Quinn knelt to massage Noodles behind the ears. Doug snuck quick peeks at the dog as he continued his meticulous work of heaping the hazelnuts onto the scale.

"I probably should have called and told you to come later. We got a little behind this morning. It's going to take Doug a while to package your order," Quinn said. "He values precision, and he doesn't like me to help."

She smiled at the bespectacled man, but Doug still did not return the smile, his attention fixed on the scale.

"He's not big on social interaction," Quinn said. "But he's an amazing worker, and, like I said, he's passionate about his ice cream."

"No problem. I will make sure we've got plenty of fresh-churned vanilla on hand."

"Fantastic. Can I get you a cold soda while Doug finishes up? I keep some in a cooler."

"That would really hit the spot."

He handed her a can, opened one for himself, and slid a bottle of apple juice on the counter next to Doug. Without a word, he poured a bottle of water into a plastic container and set it down for Noodles to have a drink. "How are you two liking Upper Sprocket?"

"So far, so good. It's quiet here—quieter than Portland, anyway."

"That's what Doug and I like about it. Things get hopping during Alpenfest and for the summer visitors. We'll be happy after the Fourth of July comes and things slow down, though it's been fun to give tours to a few nut lovers who've stopped by. Met many of the locals yet?"

"Not many so far. Though I did finally run into Juliette, at the Store Some More just today," she said.

"Ah." He didn't seem inclined to fish about her colorful past with the hometown boy or his trail of ex-wives. She exhaled in relief as he changed the subject back toward where they were both comfortable—their businesses.

They sipped their sodas. She learned that Quinn was a veteran of the Army, and the land he worked had been in his family since his grandfather's day. "We're kind of an anomaly. Most hazelnuts are grown in the Willamette Valley, but we've got a funky microclimate going on here, thanks to the shelter of the Wallowas. It's not easy. Things went south because of the filbert blight, but we're regaining momentum now that the resistant cultivars are producing." He kept up an amiable chatter. "So, tell me how things are going at the ice cream shop."

He was easy to talk to, eager to listen, and she was dazzled by his boisterous laugh. By the time they finished their visit, she was startled to see that a half hour had whizzed by. When was the last time she had enjoyed such a genial chat…with a man? The nuts were weighed and ready to be paid for. Quinn insisted on carrying the buckets to her car, which both thrilled and embarrassed her, though she couldn't say why.

"We'll see you in town soon, then?" Quinn said.

She nodded. "Bring all your ice cream–loving friends and neighbors."

He laughed, eyes flashing a breathtaking blue. The hue seemed to her to be the exact shade of the lush hydrangeas Papa Luis grew in his greenhouse. "You bet we will."

She thanked him, returning his cheerful wave out the window as she drove away.

Back in town nearly three hours after she'd started her nut errand, the tantalizing scent of caramel and kettle corn wafting from Kevin's Popcorn Palace tickled her nose. Caramel. Maybe she would concoct a caramel and vanilla crème shake, since she'd already decided to crank out a batch of her special french vanilla for Doug. *One masterpiece at a time,* she told herself. She couldn't wait to get started on the brownies, which would be the crowning glory of the Fourth of July Freakshake. She recalled the days she'd spent with Papa Luis hand-cranking a mound of vanilla, which they'd eat straight from the dented churn before it had even set. He was the one who had always inspired her ice cream dreams.

"This is happiness," Papa Luis always said with a wave of his spoon, and she'd agreed. Childhood, the love of her darling grandfather, and spoonfuls of creamy bliss. Happiness indeed. But Papa had seen plenty of bitterness, too, including the death of his son, her father, two years prior. Blinking back tears, she decided she would take some pictures of the shop to send to her mother, brother, and Papa Luis.

Her shop. Delicious and unaccustomed excitement buzzed in her belly. Never in a gazillion years would she have imagined herself as an entrepreneur, but then again she'd not pictured herself being divorced, either. It was as if she were a small child, standing for the first time on shaky legs. Fresh doubts assailed her. What if there weren't enough people willing to pay for her amazing shakes? Who would keep the heat on in the winter and kibble in Noodles's bowl? She held onto Quinn's encouragement. *It'll be a huge hit; don't you worry.*

Swallowing hard, she got out of the car and hauled out the buckets.

Across the street, a man pulled up in a green van with VINTAGE THEATER COMPANY stenciled in peeling paint on the side. He chewed a string of black licorice clamped between his teeth.

"Help you with that?" he said.

The man was familiar, the genial smile almost swallowed up by his wide, fleshy cheeks. She'd seen him at the grocery store, she recalled, chatting with the employees about fishing. "Oh no, thank you. That's kind of you to offer." She was still getting used to the helpful Sprocketerian spirit. Nut farmers offered sodas and water for dogs. Van drivers stopped at a moment's notice to help schlep buckets. What a place.

He chomped the rest of his licorice twist and extracted his portly form from the van. "No prob. I got to let my engine cool down anyway. Darn van overheats at the drop of a hat, and the way back from the printer's seems like it's all uphill." He approached her. "Name's Warren Wheaton." Warren wiped his palms on his pants before he extended a beefy hand. Everything about him was beefy, his stomach pushing against the confines of a T-shirt and overlapping the belt of his jeans. The top of his head shone white and slick as a fish belly with a fringe of wispy hair clinging to the circumference.

"Trinidad Jones," she said, giving his palm a shake. "I'm opening a shop here in town." She floundered around for something else to say before she gestured to the dog. "This is Noodles."

Warren cocked his head. "Hang on. Are you the woman working on the ice cream joint? But that was Gabe Bigley's storefront. I heard he turned it over before he went to jail. Seems like Sprocket gets a new business for every one of Gabe's exes." His cheeks went red. "Oh, wait. You're not..."

"One of the bunch," she said, feeling the flush creep up her neck. "I moved to town six weeks ago and started my own business."

He looked from his scuffed boots, to the dog, to the van, and finally settled on her kneecaps. "Oh, well. Welcome to Sprocket."

"Thank you," she said brightly, wondering if her decision to stay in Sprocket meant that she would be perpetual fodder for the rumor mill. Would she forever be known as a Bigley ex-wife?

"Real interesting name you got, Trinidad. Family thing?"

"I'm named after a town," she said.

"Let me guess...a town in Trinidad?"

"No, the town of Trinidad in Cuba."

He blinked. "That right? I'm named after my no-good uncle Warren. He pickled himself with too much drinking, but he sure was entertaining at family parties." He laughed. "I'm a landscape guy, but I help out the theater company. Right now, I got a cargo area full of flyers. Hot off the presses, or at least the copy machine. Haven't even looked at 'em, but I sure hope this batch doesn't have a typo. Last time, they said our production was called *Our Floundering Fathers*." He chuckled. "We're doing a big patriotic show starting mid-July, and hopefully there will be no floundering involved. You should check it out." He winked. "I'm playing Benjamin Franklin. I got just the hairline for it, don't I?"

She laughed. "Perfect."

"Anyway, since you don't need my help, I'd better scoot," he said, with a chagrined smile. "Welcome. Hope to see you around." He gave Noodles a pat before he returned to his vehicle.

She hauled the first bucket to the closed door of the Popcorn Palace, Noodles following. The structure was a boxy cinder block building painted brilliant white with black trim, nestled alongside a wide graveled drive. The hours on the place said, 11:00 A.M.–7:00 P.M., MONDAY THROUGH SATURDAY, MAY THROUGH NOVEMBER. The sign included a color picture of Kevin Heartly wearing a goofy grin and sporting a hat that resembled a giant, fluffy popcorn kernel. The monthly special was a festive Fourth of July kettle corn that looked to be streaked with drizzles of red- and blue-tinted white chocolate.

Kevin had told her when they first met that the Popcorn Palace had been in his family for fifty years. The caramel corn hazelnut combo was a favorite all across the state with some people driving hours to stock up when the Palace opened after the spring thaw. Demand for the sweet, salty delicacy would be high during the upcoming Fourth of July holiday weekend. And, after they'd tried the Popcorn Palace's offerings, they'd be sure to stop for a Freakshake, she assured herself.

Trinidad rapped a knuckle on the door, which she realized was not quite closed. It swung open a few inches. "Kevin? It's Trinidad. I've got your nut delivery."

The interior was quiet and dark. Cool air whispered through the front door. Kevin must have had the air conditioner running to combat the summer heat. The sun blazed down on her back, dampening her T-shirt. Noodles oozed into a puddle in the shade of the ivy that grew nearly to the height of the shop's low roof. A neatly packaged rosebush with a spray of pink blooms leaned against the porch step, ready to be potted or planted. The label said, "Pink Princess." Trinidad didn't know a thing about roses, but the Pink Princess variety puffed a lovely fragrance into the air, which mingled nicely with the sugary caramel corn smell. *A person didn't get this kind of olfactory bonanza in the big city,* she thought. "Kevin?" she called again, louder.

Still receiving no answer, she decided to stall, going to her car and lugging over the second bucket of hazelnuts, marveling at how easily Quinn had carried them. This time she rapped so hard on the door it flew wide, opening the shop to her.

She debated. Should she load the nuts back into the car and return later? But she'd hoped to have the delivery done by two and it was already approaching three thirty. He would want it before closing up, wouldn't he? She could leave them on the doorstep. The crime rate in Upper Sprocket was probably close to nil, so nut theft wasn't on the radar. Still, she was hoping to collect his half of the payment.

"Maybe I'd better put them inside at least and close the door," she said to Noodles. Since he did not detect the words "walk," "treat," or "vet" in the comment, he apparently felt no need to weigh in. "Okay, it's nuts or never." She half-lugged, half-rolled the buckets into the store. The dog followed.

Inside was a small counter set up near the window where Kevin or his helpers could take orders without leaving the building. A second window was for product pickup. Big roll-down shutters would allow Kevin to whip up his kettle corn delicacy with sufficient ventilation. Behind the counter was a pristine tiled floor. A stove hugged the wall topped with small copper pots. Caramel fragrance hung heavy in the air.

An enormous iron kettle stood centered on the tile, which must be where Kevin worked his corny magic. She thought she heard a noise, a scrape from the rear of the building. Perhaps Kevin was working in the lot behind the store. Her mood improved at the thought of picking up his half of the $200 payment.

She slid the buckets toward the wall to keep them out of the way and headed behind the counter. As she went to the back door to find him, she stumbled on something. A wooden device with a long handle like an oar for a rowboat, lay at her feet. She realized it must be the tool he used to stir the kernels in the kettle.

Weird, she thought, for Kevin to leave the tool lying on the floor, even though at first glance, the floor looked fairly clean. Except for a few drips on the tile dark against the white, glossy in the unlit space. Caramel perhaps?

She followed the drips with her eyes, tracing their path, which seemed to extend from the wooden paddle across the tile floor and up the side of the massive iron kettle where the droplets had morphed into dribbles that ran down the rounded metal sides. Something cinched tight in her stomach.

This is Upper Sprocket, she told herself, *not a bustling city,* and she was in a popcorn shop, not a seedy back alley. Still, her body whispered some nonverbal alarm that sent the hairs along her arms standing at attention.

"Noodles," she whispered as she drew near the kettle. "We should go."

But, inexorably, she moved close and closer until she fingered the rim, solid and smooth. When she peered over, she nearly touched her nose to a shoulder. The shoulder was attached to a body, curled up in the fetal position inside the kettle. The body was bloody and still.

When she shot backward, she overturned the nearest bucket, which sent hazelnuts rolling all over the floor. Scrambling over the nuts and Noodles, Trinidad stumbled to the front porch, nausea almost making her retch.

Kevin Heartly had popped his last batch of corn.

Her scream exploded like an erupting kernel in his iron kettle.

Chapter Three

"SHE CAME OUT SCREAMING AND keeled over like a felled pine," Warren Wheaton said as Trinidad achieved a sitting position.

She wasn't sure who he was speaking to. Her head spun and her skin prickled with goosebumps, though the temperature was still in the lower nineties. A leaf dangled in her frame of vision, stuck in her frizzy bangs. Warren was kneeling next to her. "I figured something was up when you screamed, so I went in and… uh…well, you already know what's in the kettle."

The kettle. A chill swept through her nerves.

"Yes," said a calm voice. "We do. Miss Jones, do you need an ambulance?"

She looked up to see a tall, uniformed woman with brown eyes staring down at her. Something about the thin nose and the fringe of dark lashes was familiar. "No, no, I'm okay. I just got lightheaded for a minute and tripped over my feet, Officer… uh…"

"I'm Chief Cynthia Bigley of the Sprocket Police Department."

Bigley? Trinidad blinked and swallowed, throat dry as dust. "You aren't another ex-wife of Gabe's, are you?" *Had she actually said that aloud?*

The chief cleared her throat. "No, ma'am," she said slowly. "As far as I know, he only married three. He's my baby brother."

Trinidad gaped. This woman couldn't be Gabe's sibling. She must have heard wrong. "The sister who stole cars?" she squeaked, overriding her brain's warning Klaxon.

Warren's mouth fell open with an audible plop. She wished feverishly to cram the words back in her gullet. Why, oh, why hadn't Juliette mentioned that the chief of police was their former sister-in-law? Noodles, picking up on her tension, applied his wet nose to her chin with a plaintive whine.

"People change, ma'am," the chief said after a beat. "I don't steal cars anymore. The Army set me on the straight and narrow. They're pretty good at helping a person reconfigure their priorities." She cocked her chin. "I've met Juliette and Bonnie. I didn't plan on getting to know the remaining ex-wife at a murder scene."

Through her spinning senses, Trinidad made note of the slightly sarcastic delivery of "the remaining ex-wife."

"Juliette has plenty of mud to sling around about Gabe. You, too?" said the chief.

Trinidad started to reply when the chief waved her off. "Never mind. Not the time. Are you sure you don't need an ambulance?"

Trinidad felt like she needed a sweat sock to stuff in her mouth instead. She shook her head and gave the dog a reassuring pat. Noodles trotted off and returned a moment later carrying a warm bottle of water he'd retrieved from the Pinto. It had taken him a while to master how to open the front door, but now he was a pro. He dropped the bottle in her lap, this time swiping his tongue across her forehead. She leaned her cheek against his furry side to steady herself.

"Well, would you look at that," Warren said. "Dog's smarter than some of my kinfolk. He opened up that car door slick as a whistle."

She didn't have the strength to explain that Noodles was a service dog flunk-out in his younger days, according to the shelter where he'd been dumped in favor of a new puppy. After a steadying breath, she said, "Chief, I am sorry about the car theft crack. Um...Gabe said a lot of nice things about you, too." In truth, he'd gushed with pride to speak of how she was turning her life around, his darling big sis, how close they were. Never once had she heard him mention his sister had gone into law enforcement in Sprocket, of all places.

"Apology accepted," the chief said. "I adore my little brother, but he can talk the paint off the walls, and nothing is out of bounds. Let's get you into the shade. We can stroll down memory lane when we don't have a dead body to process."

Warren gripped her elbow as he and the chief led her to a tree, which screened the sun. Noodles crowded along, too.

"Stay here," Chief Bigley commanded. Warren, Trinidad, and Noodles followed directions while the chief reentered the Popcorn Palace.

"I've never fainted before." Trinidad lifted her mass of curly hair away from her perspiring neck.

Warren quirked a smile. "You probably never saw a murdered guy before."

Her stomach turned over. Murdered. Though she'd efficiently recorded the details of many murder trials in her stenography work, it felt unreal that a human life could be violently ended in picture-perfect Sprocket.

"Must have been a stranger passing through. I mean, Kevin was a real stand-up guy, ran a tight ship in the way of business matters. No one had beef with him." Warren paused. "Well, except maybe the fella who clobbered him."

Trinidad groaned.

Warren patted her hand. "Terrible you should have had to find him, and you being new in town and all." His sigh turned into a chuckle. "Funny, though, you accusing the chief of being another of Gabe's wives. That was a hoot."

Trinidad glugged some water. It wasn't exactly how she would have described her mortifying slipup.

The chief summoned another officer with a camera and one who stayed outside jotting notes before she returned to Trinidad.

"Did you see anyone else on the property, Miss Jones?"

"No, but I heard someone out back. I thought it was Kevin, at first, but, um, he was in the kettle."

"I've got a cop out back right now, checking. Bunch of boxes there from the flea market. Looks as though they've been gone through. They're junk as far as I can tell at this point." She continued asking questions.

Trinidad explained in spurts and gushes. "I was delivering nuts. We split an order. I'm opening a store. It's called the Shimmy and Shake Shop, and we're going to offer giant Freakshakes. They're sort of hard to describe. Shakes, but mega-sized. You know, served in really huge mugs with all manner of goodies stuck to the sides and on top. Only, it's much more amazing than I'm making it seem," she babbled.

Warren nodded enthusiastically. "Great idea. Nice town like this needs an ice cream shop."

A nice town like this? Where people are murdered and stuffed into kettles? She felt the chief's gaze roving over her face. Warren's words rang in her ears. *Must have been a stranger.*

Was the chief thinking she fit that bill? She was new to town, the first to discover the body. She'd touched the kettle; her fingerprints would be there to be harvested by the police technician.

Surely not. Chief Bigley couldn't think that. Or could she? Mightn't there be just a tiny bit of bad blood since Trinidad had willingly cooperated in the fraud case against the chief's baby brother?

The chief's face remained impassive, but her brown eyes were calculating. "If you feel up to driving, you can go along home now, Miss Jones. We'll be in touch."

Trinidad nodded, grateful that her legs seemed steadier as she opened the car door and allowed Noodles to slide in. Something scuttled under the front tire, borne by the warm breeze, flattening itself against her shin. She bent to retrieve a crumpled leaflet and jammed it into her bag, anxious to leave the Popcorn Palace and its grisly contents far behind.

Trinidad peeled one eye open the next morning. For a moment, she could not place herself in space and time.

Gabe. The memory of him banging around in the kitchen was so vivid. It was a cruel trick her brain played on her most mornings, dredging up that past life until it ebbed away with the intrusion of reality. *Gabe was not here,* she reminded herself for the millionth time. Gabe was a liar and a cheater. Gabe was in jail. He was the reason she'd landed in Upper Sprocket.

Her senses staggered back online and recorded the knotty pine peaked ceiling of the loft a scant few feet from her forehead and the buttery sunshine warming her toes.

The facts fell into place. Fact: she was occupying a two hundred square foot tiny house she'd rented on the outskirts of Upper Sprocket. Fact: Gabe was in prison. But there was something new nibbling at her consciousness—a dreadful nightmare.

Fact: There was a dead man in a massive iron pot.

That last thought got her sitting up so quickly her vision sparked. Not a nightmare. She really had stumbled upon poor, dead Kevin Heartly. She wanted to pull up the covers, burrow deep in the bed, and stay there until it all went away. Over the whirlwind of memories, she considered that Noodles was counting on her. Not to mention she had a shop to get ready for opening. It was enough to propel her down the ladder and into the miniscule shower, but the hot water did nothing to dampen the memory of her grisly find at the Popcorn Palace. Her stomach roiled too much to think about breakfast. There was only one thing to snap her mind out of its dizzying acrobatics. Work.

An hour later, as she let herself into the Shimmy and Shake Shop, she kept her eyes away from the yellow tape cordoning off Kevin's shop. It was somewhat of a relief that the twins were home today helping their mother with a wallpapering job. The murder was no doubt the top news item on everyone's lips. Noodles took up his spot on his cushion, and she soothed herself by diving into ice cream preparations.

She'd planned on making a rich custard base speckled with flecks of real vanilla, the perfect palette for a myriad of Freakshake options. She'd just scraped the flesh of the vanilla beans into a pot, added milk, and begun to scald the mixture when a tap on the door made her jump. She stood frozen until she saw Quinn Logan peering through the glass. With a sigh, she unlocked the door and welcomed him and his brother inside.

Quinn's smile made her temporarily forget her ice cream prep. He wore pants with the knees thin as paper and a T-shirt that had seen better days. Again, an unopened package of cigarettes occupied the back pocket of his jeans. He presented her a cup of coffee while Doug stood with perfect posture, staring over her shoulder at the ice cream machinery.

"Saw you in here, and we figured you could use a dose of java," Quinn said. "Stan Lawper owns the Full of Beans coffee shop across the street. Met him yet?"

"Pinching pennies means I make my own coffee, mostly." She didn't want to tell him that none of the local coffee she'd tasted compared to her father's Cuban concoction served in tiny porcelain *tacitas*. A few of his robust brews, he would proclaim proudly, would grow hair on any chest. "I went in a few times, but he was pretty busy so we've only exchanged a few words."

"He's British, sort of a Renaissance man. He was a butler while he worked his way through law school, if you can believe it, but now he's helping run his sister's coffee shop." Quinn chuckled, and she noticed a dimple on one side of his full mouth. "Fits right in here in Sprocket. We're an eclectic bunch."

"Thank you for the coffee," she said gratefully. "I didn't sleep too well last night."

His smile vanished. "I heard about Kevin. Real sorry. No one deserves to die like that. I don't even remember hearing of another murder in Sprocket. Can't imagine why anyone would want Kevin dead." He raised a brow. "Real sorry you had to be the one to discover it."

"Me too," she said with a shudder.

He inhaled. "Smells like vanilla in here." He shot a look at his brother. "Excited, Doug?"

Doug nodded but kept his gaze on the machines.

"Anyway, I know you're real busy but…" There was something uneasy in Quinn's tone.

"What is it? Do you want to sit down?"

"No, uh…" Quinn's forehead creased in thought. "Um, it's none of my business, really," he said, "but, when I was buying the coffee just now, I saw Juliette in there. She looks, um, real upset. The rumor mill is churning at full force, and she hasn't got many friends that I know of, except Bonnie, and she's out of town. You said you'd met her, so I figured maybe you might…"

Trinidad was already turning off the stove and hanging her apron on the hook. "I want to get to know this Renaissance Stan, anyway," she said. "Might as well be now."

He heaved a relieved sigh. "Excellent. I'll introduce you."

Noodles followed Doug and Quinn across the street. A courtyard outside Full of Beans was lined with rosebushes heavy with blooms. Their fragrance mingled with the rich aroma of coffee. Inside, the quaint shop sported mismatched tables scattered across a scarred, planked floor. Wee vases offered a fresh blossom at every table. Trinidad was greeted by a gentleman with a thick head of silver hair who introduced himself with a polite handshake and a slight bow. His English accent was as charming as the blue checkered bow tie above the apron tied around his slim waist.

"Welcome to Full of Beans. I see you already have coffee," he said, pointing to her cup.

"Yeah, but I'll bet she'd like something to go with that," Quinn said.

Stan smiled broadly. "My sister Meg has prepared some marvelous lemon scones and banana squares with browned butter icing. May I interest you in a sweet?"

Trinidad grinned. "You had me at browned butter." While Stan rang her up on the antiquated push-button cash register, Quinn casually bobbed his head toward the corner where Juliette sat staring at her phone. "Make that two banana squares," Trinidad said. She took the little white bag he'd filled, her mouth watering. She felt uncertain as she shot a glance at Quinn. "Or maybe I should have asked for four? Would you and Doug…um…I mean, like to join us?"

Quinn shook his head. "We wouldn't intrude. I'll…" Then his gaze went to Juliette. To Trinidad's horror, the woman stood and swayed as if she was going to faint, her face paling to the color of marshmallow cream. Trinidad rushed over with Noodles, but Quinn got there first. He guided Juliette back into a chair.

"Deep breath," he said calmly. "Doug…" he started, but Doug had already fetched a glass of water.

"You two are amazing," Trinidad couldn't help but say.

Quinn lifted a shoulder, keeping his attention on Juliette. "I had some problems when I got back from Afghanistan. Doug learned just what to do, didn't you, Doug?"

Doug nodded.

Juliette sipped the water, which seemed to revive her. "Thank you. I'm so sorry. I was reading the news report again about Kevin… It was such a shock. We…we argued because I found out he was dating someone else. Last time I saw him, he brought me a gift, as an apology. I threw it on the floor. I was so angry."

Trinidad remembered the crunchy bit she'd stepped on at Juliette's office. It had indeed been a peace offering from Kevin.

Tears pooled in Juliette's eyes. "I guess it was normal, people do date more than one person at a time, but he didn't tell me, and, after Gabe…" She gulped. "After we got married, I found out he had been pursuing me while he was still married to you, and then I discovered he had another ex-wife neither of us knew about…" Her eyes beseeched Trinidad. "You understand, right? You get why I was so angry and hurt?"

Trinidad took her hand. They stayed locked together for a moment, fingers clutching, a bridge building between them that Trinidad somehow knew would be unbreakable. "Yes, I do understand," she said, through a thickening in her throat. "Completely."

Juliette sighed and followed Quinn's suggestion to sip the water again. "I think the chief believes I had something to do with Kevin's death. We…had a few disagreements recently. My last argument with him was pretty public, and she's not my biggest fan to begin with. I haven't spoken very highly of her brother around town. I should have been more discreet."

Trinidad shook her head. "None of that makes you guilty of Kevin's murder."

"I feel guilty, anyway, about my last words to Kevin." Juliette teared up. "I feel so alone. Like everyone suspects me. But I didn't hurt him; I never would."

Loneliness was something Trinidad was painfully familiar with. She was reminded when she saw couples hand in hand, chasing after little ones, building families like the one she'd dreamed of. "You're not alone," she blurted out. "I will help you get through this."

Juliette's eyes rounded in wonder. "You will?"

The naked vulnerability in Juliette's face struck her to the core. She found herself nodding, determination filling her. "Absolutely." She said the words that rose straight from her heart. "I understand how you felt, and Kevin should have been honest with you."

Finally, Juliette sighed and took the coffee cup, holding it as if it were a life preserver.

"Thank you," she said. "It means a lot. I need a friend right now."

A friend. There was something very sweet about that word.

Quinn patted her shoulder. "Doug and I are happy to help, too, if there's anything we can do."

Doug nodded soberly.

Trinidad's emotions swelled at the kindness. "See? It's going to be okay."

Juliette blew out a breath. "I sure hope so, but I have a terrible feeling in the pit of my stomach."

They chatted for a few minutes until the door banged open and Tanya Grant, Kevin's motorcycle companion, stalked in. Her eyes slitted as she spotted them and strode over. She wore low heels and a breezy dress of pale sage that brought out her emerald irises. She glowered at Juliette. "You did it, didn't you?"

Juliette's mouth fell open. "What are you accusing me of?"

"Don't play dumb."

"Ms. Grant," Stan called from behind the counter. "May I show you to a table? Make you an espresso?"

Tanya ignored him. "I know you followed me and Kevin when we drove to the lake Tuesday night, Juliette. I heard the angry message you left on his phone. You hated that he was going to dump you for me." Her lower lip quivered. "Why did you have to kill him?"

Juliette gulped audibly. "I didn't even know you were together until a few days ago. He said you'd dated, but you'd broken up. Yes, I followed you, I'll admit it, but I didn't hurt him."

"Liar. You wanted him for yourself, and you couldn't stand that he picked me, so you killed him."

Juliette bit her lip, seemingly unable to reply.

Trinidad finally found her voice. "That's ridiculous. You have no right to barge in here and accuse Juliette of murder. She would never do such a thing."

Tanya glared. "And you would know this how? You just blew into town a few weeks ago to open your little ice cream store. Or maybe you think you know her just because you two were dumb enough to marry the same crook. That gives you a sisterly bond or something?"

Trinidad was too shocked to rustle up a response.

Quinn moved forward, palms up. "This isn't the place, Tanya."

"You shut up, Quinn. Juliette's a murderer, and the sooner everyone knows it, the better."

A cry escaped Juliette, and Trinidad moved closer, fearing she might faint. She rubbed comforting circles onto Juliette's back.

Quinn opened his mouth just as Chief Bigley marched through the door, took in the cluster of people, and beelined over.

"Chief," Tanya said, a smile of satisfaction forming on her lipsticked mouth. "Perfect."

"Ms. Grant, I'd like you to step outside for a moment, please," Chief Bigley said.

"No way," Tanya spat. "Juliette killed Kevin, and I'm not leaving until she admits it."

The chief seemed to grow a few inches taller as she stared Tanya down. "I wouldn't want to have to take you out of here forcibly, Ms. Grant," she said quietly. "But I will if you give me no other choice. I'm not asking you to leave. I'm telling you."

Tanya held her angry stare for a moment longer before she

whirled to the door. Doug drew close to the counter to avoid any contact as she hustled past.

"I'll speak to you soon," the chief called to Tanya before she slammed out.

"Thank you so much, Chief," Trinidad said. Trinidad handed Juliette a napkin to wipe the fresh tears that had begun to pour down her cheeks. "Tanya just ran in here, spouting wild accusations."

"Not so wild." Bigley's tone was infused with an odd inflection.

Quinn, Trinidad, and Juliette all jerked their heads to look at her. Even the unflappable Stan seemed startled at the chief's words.

"The initial reports from the crime scene came back," Chief Bigley said. Her gaze locked on Juliette's, her expression hard as steel. "Juliette Carpenter, I'm arresting you for the murder of Kevin Heartly."

Chapter Four

SECONDS TICKED BY IN EXCRUCIATINGLY slow motion. The chief walked Juliette outside. Trinidad and Quinn followed as if in a trance. Noodles stayed inside with Doug who seemed uncertain whether to stay or follow. On the way, Bigley read Juliette her Miranda rights.

Trinidad's brain clouded as if she was trying to surface from the bottom of a deep, murky pool. What was happening? She must be in the grip of a nightmare.

You have the right to remain silent...

Anything you say can be used against you...

Lawyer...

Questioning...

The snap of the handcuffs securing Juliette's wrists jarred Trinidad out of her stupor. "But, Chief..." she started.

Chief Bigley ignored her, guiding Juliette into the back seat of the squad car.

Juliette gulped in some air and looked at Trinidad full-on. Her voice came out in a hoarse croak. "I was jealous and spiteful, I will admit that. I was furious at Kevin, and I should have behaved differently, but I did not harm him in any way. And that is the absolute truth." Her voice broke on the last word.

Trinidad considered the woman before her—young, pretty, hurt—fear tumbling across her face in rolling waves. Before Gabe, Trinidad had thought she was a good judge of character, able to read the hearts of the people she met in spite of their exteriors. Her father always said she was a "wise, old soul" when it came to people. She felt, down in her bones, that Juliette was being honest, but could she still trust herself to make a judgment when she'd been so profoundly fooled? She tried to reach back to the time before Gabe, to feel the confidence in herself again, the courage to believe in someone.

Sucking in a deep breath, she let the words out. "Juliette, it is going to be okay. I believe you, and I am going to help you however I can."

An unsteady flicker of a smile showed on Juliette's face before the chief closed the door. Quinn and Trinidad stood silent as the chief's car vanished in the distance.

"I can't fathom what just happened," Quinn said.

"Me neither. Juliette is not a killer."

"Yes, she is."

Trinidad had forgotten all about Tanya who was watching the proceedings. Her eyes were red-rimmed and puffy as she turned to them, arms crossed in front of her like a shield.

"I'm sorry," she said. "I shouldn't have handled it like that, especially in a public place, but I was so… I mean, he's dead, and I thought we were going to be together for the rest of our lives." Her mouth trembled and tears shone on her lashes. "Stupid me. I thought I'd found my soul mate."

Trinidad inhaled a steadying breath. "I'm sorry for your loss, truly, but Juliette didn't kill him."

Tanya's brow furrowed. "Look, I know you're trying to befriend her, but you need to see the truth. She found out that Kevin was still dating me. He tried to let her down easy, even went to see her at her work yesterday morning, but she couldn't deal with it. He told me she threw something at him and demanded he leave. She left an angry phone message on his cell. The breakup probably tipped her over the edge after what happened with her low-life ex-husband."

Trinidad stayed quiet for a moment, fighting for control. "She was upset. Betrayal will do that to a person, no matter what their history."

Tanya's lips tightened. "Juliette will go to prison for what she did. If you were smart, you'd be careful about befriending a woman like that. After all, what do you really know about her?" Tanya walked away, shoulders hunched, arms still wrapped around her torso.

"This is unreal," Trinidad said, her body beginning to shake.

Quinn put an arm around her shoulders. "Let's go back inside, okay? You need to sit down, and there's someone we should talk to right away."

"Who?"

"Stan."

Trinidad was momentarily confused until she remembered. The person Juliette most needed in her corner now was a lawyer, and Stan was the only lawyer in Sprocket as far as she knew.

Quinn held the door open as they returned to the coffee shop. Noodles sat by Doug's side, accepting worried pets from the man. Stan greeted her with a pair of tongs in one hand and a tray of pecan tarts in the other. Every patron in the shop stared at them, obviously having been riveted by Tanya's outburst and Juliette's arrest.

Stan's sister Meg hustled up, the customary pencil tucked behind her ear. "I'll man the helm. You will need some privacy."

Stan acknowledged her with a grateful pat on the arm. "Meg will take your orders," he said to the patrons. "Do try the strawberry tartlets, won't you?"

"Can you watch Noodles, Doug?" Quinn called.

Doug replied with one firm nod.

With that, Stan ushered Trinidad and Quinn to a tiny office. "I believe I know what you are after, and I must tell you that my lawyering skills are rusty. I've been spending more time with lemon bars than litigation, though my license is still current."

Quinn chuckled. "You helped me work through that incident when that guy tried to sue us for knocking over his fence with our truck." He shot a look at Trinidad. "We didn't do it, by the way, and Doug didn't appreciate all the profanity from the man. I sure couldn't stomach him upsetting my brother." There was hint of ferocity in his words. Quinn would not accept anyone mistreating Doug, she surmised. "Anyway," he continued, "Stan worked it all out, and it didn't cost us anything. He's a genius."

Stan waved the praise away. "I appreciate the compliment, but it is a long way from a possible misdemeanor to a murder defense."

Vince Jr. appeared in the office doorway, quieting the threesome. His arms were filled with books, and there was an unmistakable scent of garlic and basil emanating from his Pizza Heaven T-shirt. He risked letting go of the book pile with one hand to hike up his pants. "What's going on? I just saw Juliette in the back of Bigley's squad car. Meg said not to come back here, but I had to know."

Trinidad figured they had to give Juliette's part-time storage facility employee some sort of information. "She has been accused of something she didn't do. She needs a lawyer."

His eyes rounded to Oreo size. "Is she being arrested? For what?" He blinked. "Is this about Heartly's murder? I heard all the gossip at the pizza shop, people saying she was spurned in love or whatever. No way was she involved with a murder. What can I do? How can I help?"

"We'll let you know," Stan said with a reassuring smile.

"But I'm sure I can do something. I know I can."

Trinidad looked at him closer. There was something in his words, a hint of desperation that made her think Vince might have feelings for his employer that exceeded the bounds of a work relationship. "I'm sure she's really going to appreciate that, Vince. If there's anything you can do to keep things going at Store Some More, when you're not working at the pizza shop, I know that would mean a lot to her."

He nodded hard, shoulders lifting. "Okay. I can do that. I'll keep track of the mail and bills and answer phone calls and stuff." He scribbled his cell number on a paper napkin and thrust it at Trinidad. "Call me if you think of anything else."

He seemed hesitant to leave, but Stan rose and eased him out the door.

Vince left with more vehement promises to help.

Stan sighed. "I have to be going as well. Juliette will need a friendly face when she's finished with booking."

Booking. Trinidad swallowed hard. She knew what that meant from having been a courthouse stenographer. Her new friend would be fingerprinted, undergo a DNA swab, face a humiliating body search, have her photo taken, and relinquish all her personal belongings. Then she would be locked in a holding cell, a cold, cement room with a stainless steel sink and a commode in plain view. Goosebumps prickled Trinidad's skin.

"Bail...?" she squeaked.

Stan stopped her with a gesture. "Sometime in the next twenty-four hours, the judge will hear her bail request. There's nothing we can do to speed up the process. For now, we'll all need to be patient. I'll let you know as soon as I've met with her."

Trinidad's stomach heaved as she watched Stan go. She felt Quinn's palm on her back. "Speaking of which, is there anything I can do for you?"

She gulped in a breath. "Tell me you don't believe Juliette is a killer."

He paused, head cocked, blue eyes glimmering. "For what it's worth, I think she's completely innocent."

Trinidad let out a breath she hadn't known she was holding. "I am so glad to hear you say that."

"But my opinion isn't worth much."

"We have to dig up something to help her, an alibi or witness or even someone with a motive to kill him besides Juliette."

He frowned. "I don't really know how to go about rooting out important evidence. I'm a nut farmer, which doesn't really lend itself to the detective stuff. Before that I was an Army mechanic who barely made it through high school. Not real well qualified for sleuthing."

"Well, I'm an ice cream vendor, so I don't have the credentials either. But I am going back to my shop, and maybe something will come to me. I do my best work surrounded by sugar and cream." She hugged herself. "Besides, right now I can't think of anything else to do here." She noticed Vince had left a textbook on the coffee shop table. She gathered it up, figuring she could drop it at the pizza place, since she didn't know where he lived.

Quinn shoved his hands into his pockets. "Maybe we can brainstorm together. Want some help at the store?"

She let out a gusty sigh. "I would love it. The twins aren't able to work today, so I'm on my own."

Truthfully, she did not want to be alone to wrestle with her thoughts in solitude. The shock of what had transpired was too much to be borne in solitude. They let themselves out of the shop, Doug holding the door for their exit. She'd expected Noodles to be right behind, but he wasn't. She led them out and saw him trotting up the sidewalk, the forgotten bag of banana squares clenched in his teeth.

"Thanks, Noodles," she said, carrying the bag inside.

Quinn watched in wonder. "Your dog brought you the treats?"

"In his younger days, he was trained as a service dog, but he flunked out. His life goal is to be helpful, and I never know what form that will take. He gets confused, but he always means well."

She stored the treats for later.

Job done, Noodles flopped on his cushion in front of the counter, and she donned an apron, handing one to Quinn. Doug settled in at a small table and began to use the paper cutter she'd left there to trim the flyers.

"Oh, thank you, Doug. The boys didn't have time to get that job done."

Doug nodded, but did not look at her.

Quinn took the wooden spoon she offered and stirred the whole milk, heavy cream, sugar, and scraping of vanilla bean she added to the pot while she set it on the burner to heat.

The rituals of the kitchen soothed her. While Quinn kept an eye on the warming cream, she combined eggs, sugar, and salt. She was deep in thought about Juliette when she realized Quinn was talking to her.

"Oh, sorry. What was that?"

"I said this ice cream business is more of a science than I realized."

"The difficult part is making the base. After that, it's up to the machinery." When the milk mixture was almost simmering, she removed it from the heat. "Has to cool now."

He sniffed. "Smells good. How do we know when it's cool enough?"

She handed him a rubber glove. "Stick your finger in there for ten seconds. If you can stand it, it's perfect."

He laughed. "And I thought nut farming was difficult." When he pronounced the temperature tolerable, she directed him to add it, in a slow stream, to the eggs to temper them before she dumped it all back into the milk mixture.

"Stir in an 's' pattern," she directed Quinn.

"Why?"

"Because that's how my grandpa always did it. Papa Luis said if you pick any other letter, it doesn't turn out right."

He grinned. "I think I'd like to meet your Papa Luis."

"Maybe when all this settles down and I get the shop up and running, he can come for a visit. He'd like you, I think."

She realized he would, too. Papa Luis appreciated hard work, humility, and a deep commitment to family. Of course, there were few people Papa could not get along with.

When the custard was done, she poured it through the funnel into the ice cream mixer and started the timer for ten minutes. The machine spun along with her thoughts. What was Juliette enduring? Kevin's family? Was there a killer tucked in amongst the people of Sprocket, or had it been a crime of opportunity by a stranger passing through?

After the timer dinged, Quinn held the stainless steel container while Trinidad scraped out the ice cream. Before she put it in the walk-in freezer, she dished them all up some of the delicate concoction.

"Thinking food," she said. "Consider it soft serve."

Doug cupped the paper bowl and admired the glistening, white dessert, speckled with flecks from the vanilla pods. His whole demeanor was alive with wonder. It reminded her of the moment when Papa Luis would open the top of the old, battered churn, and they would dive in with spoons while her mother wasn't looking.

Quinn rolled his eyes after a mouthful and his reaction made her heart beat faster. "Fantastic. Best I've tasted, and, believe me, I've packed down a boatload of vanilla ice cream since Doug came to live with me."

She chuckled. "When was that?"

"About twelve years ago. I thought I was going to be a lifer in the Army, but, during my last tour, my dad died, and Mom couldn't manage Doug's care on her own. So he went to a group home."

Doug stared at his ice cream, but he suddenly grew very still.

Quinn laid a finger, feather light, on his brother's arm just for a moment. "It wasn't a good fit. As soon as I came back here, I moved him in with me. There's a little ramshackle structure on the farm property we fixed up for the two of us. Mom passed a month later." He blinked, and she thought she caught a glimmer of moisture in his eyes. "I sure do miss her; we both do. We had a lot to learn about each other, and it was rough going in spots, but we're past that now. Doug and I are a great team, aren't we?" He nodded to his brother. "We've kept the farm running and even turned a small profit."

Doug scooped another spoonful into his mouth without responding.

"Got siblings, Trinidad?" Quinn said.

"One brother. He lives with my grandpa and my mother in Miami." When he wasn't creating havoc elsewhere, she didn't add. "He's a free spirit. I always admired his fearlessness, but he gave my parents fits over the years. My dad's gone now, so it's just Papa, Mother, Yolo, and me."

She felt the ache at being apart from them. They fell into silence until the ice cream was all gone.

"You know," Quinn said slowly, "I've been thinking about Juliette's situation. I don't like to gossip, but I remembered just now that Tanya dated someone else here in town for a short while. Actually, it might have been while she was seeing Kevin."

"Who?"

"Guy named Sonny Petrakis. He owns a painting business. Friend of Kevin's, I think. High school buddies, maybe."

"Is it possible that Sonny killed Kevin because he was jealous?"

"Possible, I guess. From what I hear, Sonny upset Tanya's father somehow and got himself banned from the house."

"How did that come about?"

"I don't know the particulars. Makes me think, though."

"Think what?"

Quinn pursed his lips in thought. "If Kevin found out Tanya was unfaithful to him, maybe they got into some sort of altercation and..."

"And Tanya killed him. But wouldn't she have left some evidence behind?" Trinidad mulled it over.

"Far-fetched, I guess."

"At least it is something to consider." Could Tanya's insistence that Juliette was the killer be a smoke screen? Could she really lie that convincingly? *You should know people can be brilliant liars, Trin,* she thought sourly.

Quinn looked at the wall clock, a cheerful item with a cone-shaped pendulum and each hour represented by a different colored scoop of ice cream. "Thanks for the dessert. Doug and I'd better head back to the farm."

"My pleasure. Thank you both for your help," she said.

He tipped an imaginary cap. "Anytime, ice cream lady." His smile wavered. "People in Sprocket are good folks. Sorry your introduction to town has been so rough."

More like murderous, she thought, as she watched the door close behind them.

Chapter Five

SINCE NOODLES WAS NOT EXACTLY a morning pup, she coaxed him to the Shimmy and Shake Shop Friday before sunup with a full arsenal of treats. In order to sweeten the canine pot, she had replaced his thin dog cushion with a yard sale beanbag chair, which she set up in the front counter area. He immediately flopped into the squishy depths and began to snore. Stan had texted late the previous night, asking her to stop by the coffee shop before it opened. She hoped it might possibly be good news, but her gut told her she was dreaming.

Vince's forgotten textbook still lay on the counter. Scooping it up, she hurried to Full of Beans, rapping on the front window. Stan unlocked the door and greeted her with a genial smile and a cup of coffee.

"Did you talk to Juliette?"

He nodded. "She's holding up okay, under the circumstances. I have accepted a $1 fee, and I am officially representing her."

"What about bail?"

He frowned. "The judge is not inclined to issue bail in this situation."

"What? Why? She has no prior history of violence."

"He believes her to be a flight risk."

"That's ridiculous."

He shrugged. "There are some things we can influence. This judge is not one of them. Juliette's arraignment is in a couple of days, where we will enter our not guilty plea. A trial date will be set, and we will begin several rounds of pre-trial conferences to discuss admissible evidence, witnesses, etc. From there, the pre-trial hearing..."

"Stan," she wailed. "This could take months."

He sighed. "Yes."

"I want to see her."

"She submitted your name for a jail visit. I can describe the particulars later, but let me tell you about your new job before..."

The knock on the shop door startled them both.

"We will have to wing it, as you Yanks say." Stan unlocked it to allow Chief Bigley to enter in sweatpants and a T-shirt.

"My morning off," she explained. "On my way for a run, but I thought we might as well chat and get it over with. This is a favor to you, Stan."

"Thank you for stopping by. I would greatly appreciate hearing on what grounds my client was arrested."

"Your client? So that's official now?"

"I am Juliette's counsel, yes. We formalized our agreement a brief while ago at the jail."

Bigley smiled and accepted the cup of coffee he handed her. "Well you've got to be the most polite lawyer I've ever met."

Trinidad secretly agreed.

Stan nodded graciously. "Mother always said there's never an excuse to behave like less than a gentleman. In all my twenty years practicing law in New York, I have not had occasion to disappoint Mum." He gestured to Trinidad. "This kind lady is acting as my paralegal."

Paralegal? Was that the new job Stan hinted at? Well, she'd

certainly observed enough of the justice system during her disaster with Gabe and her stenography work to make an honest stab at it. Embracing her role, she pulled a notepad from her purse, flipping past the first page, which was a running list of ice cream shop needs. She licked the tip of her pencil, just for effect.

Bigley raised an eyebrow. "So, you're a paralegal now, too?"

"Unofficially," Stan and Trinidad said at the same time.

Bigley chuckled and then her smile vanished. "Believe me, this brings me no pleasure. You'll see it in the file soon enough, and we'll discuss it at pre-trial. Juliette admits that Kevin Heartly came to see her Wednesday morning around nine at her place of business to apologize for an argument they'd had because she'd gotten wind he was dating Tanya Grant. She became angry and told him to leave, by her own admission."

Trinidad thought about the popcorn bit she'd found stuck to her shoe. Angry enough to hurl his popcorn offering in his face.

"All right," Stan said. "So, Mr. Heartly was in fine fettle when he left Juliette's at nine a.m."

"He picked up Tanya for a ride and returned her about noon, which is when you spoke to him, Miss Jones. Correct?"

Trinidad nodded. "Yes. He went into his shop and slammed the door. I drove to Logan's Nut Farm and returned several hours later. I took the nuts over to Kevin's about 3:30. Warren drove up, and I entered the Popcorn Palace and…found him."

She nodded. "Yes. We checked all that out."

Trinidad swallowed. The chief had been looking at her as a suspect too, of course.

"There was a threatening message on Mr. Heartly's recovered cell phone recorded on Tuesday night. Juliette admits to leaving it."

"The phone call, the message, that's all circumstantial," Trinidad surprised herself by saying. It seemed to surprise Stan as well.

"As a matter of fact, it is," he agreed. "But the chief is good at her job, so I will wager there is more coming."

Bigley cocked her head, considering. "I could tell you to wait for the report, but, like I said, I take no joy in this. The wooden paddle found at the crime scene..."

Trinidad pictured that enormous stirring paddle, the one she'd found on the floor, smeared with Kevin's blood.

"The supposed murder weapon," Stan prompted.

"The soon-to-be proven murder weapon, says the coroner who extracted splinters of it out of Kevin Heartly's cranium. He'll make it official when he concludes. I promised him I'd share my secret trout fishing spot if he gave me his thoughts early." She shrugged. "The benefit of small-town connections."

Trinidad's lungs squeezed tight. She could almost feel the grenade about to explode right there.

Bigley continued. "Kevin was kind of protective about that paddle. He never let anyone else touch it. There were only two sets of fingerprints on it: Kevin's," she paused, "and Juliette's."

Her heart fell. Juliette's fingerprints were on the murder weapon?

The chief got up. "So you can see, we had plenty to make an arrest. That's all I can say right now. The remainder will be in the report."

Trinidad shot to her feet. "Is she okay?"

Bigley shrugged. "No better or worse than any other resident of county jail. If she puts you on her visitor list, you can go see for yourself."

Trinidad could only imagine how terrified Juliette must be. She clutched her notepad and pencil to still the trembling in her fingers.

Stan, on the contrary, seemed perfectly in control, as if they were chatting about the upcoming Fourth of July festivities in Upper Sprocket. "Thank you for your time and cooperation, Chief

Bigley. We are so very appreciative. By the way, do you happen to have a time of death worked out?"

"The coroner will issue his findings, of course, but he had to have been killed between the time Trinidad greeted him and Tanya and the time she returned to find his body. Juliette says she was at work during that whole window, but there's no one to corroborate that since Vince Jr. left to deliver pizzas."

No alibi. Fingerprints. The walls seemed to move a few feet closer, within smothering distance.

"I understand and appreciate the information, Chief Bigley. Thank you again. I will need to talk with my client."

"You know where to find her." The chief shrugged noncommittally, but Trinidad caught the gleam of something very much like satisfaction. Was she pleased to have made such a quick arrest? Or was it a touch of pleasure at having arrested the woman who had vociferously renounced her baby brother? Tit for tat.

"I take no pleasure in this..." Or did she?

The chief excused herself. Stan walked Trinidad to the door. She shivered in spite of the heat building. "What's going to happen now?"

"I will read through the file when it's released to me and see what else I can find out."

"She didn't do it, Stan."

He gently squeezed her wrist. "Then we will use all the legal means at our disposal to make sure she's released."

"Do you think you can defend her?"

"If I can't, I will advise her to hire a lawyer who can do better." He walked with her through the rose-scented courtyard, which still preserved some of the morning cool.

"In the meantime, we will stay quiet about what's gone on here, and I'll let you know if there is anything specific you can do to help. Quinn also."

Trinidad mulled it all over as she slung Vince's textbook under her arm and walked back along the sidewalk. Thoughts gurgled through her like ice cream in a milkshake machine. Snippets of Juliette's angry phone threat, her lack of alibi...

Gritting her teeth, she strode along. Up and down Main Street, preparations were being made for the upcoming Fourth of July extravaganza. The owner of Bait and Tackle Too was unfurling some red, white, and blue bunting to hang under the canvas awning. On the empty lot at the corner, three young men were constructing a fireworks booth, advertising explosive fun of the safe and sane variety. She harbored doubts. Lighting something on fire and shooting it over the dry grassy hills around Upper Sprocket did not sound safe or sane.

Pizza Heaven, a neat, stuccoed building with an enormous painting of a pizza slice on the front was not yet open. When she bent down to leave Vince's textbook on a bench by the front step, a flush-cheeked, round woman tugged open the door.

"Good morning," Trinidad said.

"Back atcha. I'm Virginia. My husband Vince and I run this cozy nest."

"I'm Trinidad. I know your son, Vince Jr. He left his book, so I thought I could return it here for him."

"That's my youngest, all right," she beamed. "He does deliveries for us when he isn't in school or working at the storage place."

"Which is practically never," boomed a voice from inside.

Virginia offered a rueful smile and patted her bun of silver-streaked black hair. "That is Vince Sr. We have another son, Vance. He's in medical school."

Trinidad smiled. "All V names?"

"Yes, that way we won't forget our names when we're old."

"We're already old," the voice shouted from the back.

She lowered her voice. "Vince Sr. is cranky today. His doctor told him to go on a diet, and he's been off carbs for approximately fifteen minutes and change. You'd think he was being shot with arrows."

"I need these boxes folded. Where is that kid of ours?" Vince Sr. thundered.

Virginia rolled her eyes. "Vince had some studying to do, as I already explained to my husband." She hesitated. "Or he might be putting in more hours at the Store Some More. He is convinced that Juliette Carpenter is innocent as the sunrise."

"And you aren't?"

Virginia hesitated. "My son is always wanting to defend the underdog, whether they deserve it or not. I think she may not be completely innocent, but Kevin probably had other enemies."

"Ginny," Vince Sr. hollered from the kitchen. "Where's the new box of sausage? I'm in the freezer, and I'm getting frostbite on my…"

"Coming!" Virginia shouted hastily. "Sorry. He's not usually this cranky, but there's the diet, and Vince Jr. has been preoccupied. Truth is, he just doesn't want to have anything to do with the family pizza business."

Trinidad knew exactly what it felt like to fail to meet a parent's expectations. Her mother Claudia was lovely, a Miss Chicago in her youth, a genteel hostess and jewelry designer. Unfortunately, her daughter had arrived resembling her stocky, shuffling father. It must be true that opposites really did attract, because her plumber father Manny was more at home under the sink than anywhere else.

She remembered her mother's advice, delivered in those precise, musical tones.

"Can't you clip your hair back, Trinidad? Stand up straight. Put on something with a waist. It's like you're trying to wear a disguise."

Trinidad's puff of hair, her short arms and legs, the chin that was somehow too wide, too square, left her far short of her mother's beauty. Maybe she was trying to wear a disguise, something to make her invisible, since she could not make herself beautiful.

When she'd announced her intention to become a court stenographer, her mother's expression had gone from troubled to optimistic.

"Ah. I see. Lots of eligible men in the courtroom; just steer clear of the criminals."

The irony was, she'd met and fallen for one of those eligible men while he was there giving a statement, and he'd turned out to be a criminal, and an unfaithful spouse to boot.

"Terrible what happened to Kevin." The comment snapped Trinidad back to the present.

Trinidad nodded. "You said you thought he might have other enemies. Why would you say that?"

She flushed. "Oh, I shouldn't talk out of school."

Trinidad stayed quiet, a sure way to get someone to start talking, she'd heard a cop say.

Virginia lowered her voice. "Anyone who loves gambling, you know…"

"Gambling?"

"Yes. Kevin would get together with his friend, and they'd play online poker. I only know because he said as much when he picked up pizzas for him and his friend, double thick crust, one combination and one pineapple, sausage, and onion. It wasn't just a one-time thing, either. They ordered poker pizzas at least three times a month. What do you think happens to people when they gamble? Sooner or later they lose, and they have to pay the piper."

A noise from the back made Virginia roll her eyes again. "I have to go. Nice to meet you."

Trinidad handed over the textbook.

"Vince will be appreciative. Thank you on his behalf."

"No problem." Before the door closed fully, Trinidad stopped it. "Virginia, you said Kevin used to gamble with a friend. Someone local?"

Virginia sniffed. "As local as they come. Warren Wheaton, Mr. Pineapple and Sausage himself."

Trinidad was left alone in a waft of garlic-scented air.

So, Warren was a good buddy of Kevin's, a gambling buddy at that. Funny how he'd neglected to mention that when he'd been waiting with her while the police examined the body. He certainly hadn't looked too devastated to find out his friend had been murdered.

She took a frontage road that paralleled a sleepy residential area on one side and a stretch of apple orchard on the other. The scent of fruit drifted through her open window. Three blocks further she passed a house that had to be Juliette's since it was buzzing with police activity. Two police officers carried a computer monitor and a laptop out her front door. A cluster of people were gathered there including Warren, Vince Jr., and a whip-thin woman with a chop of silver hair.

She braked to a stop, parked and hopped out.

Warren noticed her immediately. "Terrible, isn't it?"

"News travels fast," the woman with him said. Her black T-shirt was fringed at the edges, black beads added for flair.

"This is Cora Fieri," Warren said. "She's the theater manager in town."

"Welcome to Sprocket," she said dryly. "It's a nice town, murders aside. Never would have thought Juliette would be accused."

"She didn't do it," Vince said stoutly.

Warren stroked his lower lip. "The police are all over her place, though. They must think they're gonna uncover something incriminating."

"How did everyone find out so quickly?" Trinidad said.

Cora snorted. "This is the biggest news since the laundromat caught on fire. Folks in this town are gonna notice in a hot minute."

"Do you both live around here?"

He pointed to a narrow house on a small lot, rich with a range of flowering plants. "Right there. It was built in the seventies. It's got the mustard carpet and avocado-green phone to prove it."

"He's not lying," Cora said. "I live in the townhome right behind him, and he resists my every effort to help him bring his decor into the next millennium."

"Not everything has to be painted, stenciled, or repurposed, Cora," he said.

"I could revamp that old bookshelf you got in a heartbeat. The paint's on sale, too. I called to tell you." She glared at him. "Why aren't you answering your cell, anyway?"

He shrugged. "A man needs a break from his technology tether."

"You lost it again, didn't you?"

He shrugged. "Nah. Left it at the nursery over in Brighton. I'll get it tomorrow after they open."

Another police officer walked by with a box of what appeared to be papers. Cora's gaze drifted over the taped yard before her attention snapped back to Trinidad. "Wagging tongues in town say you and Juliette are friends. Did she kill him?"

The bluntness of the question left Trinidad sputtering for a moment. "No," she and Vince said at once.

"Certainly not," Trinidad added for emphasis.

Vince's cheeks went dark. "I mean, this is insane. Juliette had nothing to do with Kevin's murder. He wasn't worth her time to date, let alone kill." His fuzzy upper lip quivered as though he might be about to cry. Warren clapped a hand on his back. "Keep steady, son. If the cops have enough evidence to arrest her…"

"Don't say it, Warren," Cora said severely.

He hiked up a shoulder. "My uncle Jerry was a cop, and he said he never did arrest anybody who didn't deserve it."

Cora sighed. "Your uncle Jerry lost his shirt betting on the ponies, like someone else I know."

"Yeah, but he was a good cop, other than his gambling problem. Maybe Juliette had her reasons. Kevin was dallying around with her and Tanya at the same time, and, well, considering Juliette's history with men..."

Trinidad went cold and then hot. She wanted to turn and walk away, but Juliette's past was her past too, her reputation, her friend to defend. "Juliette and I married the wrong man," she said. "That is not a crime."

"Too true," Cora chimed in.

Warren scratched at his eyebrow.

"Have the police asked you about your relationship with Kevin?" Trinidad said to him.

Warren jerked. "Me? We were pals, is all."

She was still irate at his earlier comment. Time to put manners aside. "Weren't you gambling buddies?"

His cheeks went rosy. "Man, you sure didn't waste time shoveling up the town dirt. Yeah. We enjoyed some online gaming. That's not a crime, and, if the chief asks me about it, I'm happy to fill her in, chapter and verse."

Trinidad made a mental note to be sure the chief knew everything about another possible suspect. Warren had assumed his affable smile. "Got bigger crimes going on in this town besides some harmless gambling. Looks to be more of a love triangle thing to me."

Vince shouldered his backpack. "Juliette wasn't into Kevin anymore, anyway. She broke things off when she realized he was dating Tanya. I heard her. She said she wouldn't go out with him anymore if he were the last man on the planet."

"When did you hear her say that?" Trinidad pressed.

Vince shifted. "Tuesday night. I went by late to get my paycheck. She was talking on the phone, real angry. I figured she was talking to Kevin or maybe leaving him a voicemail." He grinned. "Told him off good and proper for going to the lake with Tanya."

But that wasn't the end of it. Kevin showed up at the Store Some More with a peace offering the next morning that had infuriated Juliette, and then he likely called her cell while Trinidad was there.

Vince looked crestfallen. "I told the police that she broke up with him." He sighed. "I thought it would clear her, but I don't think it helped at all."

"How long were you at the office the day Kevin was murdered?" Trinidad asked.

"Wednesday? Only until a few minutes after you left. Then I had to go help deliver pizzas." He groaned. "If only I'd stayed, she might have had an alibi."

"Easy son," Warren said. "Don't worry. It will all come out in the wash. I guess, though, you probably need to look for a new second job unless you can run the storage business while she's in the clink."

Vince colored. "I know some stuff. I can enter computer data and keep the place secure and all."

But Warren wasn't listening. He raised a brow at Cora. "Is there any work at the theater? Besides him advising on the props for the play, I mean?"

"We don't need any more advice," Cora snapped.

"Ah, let the kid use his smarts. He's learned all that artsy stuff, right? Might as well find something to do with all that dusty, old info. For sure he's never gonna pay the bills with it."

Vince's nostrils flared. "You sound like my father. Juliette is the only person around here who understands the significance of my field. For your information, the study of art history provides us with an awareness of economic, political, religious, and social history and the ability to think critically."

"Right. Only thing that's missing from that list is earning a paycheck." He looked at Cora. "So, we got a job for the professor here or what?"

"No need," Vince said coldly. Trinidad admired his self-control. "I am going to continue on at Store Some More like nothing's happened until I am told otherwise."

Trinidad felt like hugging the skinny kid to thank him for his loyalty.

Warren pursed his lips. "Sure, sure, no worries. And you can always boost up your hours at Pizza Heaven."

Vince's face fell, and he turned and strode away without another word.

"Sometimes you can be a class A chump," Cora said.

"What did I say? I was just trying to help."

Trinidad left the mystified Warren and the milling spectators behind. She hopped into the car, goosed the engine and caught up with Vince. "Want a ride? You left your book at the coffee shop, so I dropped it at Pizza Heaven."

He shrugged. "Oh, thanks. I have class in an hour. If you can drop me there, I can get my book beforehand. That would be great." He climbed in, and she rolled down the window to cool the car. They passed the turnoff to Three Egg Lake, stopping behind a lumbering RV.

"Plenty of strangers in town," she mused.

"They come in to camp by the lake, get a spot for the holiday weekend. The fireworks bring them here in droves." He sounded morose. "That's what passes for excitement in this place."

And a juicy murder doesn't hurt either, she thought. There seemed to be plenty of people excited about poor Kevin. "You don't want to stay here forever, I take it?"

"No way. Soon as I get my master's degree, I'm applying to teach overseas at a university. I want to travel. Juliette and I talked about it all the time. She wanted to see the world, too."

Trinidad thought of her grandpa. People could have such opposite goals in life. Her grandfather had loved to travel in his younger years, and he'd regaled Trinidad's mother with tales of the beautiful, romantic town two hours outside Havana, where he'd first encountered his future wife. Papa Luis and his bride had met on the wide cobblestone streets. It was also where he'd proposed in front of the beautiful Iglesia de la Santísima cathedral. Decades later Trinidad's mother had named her daughter after the gorgeous location.

Conversely, her father Manny was perfectly content with his head in the pipes under a kitchen sink right up until he'd died of a heart attack shortly after her marriage to Gabe.

Now that Papa Luis was settling into his eighties though, his wanderlust was waning. He was happiest puttering around the pots he'd stuffed full of garlic, oregano, and cilantro in their Miami backyard greenhouse. No man-made marvel would ever compare in his mind to the wonder of watching a fat tomato unfold in all its glistening glory. Maybe she was more like her father. At the moment, all she wanted to do was hide in her tiny house with Noodles, pull the pillow over her head, and never come out.

But that would not help Juliette.

"Vince, did you know that Kevin was seeing both Juliette and Tanya?"

Vince shrugged. "Not until I overheard Juliette on Tuesday night, but it doesn't surprise me. He was always zipping around on his motorcycle, showing off his physique with those tight T-shirts. He was a jerk."

Sour grapes, she thought. The young beanpole of a student did not get much in the way of female attention, she imagined. She stopped outside the coffee shop while Vince unloaded himself. "Is it okay if I get your cell number?"

He looked wary. "I don't need any pity jobs, if that's what you're planning."

"Not for that. In case I think of some way we can help Juliette."

He blinked, then smiled. "Oh, okay. And I'll call you if I think of anything, too. Thanks. Juliette's been good to me, and, unlike everyone else around here, she's never made fun of my dreams. She probably wasn't even serious about Kevin."

Trinidad remembered the fury in Juliette's voice when she'd threatened to kill him. Vince may not want to believe it, but Kevin was more than just a casual friend.

Vince left, and Trinidad was alone with her thoughts. A memory niggled at her. What had Juliette said about needing a guard dog? Installing fake cameras? Could that have something to do with the current situation?

She would have to find out.

And all of a sudden, Trinidad realized her assignments were multiplying rapidly. She intended to start her own investigation, for what it was worth, to try and help her friend. Ice cream maker, paralegal, and detective. Why not?

Time to start serving up some justice in Upper Sprocket.

Chapter Six

TRINIDAD WAS LED INTO THE visitation room at the county jail at precisely 2:30 p.m. She'd had a moment to buy a few snacks at the vending machine, a trick recommended by Stan.

"The snacks sell out quick," he had told her. "It's one of the few creature comforts in jail."

Juliette was led in, pale and small in a stiff orange jumpsuit. Trinidad leapt to her feet, ready to embrace Juliette until the guard barked at her to sit. Cowed, she dropped into the chair and slid the candy bar and bag of pretzels across the wooden table, blinking hard to control the tears. "I...I figured you might not be getting, you know, good food," she babbled. "Here are few nibbles. It's all that was left in the machine. Next time, I'll..." Next time? How long would Juliette be jailed? Until her trial? And what if that didn't go her way?

"Thank you," Juliette said.

Trinidad swallowed and forced a smile. "Don't worry. Stan is working hard on this, and Quinn and Vince Jr. and I are trying to help in any way we can."

She nodded, eyes dull and smudged underneath with dark circles. "Is Vince able to run things at the Store Some More?"

"He's keeping it afloat."

"Not much new business, anyway, I'm sure," she said. "Who would want to rent from a murderer?"

"People don't think that." But Trinidad feared that many Sprocketerians believed, without question, that Juliette was a killer. The outsider who'd come to town, already the spurned woman with a tarnished reputation before she even arrived? By her own admission, she'd not made friends, except for Bonnie.

And me.

"Do you want me to contact Bonnie? She would probably love to talk to you."

Juliette shook her head with some violence. "No. Let her enjoy her vacation. I don't want Felice to know anything about it, anyway. I'd rather she think I just up and moved away." Juliette sniffed, and tears pooled in her eyes. "She calls me Auntie. How can she understand that her auntie was imprisoned for killing someone?"

Trinidad itched to take her hand, but she knew the guard would disapprove. "Okay, let's focus on what we can do to get you out of here. Do you remember when we met in your office? I had Noodles with me?"

"Yes. That feels like a lifetime ago."

"You said things had been strange and you could use a guard dog. Remember?"

"I guess so."

"You said there was someone prowling around Store Some More. Can you tell me any more about that?"

Juliette blinked. "Why does it matter now?"

"Because it might have something to do with who killed Kevin."

She straightened. "Oh. Okay. I drove over late on Sunday night to file some papers."

"What time, exactly?"

"I don't remember. Maybe 10:30 or so? I saw movement. I

thought at first it was a deer; they wander through once in a while on their way to the grassland behind the property. They stop and drink out of the birdbath sometimes. When I pulled into the drive, whatever it was ran away."

"Anything else?"

"I examined the units, and there were signs that it wasn't a deer, more like a person looking to steal."

"What signs?"

"Scratches on one of the unit padlocks, as if someone had been trying to pick it. The back door of the office was open, too. I thought, at the time, that Vince or I hadn't secured it properly, but it could have been jimmied. Fortunately, all the keys are in a safe, and I'm the only one with the combination. Maybe that's why they tried to break into the unit instead."

"Did they succeed?"

"No, the lock was secure. After that I put up the fake camera… I figured it would be a deterrent."

"Did you call the police?"

She pulled a face. "I wish I had now, but the fact of the matter is I bad-mouthed Gabe all over town. I didn't really think his big sis would go out of her way to help me." She sighed. "Telling her after the fact will only seem like I'm making things up to save myself."

"I'll have Stan arrange for her to hear you out anyway. Whose unit was tampered with?"

"Edward Lupin's."

Trinidad sat back in her chair. Edward Lupin, the junk collector.

Then it dawned on her. "Sunday was the day before you auctioned off his belongings, wasn't it?"

She nodded. "But I looked in that unit myself, Trinidad. There was nothing but trash in there. Piles of it."

The guard signaled that their visit was over. Juliette was led away after one helpless look at Trinidad.

"I'll see you soon," she called, but the door was already closing.

So, Lupin's unit was of interest to a prowler. Why risk breaking in for a bunch of trash, as Juliette put it?

One man's trash, she thought, *might be a treasure worth killing for.*

After communicating her conversation with Juliette to Stan, who promised to alert the chief about the potential break-in at Store Some More, Trinidad stopped at her tiny house to get her thoughts in order and fix Noodles a snack. She plonked herself in front of her laptop and tried to think like a detective. Lupin's mysterious storage unit remained an enigma.

Sensing her unease, Noodles shimmied to the refrigerator and yanked on the towel she'd tied around the handle. She waited to see what he'd bring to comfort her. It was a source of endless amusement.

He presented her first with a bottle of ranch salad dressing.

"Thank you, hon," she said, drumming her fingers on the table. What was the first thing a detective would do?

The dog's next soothing offering was a jar of dill pickle spears. She scratched his ears. "I'll eat some later, okay?" The screen threw her own frowning reflection back at her.

Finally, when Noodles arrived with a container of guacamole, she sighed and pushed her chair back. He crawled into her lap and licked her chin. She eyed the computer screen over the top of his fuzzy head as she massaged his sides.

She knew detectives tended to "follow the money." But who would benefit from Kevin's death? His family was out of the area, but that didn't mean they weren't his heirs. She'd heard a police investigator say crimes all boiled down to three motives: greed, love gone wrong, or power.

Her thoughts wandered to Gabe. So which camp had he fallen

into? She felt the familiar confusion as memories washed over her again. He had been greedy for love, it seemed, along with the money he'd embezzled.

"*We were meant for each other. You're my soul mate,*" she recalled him saying, and how the words had flown right to her heart. That she, plain, ordinary, shy, and clumsy Trinidad, might be the whole world to someone had thrilled her to the core. When something seems too good to be true, it usually is, she recalled her father saying in her teen years. The wisdom hadn't even dented her rosy-colored view of people in general and Gabe in particular—her unshakable belief that there was good in everyone. Only her divorce had stripped the world of its beautiful hues and left it painted in bitter tones of gray and black. She remembered Juliette's revelation that her life was divided into B.G. and A.G.

Someday, when she had the courage, perhaps she'd ask Bonnie and Juliette if Gabe had babbled to them about being soul mates. But what was the point? Build a wall around today and don't climb over it, Papa Luis had told her during her darkest period. And Juliette had no doubt felt the same thing, along with a healthy dose of anger to which she was entitled. How many people agreed with Warren that Juliette's anger at being betrayed by Gabe might easily turn her into a murderer? It was grossly unfair.

"All right," she said aloud, earning a look from Noodles. "Juliette needs us, and we have to do everything we can for her." It was odd to be needed, and somehow the knowledge warmed her inside.

Opening a new document, she made three columns: greed, love gone wrong, and power.

The greed column she left blank.

Love gone wrong? Tanya Grant certainly seemed to have strong feelings for Kevin. And Bigley already had Juliette fixed under the "scorned in love" motive.

Power? She could not think a guy who made popcorn for a

living had clout enough that someone would murder him to get a leg up. Revenge maybe? That was a way someone could exercise power over a foe. Blackmail? The cursor blinked at her as she sat and thought, time ticking away and Noodles overflowing her lap.

Though she didn't feel particularly hungry at dinnertime, she was restless, so she fixed herself a peanut butter and marshmallow fluff sandwich and a bowl of kibble with a wee bit of boiled egg for Noodles. Alone at the table, her thoughts wandered again to Gabe. He'd charmed her mother, the same way he'd done with her, arriving to meet her parents with flowers in one hand and a chessboard in the other, prepared to please.

Her mother had adored him at first sight, or perhaps she was just thrilled that a successful man was courting their socially awkward daughter. Her reaction bordered on giddy. Her father was more reserved but ready to like the young man who would play chess with him. Papa Luis, a chess champion in Cuba, declined to play with Gabe, a red flag if there ever was one.

That a patient, handsome, tenderhearted man would fall in love with her, and she with him, seemed so fanciful she'd had to pinch herself on a regular basis. Too good to be true, her inner skeptic had said. She should have listened to that inner skeptic. Only her grandfather had sensed something wrong with Gabe Bigley.

But, sometimes, regardless of the betrayal, the anger and hurt that shook her to her very foundation, she missed the love she'd had, or thought she'd had, with Gabe.

Shrugging off the angst, she forced down her dinner. When the shadows crept across the kitchen floor, she resumed her computer sleuthing. She turned her attention to searching the web for information about Kevin. Her curiosity made no practical sense, but she felt a burning desire to find out more about the life of the man she'd known for only a few scant weeks before his death.

His name popped up in her Google searches several times:

when he'd assumed ownership of the Popcorn Palace a decade before and his participation in various charity events, including a motorcycle ride to solicit toys for the underprivileged. Trinidad sat up higher when she saw a photo of Kevin participating in a show at the Vintage Theater. He was dressed in a tuxedo, a smiling woman dipped in his arms. The woman was pretty with a bouncy auburn wig and lips painted scarlet, Tanya Grant. In her arms she clutched a bouquet of pink roses. The play was entitled "Princess and the Pirate."

Tanya was the Princess.

The two items of information rolled around each other in Trinidad's brain. The Pink Princess rosebush waiting to be planted next to Kevin's front porch steps. The blooms that matched the bouquet Tanya held in the photograph. Had the rosebush been intended as a gift for Tanya? The cast picture led her to a different thought. She reached for her bag, pulling the crumpled theater flyer out and smoothing it.

Our Founding Fathers, *a patriotic extravaganza, opening July 5 for two weekends only. Featuring a talented cast of local singers, dancers, and actors, graciously sponsored by the Grant family. Tickets available now.* There was a number and a website. Trinidad pulled up the website and enlarged the tiny group photo. Tanya Grant was pictured there, too, standing next to Warren along with four other actors, but Kevin was apparently not in the cast. Did that indicate a rift had developed between Kevin and Tanya? Or, perhaps, it was just a busy time for Kevin, and he could not free up his schedule for theater.

She folded the flyer and was just reaching to return it to her purse when a different thought flashed across her mind.

What had Warren said when he was stopped in his van across the street from the popcorn shack?

"Right now, I got a cargo area full of flyers. Hot off the presses, or at least the copy machine." He'd said he hadn't even looked at them.

They'd been tucked securely in the back. But, if he'd just picked them up and stopped to wait for his van to cool off, how had one come to be flying around her feet? The only way that would have happened is if someone had opened the rear van doors, someone very close to the scene of the murder. Maybe they'd stashed something inside? What about Warren himself? Could he have arrived earlier, killed Kevin and stolen something from him, then driven around the block, appearing as if he'd just pulled up?

He was Kevin's gambling buddy and not overly broken up about his pal's murder. Perhaps he owed Kevin a debt he couldn't repay and decided to kill him? Warren, Kevin, Tanya. What did they all have in common? They had all acted in plays together. It was the best lead she had, but what did any of it have to do with her brainstormed motives—greed, love gone wrong, and power?

What should she do with her strange ideas? Talk to the police? Picturing Chief Bigley's face as she trotted out her oddball ponderings was enough to discourage that notion. She needed more to offer the chief than a vague suspicion. *Head to the theater and ask a few questions tomorrow,* she told herself. What harm could it do? It would take her mind off her current worry about Juliette and her fear that her shop would fall into a sinkhole of failure.

Determined to calm her mind in preparation for some restorative sleep, she walked with Noodles outside into the yard. Noodles did his business and ambled the fenced perimeter, which was home to nothing more than scruffy grass and a lopsided tree. They stayed outside, inhaling the faint whiff of a faraway barbecue. When the sky turned dark and the shadows crept in, Trinidad began to think of Kevin Heartly's body lying curled in the iron pot. Someone in this quaint little town was a killer.

She swallowed her sudden queasiness. "Okay, Noodles. Let's go back inside."

Something cracked through the air, whistling overhead. Reflexively, she ducked. The screech and glare told her it was a firecracker, probably launched by some teens hanging out in the empty lot along Main Street. Another shot up and burst into a shower of sparkles before it screamed back to earth. Noodles stiffened, nostrils quivering, and promptly went bananas, howling and tearing around the yard in a frenzy of fear.

"It's okay, Noodles," she hollered, but the dog would not be placated. She had adopted Noodles in late July the previous year, so she had never experienced the Fourth of July with him. She watched in horror as he careened to the gate. He slammed against the wood so hard it opened. He sprinted outside, howling.

"Noodles, stop!" Her scream did not seem to register as the terrified dog bolted. She ran after him, shouting at the top of her lungs. The road was dark in both directions, a desolate country lane without the benefit of streetlights. On either side of the roadway were tall trees and thick shrubbery. She stilled herself, trying to calm her panicked breathing so she could hear which way Noodles had taken. She caught only the whisper of leaves.

What should she do? How could she locate the frantic animal in the dark? With fumbling fingers, she found her cell phone and dialed the only person that came to mind.

"Quinn..." she panted. "I'm sorry to call, but...but..." She burst into tears.

"Trinidad? What's wrong? How can I help?"

She managed to stumble through the story. "Noodles is lost," she finished with a wail.

"I'll be right there. We'll find him."

Quinn rattled up in his truck less than a half hour later, with Doug in the passenger seat. He had two flashlights tucked in his back pockets. "Which direction did he go?"

She pointed. "That way, I think, but I'm not sure."

"Okay. Not much out that direction but Store Some More and a couple of orchards. There's a kind of trail down along the creek, so he might have headed there. Doug and I will drive along the bank real slow going south. You take the road northward. Text me if you find him, and we'll do the same."

He handed her a flashlight. "In case you need it."

Doug wore a strap-on headlamp around the brim of his baseball hat, which he switched on.

Grateful to have two willing searchers, Trinidad stopped only long enough to snatch her car keys from the tiny house. Quinn and Doug had already gone when she fired up the engine.

With the windows cranked down, she drove slowly along the road. Stopping every few minutes, she hollered for Noodles until her voice was raw. What if they didn't find him? What if he got run over?

"Stop it," she told herself. Traffic in Upper Sprocket at this hour of the night had to be next to nil. He was her best friend, her dearest companion. Tears welled up again, but she blinked hard. As she passed another mile, she saw the gleam of headlights as a truck approached.

"Be careful of my dog," she wanted to scream. As she neared the other vehicle, the road pinched across a small bridge, allowing only for one-way traffic. She pulled over and let the other driver across. He stopped when he came alongside.

Warren Wheaton rolled down his window. He looked startled, but then the easygoing smile was back in place. "Trinidad. Out for a midnight drive?"

"I'm looking for my dog. Have you seen him?"

"No, did he get out?"

"He was scared by a firecracker. He took off, and I'm trying to find him."

"Oh, gee. That's too bad. I will keep my eyes peeled." He started to creep along.

A question poked through her panic. "What are you doing out so late, Warren?"

"Me? Oh, I'm just taking a drive. It helps sometimes if I can't sleep. Chronic insomnia. Darnedest thing." She noticed a glow from his front shirt pocket, the gleam of a cell phone receiving a message.

"You got your cell phone back."

"Uh, yeah. Sure. Left it at the nursery, just like I said. Can't live without it for long. Crazy how dependent on technology we are, right? Anyway, I'll let you know if I see any sign of your pooch."

"Thank you," she said faintly as he drove away. Liar. He'd told Cora he would retrieve his cell phone the following day from the nursery in Brighton, and there it was in his pocket. Maybe he was lying about where he'd dropped it? Perhaps it had been him trying to burglarize Lupin's storage unit when Juliette interrupted him? Cora had said he hadn't been picking up his calls for several days. Had it been lost at Store Some More all this time?

He drove past, and she continued over the bridge. Brushing aside thoughts of Warren, she gave her undivided attention to finding Noodles.

Her dear, dear friend and faithful companion, the one who listened to her burdens, shadowed her every move and brought her jars of pickles from the fridge to cheer her up. There was no sign of him anywhere. Should she turn around? Keep moving forward? The car idled as she spun her mental wheels. Her cell phone buzzed with a text.

Found him. Taking him back to your place.

She was so thrilled she hardly managed the reply text. "On my way." Mumbling a prayer of gratitude, she cranked the Pinto into a U-turn. She zipped back to the tiny house where she found Quinn sitting on the front porch along with Doug and Noodles. Leaping from the car, she ran to them.

Doug was bent over Noodles, stroking his heaving sides, murmuring softly.

Tears drenched her face as Noodles caught sight of her and

sprinted, taking one giant leap and hurtling into her arms. She almost could not handle the seventy-pound dog and sank to the ground, cooing and crying over him.

Quinn approached. "He doesn't seem hurt in any way, just scared. We found him down by the creek, and it took some effort to convince him to come, but Doug just sort of hunkered down and sat until Noodles calmed enough to approach."

"Thank you. Thank you so much," Trinidad said, trying unsuccessfully to stop crying. "He's everything to me."

Doug nodded. "Fireworks are scary."

She blinked. It was the first time she'd ever heard him speak. "I think so, too."

"Yeah," Quinn added. "I can't stand them. Ever since I came home from Afghanistan. We usually hide on the Fourth of July and wait for it all to be over."

She laughed and hiccupped. "That sounds like a good idea to me. Thank you. Thank you both. Would you like to come inside for some water or something? Coffee?"

"I'm sure you and Noodles are ready to hit the sack," Quinn said. "We'll see you inside safely, and then we'll take off."

As if he'd understood every word Quinn said, Noodles jumped off Trinidad's lap and galloped to the front door. Trinidad followed. "I ran into Warren driving the opposite direction."

Quinn raised an eyebrow. "What was he doing out here at this time of night?"

"He said he couldn't sleep—chronic insomnia."

"Hmmm. I've seen him sleep through town council meetings, church services, and the high school baseball championship game. Do you think he was telling you the truth?"

"No." She quickly filled him in on Juliette's adventure in surprising the burglar, her suspicion about Warren's participation, and the cell phone in his pocket.

"I'll put on my sleuthing hat tomorrow and see what I can find out. I know a guy at the nursery, so I might be able to check out Warren's story," Quinn said.

Trinidad nodded. Quinn patted Noodles. "Take care of your Mama, now, and no more running away, okay?"

"Thank you again," she said with only a small hitch in her voice this time.

Quinn smiled, and it lightened his whole face. "Our pleasure. Anytime."

After closing and locking the door, Trinidad fixed a snack of leftover chicken for Noodles. He scarfed it up, licked his lips, and trotted over to retrieve her cell phone, dropping it into her lap. Sure enough, there was a voicemail waiting. She could never understand how he knew, since she kept her phone on silent.

"Good to know your spidey senses are still intact, Noodles." She played back the message.

"Hello, Trinidad? This is Candy Simon. I own Simon Real Estate here in town. I have a business proposition I'd love to discuss with you. Can you meet me tomorrow at Edward Lupin's place?" She rattled off an address. "I think it would be a mutually beneficial arrangement. I'd like to talk to you about catering an event for me."

Excited, Trinidad texted her agreement. She'd been thinking about ways to expand her business venture into some sort of mobile service, and a chat with Candy might be the start of something lucrative. Besides, she'd heard so much about Edward Lupin lately that she was curious to see his place.

She mused as she tucked herself onto the sofa. Noodles snored on his cushion right beside her, just in case there was another firecracker. Juliette said that someone had been snooping around Store Some More just before Edward Lupin's storage unit was auctioned off. Maybe the prowler figured there was something inside worth the risk?

Prowlers? Murder? It was too much for one night.

The most important thing was that Noodles was home and safe.

Her suspicions could wait until the morning.

With one arm slung over the side, Trinidad stroked Noodles's satin ears and accepted a warm lick in exchange. For the moment, at least, everything was all right. But how long would the moment of peace last?

Chapter Seven

SATURDAY MORNING ARRIVED CRUELLY EARLY, after the nighttime dog retrieval. Noodles dragged, too, but he managed to gobble his morning kibble before they made their way to the shop. Immediately, she set about preparing the brownie batter complete with chopped hazelnuts from Quinn's farm. Gratitude for the Logan brothers' dog rescue nearly made her cry again. To think of Quinn and his brother leaping into action to help find her traumatized dog… It gave her the shivers. Something would have to be done to help Noodles through the upcoming fireworks. Hunker in place as Quinn suggested? She was not sure that would be enough, since their tiny house was so near the lake.

After the brownies were baked, she cut them into star shapes using her antique cutters and adorned them with stripes of red, white, and blue frosting before she set them aside. They would be the perfect final flourish for the Fourth of July Freakshakes. A half dozen brownie stars went in a Tupperware container, a thank-you token for Quinn and Doug, and a couple set aside for the twins.

Carlos and Diego arrived and accepted their greeting from Noodles before they wolfed down a brownie each in the name of scientific testing.

The twins took inventory of the walk-in freezer, Diego ticking off items on a clipboard. "Two gallons of chocolate, one vanilla, caramel ripple, and a banana custard," he announced. "That's not enough, right?"

"I sincerely hope not. I'll work on more vanilla and a citrus variety for the Key Lime Pie Freakshake."

"What's that gonna have on it?" Carlos asked.

"Graham cracker crumbles, a white chocolate striped shortbread cookie, and a couple of lime-candy twists for drama."

"Oh, yeah. That's gonna be a hit."

Diego affirmed with a nod. "Mom will love it. Key lime pie is her favorite."

"Mine too. I had to substitute for the key limes, which is what we used in Miami when Papa Luis and I used to make it. You gotta squeeze a lot of those teeny limes to get enough juice, let me tell you."

Carlos's eyes flew to the window when a police car rolled past the shop.

He raced to look out. "Maybe the chief's gonna make another arrest. Mom says cops always accept the jealous lover angle, and they love to pin things on the lady." He slouched as the car rolled by with no further action. "Mom's not a fan of the chief since she got two speeding tickets in one week."

"Mom's a lead foot," Diego explained. "Just ask my dad."

Carlos laughed as he submerged the detachable door of the ice cream machine into a sink full of hot, soapy water and Diego set about cleaning the insides. "Mom says it's the painter guy for sure, Sonny what's-his-name."

Trinidad jerked. "Petrakis?" That was the name she'd heard from Quinn, the one who might have dated Tanya. "Didn't he go to school with Kevin Heartly?"

Carlos extracted the machinery from the water and set it on a clean towel to dry. "Yeah. Sonny and Kevin were playing basketball down at the park last month, and Mom said they got into a brawl." His expression was gleeful. "Blood and punches and everything. Mom is a Bible school teacher, and she gave them the what for in Old Testament verses until they gave up and begged for mercy." He laughed some more. "They apologized, said they got caught up in the spirit of the game."

Diego rolled his eyes. "Who would get that excited about a sport?"

"Normal guys who think about points instead of physics," Carlos said.

"I play a sport." Diego appeared offended.

"Academic Decathlon is not a sport."

"We've got uniform shirts."

"With geek written on them. Do they issue matching pocket protectors?"

Trinidad held up her palms. "Okay, let's not get into a brawl here, gentlemen."

Carlos shrugged. "Anyway, Mom said Sonny dated Tanya Grant, and she figures maybe Sonny killed Kevin out of jealousy. But Dad says she watches too much television."

Trinidad laughed. "I've got to go to an appointment now. Will you guys be okay to lock up?"

"Sure." Diego dried his hands. "Oh, and some guy phoned for you, but I couldn't understand him."

"Did he leave a number?"

"Nah. Said he'd see you soon."

In a distracted daze, she hung up her apron. So, Sonny and Kevin were angry enough to throw punches. *Interesting,* she thought as she called to Noodles to load up in her Pinto.

"Time to focus on our business, Noodles. Murder investigations will have to wait." She had to go see Candy Simon about the "mutually beneficial arrangement," as she'd called it. Trinidad's mind raced. Perhaps she could cater small events for other businesses, earn enough to sock away for the cold weather months when folks weren't as keen for ice cream. She could use a proverbial shot in the arm instead of a sock in the jaw.

Any professional person would probably not arrive to meet a business contact toting a recently overwrought dog, but Trinidad wasn't about to leave her faithful companion alone when the twins had to go. He was still not his normal, sanguine self, evidenced by his dramatic reaction when a broom had fallen over on the shop floor. Noodles whimpered now, his silky head pressed against her thigh as they drove. He had been nothing but comfort in his own odd way, a simple, trusting soul that reminded her what goodness looked like. He would bring her every last condiment in the fridge if he thought it would soothe her. How could she care for him any less? Unprofessional though it might be, she would not leave this dog behind.

Driving past the fireworks stand again, she noted a tiny vet clinic sharing the same parking lot. She made a mental note to ask the doctor if he could suggest anything to help her quivering dog through the Fourth of July weekend. Noodles was notoriously bad at taking pills, but that was a battle for another moment.

Passing the stately home belonging to Tanya Grant, she saw the woman in a pair of trendy yoga pants with a matching shirt standing on the stamped concrete walkway that curved gracefully up to the ornate front doors. On either side of the cement were mounds of blooming roses in reds, pinks, and whites. Trinidad couldn't even maintain a silk plant, let alone a real one, but even her unpracticed eye could see that the roses were immaculately tended and a glory to behold. She thought about the pink rosebush on the front step of Kevin's shop. Was it a love token that would never be delivered, as she suspected? A Pink Princess rose for the woman who'd starred as the princess to his pirate? *Sad*, she thought. Would it wither and die there on the deserted porch step of the shuttered shop? Tanya was speaking to a rotund man in overalls...Warren Wheaton. He stood there holding a spade and a bucket.

"So, Warren's an employee of Tanya's?" she mused aloud.

Warren waved jovially when he caught sight of Trinidad. Tanya crossed her arms over her chest and permitted a brief chin bob. It was not brimming with good cheer. Trinidad's defense of Juliette had placed her squarely in the enemy camp. How had she landed in Sprocket only a few short weeks ago and already earned the wrath of the town's most prominent citizen and insulted the police chief? Taking in the luxurious house trimmings, she wondered what Tanya might have in common with Kevin, a guy who popped corn and got into basketball brawls at the park. Or painter Sonny Petrakis?

Still mulling it over, she continued to Lake Shore Drive. It was a bit removed from the tonier part of town and the Grant mansion. This was a long street, speckled with much older saltbox houses set on large plots of land. Many of the properties were overgrown with tall grasses that tickled the bottoms of rusted cars or tractors. She spotted a rusted, 1950s-era Buick up on blocks in a sprawling driveway. Her grandpa was a passionate devotee of classic cars. He would say proudly that a real Cuban man could keep any worthy car running with no more than a paper clip and a roll of duct tape. His brother Raul, who had not escaped Cuba before it fell under Castro's control, maintained a gaudy yellow Thunderbird until the day he died. Papa and Raul sent constant streams of letters back and forth, both insisting their vehicle was the superior one.

She waved to a worker at the sprawling Apple of My Eye Orchard. He was on the top of a tall ladder, stripping fruit from a heavily laden tree and deftly tossing it into a basket strapped to his back.

She rolled down her window. "Is Edward Lupin's house on this road?"

The man wiped his brow and nodded. "'Bout a mile down. Look for the mailbox." She waved a thank-you.

Continuing on, she'd almost passed the vine-covered mailbox with the name Lupin stenciled in peeling paint. It was leaning slightly to the starboard side. She took the turn that led down a graveled slope, along a thickly wooded drive. A small one-story house appeared at the end with a sleek, red two-door car parked in front with personalized plates that read, ISELLIT. The house was freshly painted, the bushes trimmed back, but the old roof was clearly in need of some repair. The sidewalk sported a network of fissures, which had probably laid out a few visitors in its time. There was a row of newly planted rhododendrons flashing some welcome color near the front door.

Candy Simon opened at her knock, smile flickering when she took in the dog. She had a perfect coif of black hair and eyes to match. A good five inches taller than Trinidad, Candy wore a neat pantsuit that hugged her trim frame.

Trinidad tried to smooth a hand over the hair straggling out from her barrettes and stood up straighter. "Hello. I'm Trinidad Jones."

Her eyes slid from Trinidad to Noodles. "I don't think we should bring your dog inside, if you don't mind."

"I apologize, but he's had a shock. I need to keep him close, but he'd be fine on a blanket in the backyard if that's okay. It's too hot in the car."

"Oh...well, okay, as long as he doesn't dig. The yard is enough of a mess as it is."

"He's not a digger."

She quirked a brow. "You know what they say, you can't take the dig out of the dog."

Trinidad wondered who exactly had said such a thing, but Candy continued.

"I think there's a latch on the gate. You can open it from the outside. Come on in through the sliding glass door when you're done."

Relieved, she led Noodles around the side yard and pulled on a half-rusted wire to open the gate. The fence was reasonably sound, having had several boards replaced that had not yet weathered to match the others. The yard was a newly mown patch of weedy grass crowded around a massive oak, which cast a wide shadow. *Gloomy,* she thought, though the shade was delicious. Trinidad stroked Noodles and filled a travel bowl of water for him. "Be right back, sweetie."

The interior of the house smelled of fresh paint and new carpets. A small living room opened into a kitchen tiled in a dated golden shade. The dark wood cupboards cramped the space even further.

Candy clacked her way into the kitchen, her low heels loud on the linoleum, a clipboard in her hands. Trinidad caught a glimpse of the neatly printed list and the series of check marks by most of the items. "Festive food" was the last note on the list, just before "dispose of ice cream equipment." She began to get an inkling of the type of arrangement Candy might be looking for.

"Thanks for coming. I'm desperate to start showing the house next week while we've got visitors in town for the holiday. I need to generate some excitement for the Monday open house. Selling this relic is going to be a challenge. People aren't exactly moving in droves to Upper Sprocket, but there's a buyer out there for everything. It would be a great house to purchase and rent out to college kids attending the university, wouldn't it?"

Trinidad didn't actually think a bunch of college students would want to live at the end of a lane, far away from the eateries and on the other side of town from the college, but she wasn't going to rain on Candy's parade.

She flipped to the second page on her clipboard. The backs of the repurposed papers were old listings. Candy was a frugal gal from all appearances. "It looks one hundred percent better than it did a week ago, let me tell you. Lupin was a collector, shall we say, by which I mean he was a yard-sale junkie. He always thought he was going to find that piece of priceless 'junkola.' There was such a mess of epic proportions to clean up, you wouldn't believe it."

"I've heard he liked to collect things."

Candy rolled her eyes. "That doesn't even begin to touch it. Everything from a busted-up candy machine to sixty-five coffee grinders. Sixty-five, mind you. When he told me he was going to sell, I strongly advised him to start culling his belongings, but he didn't make much progress before he died. After that, I boxed whatever didn't appear to be outright trash and had it shipped to his family in Michigan. That cost a chunk of change for them, I'd say."

"He had a storage space, too, didn't he? At Juliette's place?"

She tapped her pencil on the clipboard. As she did so, Trinidad noticed that the hem of her sleeve had come unraveled and was held together by a small bit of silver tape. "He did. Defaulted on the payments, so those items were auctioned off, and the remainder went to the flea market. More junk, all of it."

"Who purchased the contents at the auction?"

There was a pause. "Sonny Petrakis. He's a painter here in town."

The same Sonny Petrakis who had a fistfight with Kevin?

Candy checked her watch. "I'm sorry, I'd love to chat, but I really can't stay here any longer, so we need to get down to business. There's an antique ice cream machine in the garage. I figured who would be more interested than a person opening an ice cream shop?"

"That was very considerate of you."

"No big deal. Take it if you want it. You can access the garage through the side door. I've had it appraised, and it's worth close to $500."

"Oh, I couldn't just take it..." Trinidad began. "The family might want to sell it."

"They said it wasn't worth the cost of shipping. Besides," she flashed a brilliant smile, "I was thinking along the lines of a barter. That's the arrangement I mentioned. You take the ice cream machine, and in exchange, you provide ice cream for my open house on Monday...$500 worth of product ought to cover the event. You do the setup and cleanup, and you get to advertise your business. A win-win, right?"

"But..."

"Great. Well, it's settled then. I'll get back to you about the exact timing. I'll lock up, and you can pull the side garage door closed when you leave." And then, in a matter of moments, Trinidad found herself deposited on the front porch, listening as Candy's heels clicked a lively staccato down the front walk.

But I have no time for this... I have a shop to open and a friend to get out of jail, her mind shouted. Was an antique ice cream machine worth the cost of providing free ice cream and the trouble it would take to bring it to the open house? How would she keep a great quantity of ice cream cold enough in the July heat? Coolers? And how exactly was she going to fit a bunch of coolers in her Pinto? The logistics were dizzying.

She realized that it had been no sacrifice at all for Candy Simon to fork over something that didn't even belong to her in the first place. She'd gotten $500 worth of free ice cream. Then again, it was a chance for Trinidad to advertise the Shimmy and Shake Shop if Candy could rustle up a good number of attendees. Trying to decide if she had just stepped into a sweet business arrangement or a pile of work she had no time for, Trinidad wandered through the side gate and into the garage.

A bare bulb cast a sickly pool of light by which she found stacked boxes marked "donation" and a note for "ice cream lady" stuck atop an old machine. Trinidad's breath caught at the relic. She'd made a study of the history of ice cream, and she knew this old beauty was a Gem from the early 1900s, featuring a sturdy cedar tub that appeared to be in great condition along with the heavy metal gears. She knelt and skimmed a finger along the appliance. The Gem featured something special. The can and the dasher both revolved in different directions. It would be absolutely perfect to display in the shop. Maybe she hadn't been handed such a raw deal after all.

"You're not going to wind up in the garbage heap," she said, pulling cobwebs from the machine. "Even if it is going to cost me a boatload of work."

The garage was stifling, and she wished she had someone to share the find with. It would be presumptuous to call Quinn, wouldn't it? He'd probably think her silly, anyway, and her only other friend, Juliette, was busy with far greater concerns.

She stared at the amazing appliance with a twinge of guilt. Was it really okay with the family to take it? Had Candy been clear with them about the value?

"Who in the entire world would care about an old ice cream machine except you, Trin?" she asked herself. Trinidad noticed a box nearby that had not been taped closed yet, nor was it marked for donation. Instead there was an *S* written on the side in red ink. Curious, she flipped open the cardboard top. It wouldn't hurt to take one quick look.

Inside she found a stack of thin black bound books, a series entitled the Collector's Treasure Trove. Each volume covered a different type of collection such as coins, antique glass, jewelry, art, fine porcelain, and stamps. She wondered if Lupin was interested in any particular collection or all of them. She thumbed through one about coin collecting, or numismatics, as she discovered it was termed. The pages were yellowed and brittle, but someone had dog-eared a scattering of them and circled various specimens of old coins, including the 1955 doubled-die penny and the 1913 Liberty Head nickel.

"Maybe I should have collected coins instead of cookie cutters," she muttered. The other books were similarly dog-eared and marked up.

Another box nearby had not yet been taped. Trinidad couldn't resist a peek inside. It was full of small ziplocked bags of coins, which appeared to be all of a modern minting. There was also a stack of old china saucers, a string of dull blue beads, three antique pairs of sewing scissors, and a couple of metal thimbles. The side of this box was labeled, "for donation."

How sad, she thought. Lupin had accumulated these items and held onto them, and now they were considered unwanted junk. Had he felt unwanted, too? Tucked away in this overgrown, out-of-the-way house? She suddenly thought of Papa Luis, grateful that he was surrounded by friends and her mother and brother in the house they shared in Miami. They chatted on a regular basis, but she'd been so busy lately. She made a mental note to call and check in with him. He would love to hear about her antique ice cream churner.

Climbing to her feet, she had almost cleared the garage door threshold when she noticed a bulletin board leaning against the wall by an old lawn mower. There was a picture tacked there of a man with long bushy hair squinting into the sun, holding a fish he'd caught. It must be Lupin. The photo was damaged by age, curled at the edges. Below was a series of business cards shoved into the corkboard framing. One for Pizza Heaven, the delivery number circled, one for a local taxi service, and one more. She bent to pick it up for a closer look.

Sonny Petrakis, Petrakis Painting, the card read. There was a phone number printed on the front and a business license number. Sonny must have done the recent painting on the house when Candy began to prep it for sale.

She considered what she knew about Sonny Petrakis, one of a scant few names on her suspect list for Kevin's murder. According to the twins' mother, Sonny was interested in Tanya, or at least in her money, and fiercely competitive with Kevin. And now his name resurfaced, popping up at the home of Lupin, a consummate collector whose storage space he'd bought at auction. No other connection between the two, was there?

Her mind tumbling in untidy waves, Trinidad closed the garage and went to retrieve Noodles.

She woke him from a peaceful slumber, which seemed to have revived his spirits. Her garage snooping had taken longer than she'd realized. Afternoon shadows had begun to creep over the house, and it felt as if the fence had edged closer, or maybe the tangle of shrubbery was creeping nearer to entrap them. Spooky.

Stop being ridiculous, Trin.

Shaking free of the thoughts, she collected Noodles's water dish. He leapt to his feet and began to bark. She froze. It was not his "how about some playtime outside" bark, but a full-on danger-alert warning. Perhaps it was just a squirrel that had darted along the fence line? But the barking increased in volume into an unceasing cacophony. The scruff along his neck stood stiff. She gripped the bowl.

A clang rose over the barking. Someone was in the garage now. She was certain. Maybe Candy had returned? But why would she let herself in through the garage? Gripping her phone, finger on the emergency button, she tried to ready the bowl in case it was all she had to defend herself. With a sudden lunge, Noodles took off.

"No, Noodles," she whispered. "Stay here."

But he was off and running, electric with tension, barking for all he was worth. She heard the side garage door open and the sound of a heavy tread, definitely not a woman's.

Prickles erupted over her skin. She froze, listening as the intruder came closer, realizing that she had no place to run.

Chapter Eight

TRINIDAD OPENED HER MOUTH TO scream when a dark-haired man wearing painting overalls stepped around the corner, a box pinched under his arm. His tall, lanky frame was athletic, a tattoo peeking out from beneath the short sleeve of his T-shirt. His dark, close-set eyes were fixed on the dog.

"Easy, boy. Man, that dog scared me. You must be Trinidad. Candy said you might be stopping by here today."

She heaved out a breath as Noodles stopped barking and settled into wary silence. "Yes," she managed. "And this is Noodles."

He offered a grin and jutted his square chin at the dog. "Sorry I scared you, Noodles. I'm Sonny Petrakis. I did some painting for Candy to get the place ready for sale. I left my best brush over here." He pulled a paintbrush from his pocket with a flourish. "A man's only as good as his tools. This is Old Bessie. Can't do my job without her."

Trinidad's eyes traveled to the box under Sonny's arm. The top was folded closed, so she could not see what was inside. She noted the *S* on the side. "Are those your tools, too?"

He looked at the box as if surprised to find it in his possession. "This? Oh, no. Candy put some of my leftover paint in here for me. Never know when you might need a pint of antique white." He eyed the dog. "Sure he's out of attack mode?"

Trinidad gave Noodles a pat. He sat down, panting.

Sonny gazed at the house. "Lupin was a pack rat. When I was here priming, he rambled on about the stuff he picked up from yard sales and his trips and whatever. Never was anything worth one thin dime, probably, but he was convinced he'd found something invaluable. Saw a picture in a magazine article that made him think of an item he'd supposedly acquired a couple decades ago. Didn't tell me exactly what it was." Sonny tapped his forehead. "And he couldn't remember where he'd put it. Not surprising, since his house looked like a rummage sale." Sonny sighed. "Kinda sad, really. I guess he tore the place apart looking for whatever it was. Too bad, huh? To realize you have something worth some dough but can't remember where you put it?"

"Yes," she said thoughtfully. "That would be painful." *Especially*, she thought, *if it wasn't in Lupin's home anymore*. "Is that why you bought his storage unit at the auction? Hoping the valuable item might be in there?"

His eyes narrowed for a moment. "You make it sound like I was taking advantage of an old man or something. He was dead. What did he care? Sure, I was hoping to score, but it was all legal. I didn't do anything wrong." He paused. "I heard your friend Juliette was arrested for murdering Kevin." His voice was edged with something she could not identify. "Is that why you're giving me the third degree? Hoping to find someone else to pin the blame on?"

"No, I'm just a curious kind of person. But Juliette didn't kill Kevin."

"Police think she's good for it."

"The truth will come out."

He shrugged. "Whoever did it should pay. Kevin was a good guy."

"You were friends?"

"Went to high school together. We competed in everything, but I was the better athlete. We used to play pickup basketball at the park uptown in the spring when our businesses were running slow." He frowned. "I'll miss Kev. I used to tease him that he got everything handed to him—the popcorn business, his old man's house." He grimaced. "Not me. I had to work for every penny I ever made. Still, though, he was a good guy. Did me some favors. Someone needs to be punished for his murder."

"I agree." She was struggling to think of how to tactfully slide the conversation around to Tanya when he shouldered the box. "I should go."

No time for tact. "Were you and Kevin both dating Tanya Grant?"

He blinked, mouth open in surprise. "I didn't figure you for the gossipy type."

Though her cheeks burned, she kept her gaze on him.

His lip crimped. "No reason not to tell, I guess. I was really into Tanya a few months ago, but Kevin turned her head when they worked on a pirates and princess play together for the theater. She used me to make him jealous, only I didn't see it at the time. She would have done anything to get him to pop the question. Stupid me. Yeah, I was sorry when she dumped me, but, hey, all's fair in love and war. And Kevin won that round."

But he'd certainly lost the war, she thought. And now Tanya was available again. She wondered if Sonny was going to try and win her back.

Sonny paused, his expression calculating. "If you're playing sleuth trying to find another killer, I'm not your guy. I didn't kill Kevin."

"I didn't accuse you of it."

"Uh-huh," he said, oil-black eyes gleaming. "I hope not, but it sure sounds like you're throwing shade in my direction."

She flushed but did not answer. Sleuthing apparently required a subtle touch, which she did not seem to have.

Sonny was still staring at her. "Think about it. You're a newcomer to town, trying to get settled. It would be a bad time to make enemies."

His eyes were flat and cold. Had she goaded him too much? She forced herself not to retreat, but she gripped the phone in her pocket, heart beating wildly. "Are you threatening me, Mr. Petrakis?"

He held the hard stare for a moment longer, then his face morphed into an easygoing smile. "Nah, of course not. I'm not that kinda guy. Sorry if I came on too strong. It set me back a pace, all those personal questions. I'm not used to interrogation, especially by someone I just met." He shrugged, smile still in place. "Anyway, I guess I'd better go." He picked his way along the overgrown flagstones that led to the side gate.

He wasn't sorry, and he knew for certain that he'd scared her. Her fear at his subtle threat turned into a hard kernel of anger. "Mr. Petrakis?"

He stopped and turned. "Call me Sonny."

"All right, Sonny. Mind if I ask what you found in Lupin's storage unit?"

"Just my luck. Nothing but junk that that I passed off to the flea market: fly swatters, an old gumball machine with the red paint half-rusted off, clay pots, a cash register with a stuck drawer that held a whopping seventy cents, three toilet plungers, and such. What did anyone need with three plungers? I probably won't even make my money back. I had to look at everything in private, so as to keep the gawkers away. Sorry to disappoint, but I didn't find anything valuable." He gave her a paintbrush salute. "Anyway, gotta run. Nice to have met you, Trinidad."

The gate squealed closed behind him. She gave him a head start. Sonny Petrakis was not a man she intended to be alone with ever again. There was something hard and opportunistic about him, yet, to be fair, he had done nothing illegal, just like he said. And she had asked nosy questions. When she heard his engine start up and his truck rumble away, she and Noodles headed around the side. Reaching for the garage door handle, she found it locked. So, Sonny did not want anyone else poking around in Lupin's belongings. She'd have to get the ice cream maker another time. On a whim, she peeked through the dirty rectangular window. She scanned the cluttered space, the boxes marked for donation, the bulletin board.

One thing was missing: the old books perched on the top of the donation box. If Sonny was certain there was no treasure, why was he taking the Collector's Treasure Trove series? And why lie and say it was a box of his paint? The seconds ticked by, and she had no answer as she returned to the Pinto.

It came to her on the way home. The boxes marked *S* were being diverted to Sonny by Candy Simon. Perhaps it was all very innocent. Lupin's family didn't want to deal with sorting through the contents, as with the ice cream machine, so Candy was left to dispose of things as she saw fit.

But what if Candy was sending Sonny items so he could look through anything promising that might lead him to the valuable item Lupin had been searching for? How much did Candy divulge to Lupin's Michigan family about what she was distributing?

If Candy and Sonny were searching for something, they had not found it—not yet, anyway. A thought sizzled through her mind.

Nothing but junk that went to the flea market, Sonny had said. Why did so many details bring her back around to the flea market?

Lupin's "junk" wound up there.

Kevin had made a purchase there before he was murdered. The boxes from the flea market were piled behind his store. And she'd had the strangest sense somebody had been out there when she discovered Kevin's body. Could they have been searching through those boxes?

Was it possible that whatever Lupin had been looking for and Kevin's murder were connected? And, further, could the flea market hold the answer? Trinidad tootled along the quiet streets of Sprocket, her thoughts anything but quiet.

As she drove by the Vintage Theater, she noticed the front doors were propped open. She remembered she had to ask Warren about the crumpled flyer she'd found on that horrible day at Popcorn Palace. Maybe it would be better to talk to the theater manager instead, since Warren's credibility might be in question.

"No time like the present," she told Noodles as they hopped from the car. The dog sat on the shady front step to wait. Inside, the scent of mildew and the faint odor of spray paint hit her nose. The lobby was like something steeped in yesteryear, from the ornate wooden ticket counter to the ceiling covered in fancy wooden tiles. A yellow penny candy machine added to the vintage feel. Feet muffled by the thick carpet, she pushed through a heavy curtain. The interior was dark with velveted seats that had seen better days and a sprawling stage crowded with a backdrop painted to look like some sort of old meeting hall. It was warm, beyond warm, which probably explained the open front doors. Perspiration beaded her forehead.

Warren was deep in conversation with Cora, the theater manager Trinidad had met outside of Juliette's house. It was hard to tell Cora's age, but Trinidad guessed her to be somewhere in her early sixties. Her face shone milk-white against the dark fabric of her T-shirt, giving her head a strange, disembodied look. Trinidad suspected her dangly, beaded earrings were handcrafted like her fringed T-shirt had been.

"Those dishes are perfectly satisfactory," Cora snapped. "I just finished spray-painting them to look like rustic pottery. I even stamped them with a stripe around the edge for effect. They're fine."

Warren lifted his palms in surrender. "Don't shoot the

messenger, Cora. This is his bailiwick." He pointed to Vince Jr., whom Trinidad had not seen in the gloom.

Vince fisted his hands on his hips. "You asked me to consult on the authenticity of your props, didn't you? Those plates are way too embellished for the time period. The colonials would have plain redware or stoneware."

"Vince," Cora almost shrieked. "Who do you think we're performing this for? *Antiques Roadshow*? No one gives a Fig Newton about your fancy history facts. In act three, Ben Franklin is on stage eating from a plate that no one will even notice, so you can take your fancy history knowledge and file it under *u* for useless."

Harsh, Trinidad thought.

Vince stiffened. "But you asked me..."

"I did not solicit advice. I asked you for pizza, which you delivered, thank you very much. It was Warren here who butted in and inquired what you thought of the props." She fired an invisible laser beam at Warren, who seemed to shrink under the intensity.

"I, uh...well, I figured he could give us his two cents. Kid needs a job since his boss is in the slammer."

"He can keep his two cents," Cora snapped.

"And I don't need charity," Vince said hotly.

"Fine, since I wasn't offering any," Cora returned. "There's only one paid position in this cozy theater family, and that's mine. Everyone else is strictly volunteer, as I keep trying to tell Warren here."

"Well, we sure don't hang around here for the pay," Warren sniped.

"Come again?" Cora said. "If you have a complaint, man up, and let's hear it."

At that moment, Trinidad's phone began to buzz with a call. All three of them swiveled to see her. Hastily she silenced the phone. "I'm sorry." The look Cora gave her would have withered even a silk plant.

"There are absolutely NO cell phones allowed in this theater," she said.

"I apologize. I thought I'd silenced it. I usually have it on vibrate, but I must have forgotten."

"No. Cell. Phones. Silenced or otherwise. Didn't you see the box?"

Trinidad knew her cheeks were on fire. "Uh, no."

"No one ever notices that box," Warren said. He offered Trinidad a sympathetic look and pointed to a cardboard carton with "Deposit Cell Phones Here" stenciled in marker on the side.

"I didn't see it there."

Vince offered her a "better you than me" look.

Cora shook her head. "I prepped something fancier, but it hasn't had time to dry." She muttered as she strode up onto the stage. "Maybe a three-ton safe would be better. No one would miss that, would they?"

Warren laughed. "Good one. Cora's a real do-it-yourselfer. Loves her art projects. I wouldn't be surprised if she doesn't get hold of that three-ton safe and paint the Taj Mahal on the side or something."

"If this meeting is over, I have work to finish." Cora marched up the stage steps and disappeared behind a swish of the ornate curtain.

Trinidad sighed. "I'm sorry to have made her angry."

"You didn't make her angry," Warren said. "She was born that way. Got the disposition of an irate hornet, which explains why she was the perfect personality to work for the IRS in her younger days. Can't argue with the fact that she's a wiz of a theater manager, though. Do you want to audition for a part or something?"

Trinidad alternately gulped and shook her head. "Oh no. Not me. I'm not actress material."

"Shame. Not sure if our leading lady is going to feel up to performing since she lost her beau."

"Tanya won't be lonely long. She has plenty of admirers," Vince said, frowning.

"Besides Kevin?" Trinidad felt embarrassed asking.

"Sonny might step up again and take a swing. Tanya does love her working-class men," Warren said.

Vince shrugged. "Sorry, I have to get to my class." He scooted across a row of seats to retrieve his stack of books and scurried out.

Warren seemed in no hurry to leave. "Do you know Sonny?" he asked.

"Yes. We just met at Lupin's house."

"He and Kevin and Tanya went to high school together. He did some work for her. Now that Kevin's out of the way..."

"Does Tanya still have feelings for Sonny?"

Warren shrugged. "Probably not. Not to be crass, but Tanya's a wealthy woman, so she gets her share of attention. I work at her place, and it's chock-full of expensive goodies, artwork and such, fancy cars in the garage. Sonny could do worse than making a match with her. He was probably pretty annoyed when she dumped him and returned to Kevin."

Annoyed enough to kill? "Warren, there's something I've been meaning to ask you."

"Fire away."

"The flyers you had printed for the show."

"Yeah," he sighed. "Cora's still on my back because of that typo on the last bunch. It cost us a hundred bucks to reprint."

"I'm not talking about the typo. When I met you there in front of Kevin's place the day he was killed, you said you'd just gotten them from the printers."

"Uh-huh."

"But I found one flying around loose. I stepped on it after—I mean—after I found Kevin's body. It had a staple at the top."

"Huh. That must have been the proof stapled on the outside of the box." Warren's eyes shifted in thought. "That's weird."

"That's what I was thinking. Did you open up the rear of the van for any reason when it might have flown out?"

"No. Loaded up at the printers and drove back to Sprocket where I found you while I was having a snack and waiting for the engine to cool down. I got back in the van after we chatted and stayed there until you screamed, and then I bolted out to help you." He blinked. "I didn't open the back, so I have no idea how the flyer blew out."

"What was in the back besides the flyers?"

He looked chagrined. "A big mess, according to Cora. She tells me I am a slob of the grandest order. I guess she's right, judging by the way the rear of the van looks." He tapped his chin in thought. "So what was back there? The flyers, of course, some old theater junk. Spray paint, plastic gloves, maybe a soda can or two, and quite possibly an empty pizza box. Some cardboard. That kind of stuff."

"Is it conceivable someone stole an item from your van?"

"Don't see why they would."

They stewed on that for a while until she made her excuses and left. Warren followed her outside.

"I dunno how that flyer got out of my van, but it doesn't matter, does it? I mean, Kevin, poor gent, was dead before either one of us showed up. And…" he shrugged, "not to offend, but it seems like Chief Bigley's got your friend Juliette for the crime. Evidence doesn't lie."

"She didn't do it."

Warren offered that genial grin again. "Like I said, evidence doesn't lie."

His tone didn't quite match his friendly smile.

Evidence doesn't lie, she thought, *but plenty of people do.*

Her mind fixed on a detail, plastic gloves. Warren had them in the van. He could have slid a pair on, killed Kevin, and driven around again pretending to have just arrived. No fingerprints left on the murder weapon. It would explain how the flyer might have gotten loose as well.

She still had zero proof and plenty of speculation. As she left the confines of the dark theater, the chill seemed to linger inside her.

Murder was a cold business indeed.

Chapter Nine

AS USUAL, THE SHIMMY AND Shake Shop provided the perfect distraction. Sunday morning dawned hot and bright as she started the next round of preparations. More key lime ice cream was underway with the substituted regular-sized limes standing in for their smaller counterparts. The graham crackers added halfway through the churning process would break down and soften to a wonderful creamy consistency, the perfect sweet compliment to the sharpness of the lime.

Worry about the open house preparations hovered just under the surface as she stared into the walk-in freezer. She could haul the ice cream to Lupin's house in coolers, but how would she efficiently retrieve and scoop the stuff without everything melting into a colorful goo?

"Are you looking for answers in there?"

She screamed and whirled to see Quinn and Doug standing behind the front counter.

"Sorry," Quinn said. "Didn't mean to startle you. The door was open, so we thought we'd pop in. You okay?"

She pressed a hand to her thumping heart. "Yes, just trying to figure out how to avoid a total meltdown." She told him about her plans for Candy Simon's open house.

He laughed. "I'm not surprised that she found a bargain that didn't cost her anything. She can pinch a penny until it screams. Vince Jr. told me one time she gave him a pencil as a tip for a pizza delivery, said it would help with his studies."

"Oh, gee. Tightfisted?"

"More like a tightwad." He cocked his head. "I have an idea about how to help with the open house. Let me see what I can do, and I'll call you. It's a wacky thought, though."

"I welcome any and all help, wacky or otherwise. I'm having trouble keeping my mind on my business responsibilities with Juliette locked away in jail." Her throat tightened on the last word.

"Yeah," he said darkly. "Seems like plenty of people have decided she's guilty as charged. I heard a couple talking about canceling their storage agreements and pulling their stuff out of Store Some More."

Trinidad groaned. Could things get worse for her friend?

"Anyway, I gotta get Doug back to the farm. After he's been 'peopling' for a while, he needs some quiet time. I'll catch you later."

She said goodbye and began to wash up.

She considered her interaction with Sonny Petrakis again at Lupin's house. Could love gone wrong be the motive for murder, rather than greed or power? Tanya toyed with Sonny, used him. Was it enough to spark him to murder his rival? Relationships ended all the time, and people didn't commit murder. That said, she remembered recording a trial where the defendant was accused of killing a fellow businessman over a parking place. Tempers got the best of people all the time.

The loose flyer nagged at her, too. Someone had opened the van doors long enough for the paper to have flown out. Warren? Or someone else? And did they put something in? Or take something out? Stress made her muscles go rigid, and a headache began to build behind her temples.

She had a sudden longing to go home to Miami and sit in her family's sunny kitchen and bask in the presence of her mother, Yolo, and Papa Luis, but she couldn't face going back. Papa Luis called regularly to implore her to come home, but she knew he intended to fix her up with the grandson of his longtime Cuban compatriot, Gus. Gus's grandson Len was a fishmonger, a health food devotee who loved ballroom dancing and mountain biking. She did not think they'd have much in common. Now was not the time to go running home for a meet and greet.

It was the time, however, to head to the flea market before she started up another batch of ice cream. She wanted to know if anyone had shown particular interest in the boxes left over from the sale of Lupin's storage unit. Maybe a customer had returned a few times to prowl through the items? With some luck, she might also score some cheap coolers for the open house. Noodles was sound asleep after his satisfying tummy rub and showing no further signs of strain, so she figured it would be okay to leave him safely secured in the air-conditioned store.

The drive took only about twenty-five minutes. The flea market was located in a defunct airstrip. The old building that stood sentry over the rows of tables and pop-up tents was an ugly concrete box with a traffic-control tower sprouting out of the top. Inside the lower level, she found a man watching a baseball game on an ancient TV, his feet propped up on a peach crate. His bushy beard hung down to his clavicles.

"Help you?"

"I'm looking for what's left over from Edward Lupin's storage unit. Where would I find that?"

He pursed his lips. "That junk?"

"Yes."

"Talk to Donald, over there on the southeast corner. He

consigns for people who don't have their own booths and takes his cut, of course. Say, aren't you the new ice cream lady?"

"Yes."

"The one that's married to the chief's brother?"

She kept her expression bland. "Not anymore."

He stroked his beard. "And you're defending the other wife, Juliette Carpenter, I hear. Murder's a pretty big charge."

She steeled her spine. "She's not guilty."

To her surprise, he smiled. "Don't matter to me. If she did clobber Kevin, she had her reasons, and he probably deserved it."

"You didn't like Kevin?"

He shrugged. "I saw him around town. Too full of himself, if you ask me, roaring up and down on that motorcycle. I didn't like his pa, either. Same chip on his shoulder, like he was too good for Sprocket or something. Cleared out when he earned enough off of the locals."

Trinidad wasn't sure what to say to that, so she thanked him and left. She trudged past booths filled with a hodgepodge of items from tennis rackets to tie tacks, rolling pins, garden rakes, and a plastic Christmas tree decorated entirely with flamingos. Sadly, there were no coolers to be found. There were only a few patrons, for which she was grateful. The man, identified as Donald by his name tag, had a full head of fair hair and a beak of a nose underscored by a scraggly mustache. He peered through his reading glasses at something held out to him by Candy Simon.

Candy jerked in surprise. "Hello, Trinidad."

"Hi."

"Come to find a bargain?" Donald asked, handing back the pocket watch to Candy. She quickly secreted it in her purse. Trinidad had a fleeting thought. Could it be Candy was trying to sell something she'd found at Lupin's home?

"No, well, um, maybe. I was just wondering if all of Lupin's belongings from the auctioned unit were sold."

Candy's eyebrows formed a puzzled *v*. "Why would you want to know that? Are you trying to figure out if there is something valuable that got sent here mistakenly?"

Trinidad kept her expression blank. "I'm trying my best to help Juliette. It could be someone killed Kevin because he'd bought something at the flea market maybe, something left over from Mr. Lupin's belongings."

Candy laughed. "Not likely. I helped Sonny go through that stuff myself. No one was allowed to join in, so we had plenty of time to examine everything in peace. Then we packed it into the truck and sent it over here. If there was anything worth a bundle, we would have found it."

"I didn't realize you two were close friends."

Candy flushed. "We do favors for each other when we can. That's how life in a small town works."

"That table there is what you're after," Donald said pointing. "Feel free to peruse."

He returned to his conversation with Candy. Trinidad strolled along noting some dusty fake plants, a framed mirror, a half dozen cracked dinner plates, a box of old stamps, and three plastic umbrellas. Junk, just like he'd said. Perhaps whomever had killed Kevin had taken the item from whatever he'd bought at the flea market. But what could be worth so much? A swell of doubt dampened her enthusiasm. What was she playing at, anyway? It was a long way from court stenographer to detective. Sitting in a courtroom did not make her a sleuth any more than owning a toothbrush made her a dentist.

The adjacent table was piled high with objects, and scooted underneath were cardboard boxes. Familiar blue tape stuck to the side caught her attention.

"Are these also from Store Some More?" she asked Donald.

Candy jerked her head at Trinidad.

"Yeah," Donald said. "They belonged to Lupin, too."

She noticed Candy twitch a bit at the name.

Donald nodded. "That's more leftovers from what Sonny didn't want from the storage unit."

Candy sniffed. "It's all aboveboard, you know."

"Of course." Trinidad noticed a sheen of perspiration on her upper lip. The boxes were stuffed with piles of magazines, rusty tools, and old rotary telephones. Again, nothing of note that she could tell. "So the things you've cleaned out of his house wound up here, too, in addition to the unwanted storage unit things."

Candy nodded. "Except anything of value from the house. We shipped all those things to his family."

Things of value...like the pocket watch she'd so quickly concealed from view? Trinidad had heard enough lawyer talk about body language to know a "tell" when she saw one, the sudden look away, the pursing of Candy's lips. She knew more than she wanted to reveal.

"Really a shame about Kevin," Donald said. "I mean, I just saw the guy here at the market on Tuesday. He bought a box of junk."

"What junk?" Candy and Trinidad said in unison.

Donald looked at his receipt book and frowned. "Same question Chief Bigley asked me. I dunno. I wrote down 'miscellaneous.' Can't remember what exactly."

"Did he seem upset about anything?" Trinidad asked.

"Nah. He was a happy-go-lucky guy, happier than usual, even."

"Do you recall anything he said to you?"

"He just whistled a lot and said he was excited about the July Fourth festivities."

"Nothing else?"

Trinidad noticed Candy was nibbling on her painted thumb nail as she listened.

"Not that I can remember."

Trinidad thought about the few moments before she'd discovered Kevin's body. She'd had the strangest notion that there had been someone in the storage area behind his store. The killer? Searching for something Kevin purchased at the flea market? Something that once belonged to Lupin, that was mistakenly labeled as junk? It had to be.

Candy straightened. "While we're face-to-face, I'm hoping to get forty people to the open house. I've put the info out as many ways as I can think of. Two or three flavor choices for the ice cream ought to do it. Small scoops. Cones or cups, your choice. From noon to three. You can come as early as you want to set up, okay?" She did not wait for Trinidad's reply as she strode away.

Donald shook his head. "That lady doesn't miss a trick, does she?"

"Have you known her long?"

"She moved to town about five years ago after her fancy-pants realty office in California dried up." He leaned forward. "She likes to play the business mogul, but she's got plenty of debts, just like the rest of us." He lowered his voice. "Virginia at the pizza joint told me her car is leased and heard her fussing on the phone with someone about a missed payment. No secrets in this town," he said.

Trinidad felt more like the opposite was true.

Everyone in Upper Sprocket had a secret.

Chapter Ten

SHE'D JUST TURNED A NEW batch of key lime into the mixer when Quinn rapped on the door. Heart ticking up a notch, she opened it, wishing her hair was not secured in an unattractive pile by her favorite decades-old hair band. Maybe she should look into getting a haircut, if she could find someone in town who was skilled in styling boisterous curls.

"There's a call for you at Stan's."

"At Stan's? Why?"

"Tell you on the way, okay?"

She slipped off her apron and they hustled out. Doug walked with Noodles, and all four of them made their way to the coffee shop. "It's Juliette," Quinn explained. "She can only call collect from jail, so she couldn't ring your cell phone. She's desperate to tell us something."

Trinidad's breath hitched. Stan waved them all to the back office, a cramped but impeccably neat space with an old-fashioned rolltop desk sporting a new-fashioned computer. Stan picked up the receiver from a wall phone that looked like it had been there since the second world war.

"All right, Juliette. You've got all of us now. I'll hold out the receiver, so speak up as loudly as you can."

"I only have a few minutes," Juliette said, voice tense, "but I had to tell you."

"What is it?" Trinidad found herself leaning closer.

"You were asking me about Lupin's storage unit."

She tensed. "Yes. Did you remember something about what you saw in it? Something that might have been valuable?"

"Not a thing."

Trinidad's heart sank.

"But I remembered that I took pictures."

Quinn's face lit up, mirroring the elation Trinidad felt. "You did?" he said.

"Yes. When I took over the business, I inherited a bunch of those small disposable cameras. Do you remember those? The kind people used to put out at weddings and such? Someone kept boxes of them, and I guess Gabe's manager took possession of the unit for nonpayment, because there was a whole shelf of them in the office. Dozens. I figured I might as well use them up. Since we were foreclosing on Lupin's unit, it seemed prudent to document the contents in case there were some questions later from the family."

"So, you took pictures?" Trinidad squeaked.

"I took pictures." Her tone was triumphant. "How about that?"

"Where are they, Juliette?" Stan asked. "There was no police record of them in your office or from the contents confiscated from your home."

"That's the best part. They aren't in either of those places. I forgot to pick them up. I had to take them to a shop in Scotch Corners to get them developed, and it just flat-out slipped my mind. They're probably still there waiting at a place called Be Well. It's a drug store with a photo kiosk in the back. They still develop old film rolls."

Trinidad and Quinn got to their feet at the same moment.

"I have to go now," Juliette said. "I hope it helps." She disconnected.

Stan held up a cautioning palm. "We will have to share these photos with the police."

"But not until we take a good look at them first," Trinidad said firmly. "Due diligence, right?"

Stan crooked a smile at her. "My thoughts precisely."

Trinidad did a quick search on her phone. "The place closes at five on Sundays."

Quinn checked his watch. "It's already close to three. We'd better get moving. Can we take your Pinto? I think we exceed the maximum occupancy for my truck."

Did she have the time for a road trip with the open house looming the next day? She took a calming breath. "Sure. We'll go right now."

"Phone me the moment you get them," Stan called as they threaded through the patrons and left the shop.

Trinidad and Quinn sat in the front seat with Doug and Noodles in the back. Quinn patted the cigarette packet in his pocket before he searched for directions on his phone.

"It's about a forty-five-minute drive, so we'll be there way before quitting time," he reassured her.

Trinidad realized she was gripping the wheel. "This might be the clue we've been looking for. How can you be so calm?"

He chuckled. "I've learned the hard way. I was coiled pretty tight after I got out of the Army and came back here."

"Was it hard slipping back into country life?"

"Yes, for both me and Doug. I found out, the more agitated I got, the more he did, too. It didn't solve any problems, and it made things more difficult between us. Things are much better now. Doug's been good for me."

Doug nodded from the back seat.

Trinidad smiled. "That's what family's for, right?"

"Are you close with your brother?" Quinn asked.

"I adore Yolo, but he's as opposite a personality from mine as possible. He's a risk-taker, outgoing, always optimistic, and he can charm the scales off a snake. He is sometimes...unreliable, except when it comes to taking care of Mother and Papa Luis. He stepped up when my father died, so I'll always be grateful for that since I was...um...kind of in a bad place at the time, after I found out about Gabe."

Quinn nodded thoughtfully. "I get it. The heart can only handle so much at one time."

She glanced at him. "May I ask you a question?"

"Sure."

"Are you a smoker?"

He blinked. "Me? No, not for twelve years now. I was a couple-of-packs-a-day guy, but Doug kept getting these real bad chest colds. The doc finally got it through my head that my smoking was making things worse for him so I quit. One of the hardest things I ever did. I was a bear for a good six months."

"If you quit, why do you carry a pack of cigarettes wherever you go?"

He laughed. "Oh, that. When I was trying to detox, I'd just grab tight to that package and squeeze it for dear life. I figured, if I could hold onto a pack without opening it and lighting up, I'd know I'd really kicked the habit."

"And it worked?"

"Yep, but I carry around a pack as sort of an encouragement to myself, or a reminder. I'm not sure which." He shot her a sideways glance. "I guess that sounds pretty odd, huh?"

"I—" She broke off as an RV with a MONUMENT VALLEY OR BUST bumper sticker came to a hard stop in front of her. She braked. "Why in the world is he stopping in the middle of the road?"

Quinn was already unbuckling. "I'll go find out."

She saw in the rearview mirror that Doug was checking his watch. She knew he was thinking the same thing she was… They had only a short while to get to the photo store before it closed.

Juliette was counting on them.

Hurry up, she silently begged the RV. *This may be a matter of life and death.*

Trinidad hopped out and caught up with Quinn. "Maybe it's a deer in the road or something," he said as they approached the stopped RV. "Do you need some help, sir?"

A very small man dislodged himself from the enormous vehicle. "Not me. That guy. Take a look." He jerked his thumb towards the front of his bulky rig. They hastened to a familiar dented gray truck stopped in the road. She'd seen it before, parked at the gas station. Nearby, on its side, was an overturned wooden crate.

The cacophony was impressive…chickens, fluttering puffs of screeching white, leapt and darted every which way. Before she and Quinn could react, several more birds erupted from the gap in the crate left by a couple of planks that must have detached when it toppled.

Mr. Mavis, the gas station owner and bicycle enthusiast, stood with hands jammed into his pockets. "Oh, howdy, Quinn, Miss Jones. I've got myself into some trouble here."

"So I see." Quinn reached out to capture the closest chicken, which was beelining for the shrubs, and received a peck for his trouble.

"I was doing a favor for my cousin Larry," Mavis said. "Seems like his chickens get mighty upset at the fireworks, and they stop laying, so I was taking them up to Aunt Lucy's in Scotch Corners for him. I musta not secured the load properly. I think the rope snapped, and over she went." Mavis sighed. "Chickens never cooperate."

Trinidad could practically hear the clock ticking down until closing time at the Be Well shop, but there was no other choice.

They were stuck on the road behind an RV and surrounded by fugitive chickens. Even if there had been a way out, she could not, in good conscience, leave Cousin Larry's birds to their fate. Noodles barked to be let out of the Pinto. Trinidad had no idea how his herding instincts were, but Noodles was a dog of many talents, and she trusted him implicitly. She released him from the back seat.

Doug's mouth was pinched in a tight line.

"We've got to retrieve some chickens, Doug. Do you want to help?"

She thought he looked frightened as he got out of the car. Noodles trotted eagerly into the fray and, to her surprise, Doug climbed up onto the roof of the Pinto. "There," he said.

She followed his pointed finger in time to see a chicken hurtling down the road. Off she went in hot pursuit. After five minutes of scrabbling through the clawing shrubs, she snatched at the bird but wound up only with a couple of feathers and a scratch on her wrist.

"You're gonna turn out to be a coyote snack if you don't cooperate," she grumped, looking back at Doug who pointed again, standing on the car like a figurehead on the prow of a ship.

This time, she corralled the chicken and managed to subdue it under her arm. She arrived at the broken crate at the same time as Noodles, who carried a disgruntled bird in his mouth. He plopped it in the crate, which Quinn had gotten upright, and Trinidad followed suit with her captured fowl. Mavis slid the plank back in place to prevent further escape.

She patted Noodles. "How did you learn to do that, sweetie?"

Noodles wagged his tail.

"There," Doug called from the crow's nest, and Noodles snapped into action, darting under a shrub and emerging, tail wagging with another chicken in his mouth. Quinn helped secure that one in the crate. Trinidad's spirits notched up. Maybe they really could still make it to the shop.

"That's a mighty good dog," Quinn said.

"Sure is," Mavis agreed. "Cousin Larry has a malamute that brings 'em back in pieces. Efficient, but brutal."

"And Doug's doing great directing the troops from on top of my car," Trinidad said.

Quinn smiled. "He doesn't like birds because they move too unexpectedly, but he's a good spotter."

"The best."

The short man from the RV hustled over with a chicken under his arm. "Nasty bugger pecked my elbow."

Mavis nodded knowingly. "Cousin Larry's chickens are tough. Thanks for the help."

"So how many birds are still AWOL?" Quinn asked.

Mavis took a moment to count beaks in the crate. "That's four in the crate, which leaves us with..." He did a quick mental calculation. "Eight left to find."

Quinn and Trinidad groaned.

"Two more," Doug hollered, pointing towards a golden tangle of dried grass.

"All right, Noodles," Trinidad said with a defeated sigh. "Let's get ourselves eight birds, posthaste."

It took more than an hour to rustle the rest of the chickens, except for one that they simply could not find anywhere until Noodles sniffed it out from its hiding spot under the front wheels of Mavis's truck, where it had been the whole time. When the flock was contained and the crate tied carefully back in place, Mavis shook hands with his poultry wranglers and patted the dog before he drove away.

Trinidad and Quinn returned to the car with Noodles and found Doug in the backseat again.

"It's four-forty," Quinn said, consulting his watch.

Trinidad groaned. "We'll have to wait for tomorrow now."

She felt like smacking her head on the wheel. "But I've got

that open house at noon. I still haven't even borrowed the coolers. I don't think I can get to the photo place until after that's all cleaned up."

"I'll do it." Quinn pointed at his cell screen. "They open at ten. I'll get there first thing and meet you at the open house."

"Are you sure?"

"Yep. Mondays are quiet at the farm. Doug can handle things until I get back. Right, Doug?"

Doug nodded and Trinidad noticed that Noodles had scooted over until he was pressed against Doug's leg.

"You two are the best," she said. "What would I ever do without you?"

"Somehow, you would survive. Oh, and that reminds me. Hold off on borrowing any coolers. We have a surprise for you. Can you drop us at my truck and follow us to the farm? We'll show you."

"The surprises are coming fast and furious around here. Can I take anymore?"

"I think you'll like this one." He paused. "How do you feel about oatmeal, anyway?"

Oatmeal? "Have you been cooking?"

Quinn mimed zipping his lips and tossing away the key.

Though she poked and guessed and pestered, Quinn would say no more about the surprise. Back in town she waited while Quinn and Doug changed vehicles, and then she followed Quinn's truck until they rolled onto the grounds of Logan's Nut Farm.

"All right," he announced after parking the truck. "You stay right here with your eyes closed until Doug and I come back. No peeking, promise?"

"I promise," she said, thinking maybe the two had whipped up a batch of oatmeal cookies or something. Sitting there with her lids pressed closed, her thoughts returned to Juliette. Had her photos captured something precious? Something that might have gotten mistakenly sent to the flea market? An item that had fallen into Kevin's possession and resulted in his murder? The notion of having to wait to find out made her stomach twist. Every day that passed was another eternity in jail for an innocent young woman.

An *ahooga* startled her. Mouth agape, she beheld a sight that her brain could not at first decipher. Quinn sat in the driver's seat of a boxy delivery-type truck painted a vibrant teal. On the top was a fiberglass mass about four feet across adorned with two dark, eyelike spots. It looked like an animated shower cap. Quinn honked the horn again and disappeared from the driver's seat, a moment later prying open a side window and peering out. "Can I take your ice cream order, ma'am?"

She got out of the car, mouth still open in shock. "What in the world…?"

Now she could see that there was writing stenciled on the side. "Orville's Oatmeal," she read aloud.

Quinn and Doug climbed from the truck. "Guy who buys nuts from me used to be in the food truck business, but it was a flop."

She gaped. "He tried to sell oatmeal from a food truck?"

"Hence the flop part."

Her gaze traveled to the shower cap. "Oh, wait. That's a bowl of oatmeal, right?"

"Supposed to be. Orville was pretty skilled with oatmeal, but I don't think he exactly blazed a trail in high school sculpting class. Anyway, the truck is refrigerated, and he said you're welcome to use it to transport your ice cream for the open house."

She felt tears pricking. "He would really let me do that? For… for free?"

"No," Quinn said.

Trinidad sighed. "How much does he want?"

"Two."

"Two hundred?"

Doug shook his head.

"Two thousand?" she squeaked.

Quinn laughed. "Two pints...one chocolate and one vanilla."

She gasped. "He will let me use his food truck in exchange for two pints of ice cream?"

"Well, I told him your ice cream was the best in the world."

Her cheeks went hot. "I hope you didn't oversell me."

"Nah. His wife's been on him for years to get rid of the truck anyway, so he figures it would be good to fire up the old vehicle and get all her juices flowing in preparation to sell her."

She pressed a hand to her wildly beating heart. "That is just the nicest thing ever." She wanted to continue to thank Quinn and Doug and the kindhearted ice cream–loving Orville, but Quinn was pulling her toward the inside to show her the setup.

The interior was all shiny stainless steel with a stove and oven on one side that she would probably not require. The other boasted a sink, ample refrigerator space, and most importantly, a large chest-type freezer.

Doug pointed to the front of the truck.

"Oh," Quinn said. "Up in the driver's area there's plenty of room for Noodles to sack out in the passenger seat near the air-conditioner vent. Doug checked on that first."

"It's perfect," she said.

"I dunno about perfect, since there's that weird oatmeal man on the roof, but at least we can make sure they get the name right." He handed a scroll to Doug, and they unrolled a hand-painted vinyl sign that read SHIMMY AND SHAKE SHOP.

"How lovely," she breathed, fighting back tears.

"I only did the stenciling. Doug was the painter."

Ducking his head, Doug looked at his shoes.

Trinidad could not wipe the smile off her face. "How can I ever repay you two?"

"Keep cranking out the vanilla, and we'll call it even."

"Deal," she said, blinking back the tears.

"We'll drive it over to your shop right now."

"Excellent. I'm on my way there. I hired the twins to work a couple of overtime hours tonight." She shivered. "I can't believe opening is only days away."

"And those fireworks," Quinn said with a wince. "Doug doesn't like them, either."

"Noodles is right there with you. Anyway, I'll pop in the coffee shop and tell Stan about the delay in picking up the photos." She walked a step towards the car and then turned. Before she could second-guess herself, she gave Quinn a hug.

Then she touched Doug lightly on the arm with one finger. He did not react, but neither did he pull away.

"I never thought I would meet such amazing friends," she said.

Quinn's smile was sweet and wide. "Welcome to Sprocket," he said. "There are some really good people here."

Something warm and comforting filled her soul. Maybe she really had picked the right place to settle, murderers aside. Trinidad felt like she floated in a cloud of excitement as she drove back to Full of Beans. She spotted Stan through the front window of the coffee shop, wiping down the tables. A wave of guilt washed over her. Here she was celebrating the loan of a food truck when Juliette was languishing in jail enduring who knew what, and the photos that might help get her out were locked up until morning. She hustled inside, enveloped by the comforting aroma of coffee.

Stan drew her into his office and pulled the door closed. When she told him about the photo excursion delay, he listened, face grave.

"Did you see Juliette today?" she inquired.

He nodded. "Yes, and I'm afraid this jail situation is wearing on her. She hasn't been eating or sleeping."

A plate of brownies flashed into her thoughts. Who wouldn't be buoyed by nature's most perfect food? "Can I...?"

He held up a hand. "No outside food, I'm afraid, otherwise I would be plying her with banana squares and pecan tarts."

She slumped. "What can we do? There has to be something."

"I've read the full police file. Juliette says she visited Kevin a few times at Popcorn Palace, and he let her stir the kettle on a lark. That's how her fingerprints came to be on the murder weapon."

"Well, that's plausible, isn't it? They were dating."

"It would help if we could provide an alibi. So far, we have only one other witness reporting that she was arguing with Kevin at her office Wednesday morning."

"Who said that? Who was the witness?"

"Warren Wheaton."

"Did he explain why he was at the office at that time?"

"Says he was out for a drive and stopped, intending to see if he could use her bathroom, but he heard the yelling and decided not to."

"Did anyone see him there?"

"Apparently not. Don't trust him?"

"Not really," she said, relating how she'd seen him driving past Store Some More when Noodles had bolted. "He just seems to turn up all over the place. I think he's been skulking around Store Some More. He might have been the one trying to pick the lock the night before the auction."

"What would his motive to murder Kevin be?"

She thought about Warren and Tanya together in her front yard. "I've heard he's a gambler. He and Kevin used to play online poker together, according to Vince's mother."

Stan drummed his fingers on the desk. "Greed is a 'one size fits all' motive. Perhaps Warren owed Kevin a sum that he could not repay?"

"Might be, but I can't shake the feeling that this has something to do with whatever was in Lupin's storage unit."

"Except that Juliette, Sonny, and Candy have all said it was nothing but junk."

"So did Donald at the flea market," she said with a groan.

"Right, so how would Kevin get his hands on something valuable when everyone else missed it? We need to pray that the photos Juliette took of the storage space contents will shed some light on the situation."

"Exactly. Quinn's going to pick them up as soon as Be Well opens tomorrow."

"All right. I'll continue to prepare her defense as best I can."

She heaved herself out of the chair. "Thank you, Stan. See you in the morning."

Reaching for the door, she saw a flicker of shadow, as if someone had been standing there, listening. Finger to her lips, she alerted Stan. Immediately he came to her side. She yanked open the door. No one was there. Hurrying down the hallway, she entered the main room of the coffee shop. It was empty except for Meg who was counting the money in the till, a pencil behind each ear.

"Did anyone come by here?" Stan asked.

Meg stopped counting. "Don't think so, love, but I wasn't paying much attention. They could have slipped out the back way."

Trinidad and Stan hurried to the door that opened into a parking lot. The space was still and quiet, no sign that anyone had passed by recently. They listened in silence to the song of the cicadas.

"Is it possible you imagined it, Trinidad?"

"Anything is possible."

The pause that expanded between them told her that Stan did not believe she'd imagined it, either.

He walked her to the curb and prepared to watch while she crossed the street to her shop. "I'm sure there's nothing to worry about." His smile was confident, warm.

But with Juliette in jail and no way to prove her innocence, there seemed like an awful lot to worry about in Trinidad's book.

The pictures would help.

They had to.

Chapter Eleven

AFTER FINISHING UP SOME COMPUTER orders, Trinidad heard Quinn arrive with the repurposed food truck. He showed her how to hook it up to the electricity and left with a jaunty wave. He'd gone to so much trouble…for her. It gave her a warm, fuzzy feeling as she set about churning new batches of vanilla bean, double chocolate, and strawberry flavors. She figured she'd stick with the ice cream trifecta for the open house. That was bound to please everybody. Her flyer would highlight the Freakshakes and the other more exotic choices like the key lime currently ripening in her freezer. She breathed in the luxurious smell of cream and sugar. The tiny spark of excitement about her fledgling business burned brightly, warring with her angst about Juliette. *Waffle cones,* she thought suddenly. That's how she would serve the open house ice cream. Much cozier than paper cups.

"It's time for you two to learn to make waffle cones," she told Carlos and Diego when they showed up for their extra hours. "And how would you like to ride in my food truck tomorrow and help me scoop? Noon to three." She saw the calculation in their shrewd teenage eyes.

"Normally we get done at 2:00," Diego said.

The time had arrived to wheel and deal. "I'll pay you extra for more overtime, and you can take the leftover ice cream home to share with your friends."

Carlos gave her a thumbs-up. "Done."

"Sweet," Diego said. "Lead us to the waffle cone maker, Coach Jones. I know I'm gonna be amazing at this. Batter up!"

Laughing, she fired up the griddle. She and the twins donned aprons and hair nets, and she showed them how to make the dark batter, which was sweetened with local honey and a scoop of brown sugar. She demonstrated how to pour just the right amount of the mixture onto the heated griddle and let it cook before unsticking it with a plastic knife and quickly wrapping it around the cone mold. Only two overflows and one misshapen cone later and Diego was a pro.

She showed Carlos the chocolate recipe. Under her supervision, he prepped the next container of batter. Soon the shop was redolent with the delectable smell of crunchy, golden waffle cones. The twins happily sampled one of each.

"Awesome," they both said at exactly the same moment.

When the cones had cooled, Carlos stacked them gingerly into cartons and carried them to the food truck.

He frowned as he examined the vehicle in the growing twilight. "It's fine and all, Miss Jones, but why's it got a bowl of sawdust on the top?"

"I think it's scrambled eggs," Diego corrected.

"Actually, it's oatmeal," she said, earning a sharp look from both of them.

"Should have gone with scrambled eggs," Diego said with a solemn nod.

"Probably," she agreed. "But it's just a loaner, and it's all we've got. Let's get her buttoned up for tomorrow." Rolls of paper towels, a half dozen ice cream scoops, packages of paper napkins, kitchen cleaner, and Doug's trimmed fliers were stocked when the twins left. By then her body was clamoring for a rest.

In an effort to soothe her complaining feet, she eased down on the floor next to Noodles. She scratched him behind the ears until he fluffed his lips in pleasure. "You're really patient to sit here for so long watching the world go by, Noodles. Other dogs would be demanding coffee breaks and vacation days."

Noodles offered his tummy for scratching. As she stroked his velvet belly, a white piece of paper peeking from underneath his bean bag caught her attention. She pulled out an electric bill. "Oh, dear."

Reaching in deeper, she retrieved four more envelopes. "So that's where the mail's gotten," she groaned. "I thought the bill collectors were taking the week off." She sighed and rubbed his head. "You've been helping again, haven't you?"

He swiped a tongue across her cheek.

Noodles would often assign himself random jobs. When she'd first adopted him, he would cheerfully abscond with every writing utensil he could find, secreting them behind a potted silk ficus without her knowledge. When she'd finally cry out, "Where have all the pencils gone?" Noodles would magically produce one with Houdini-like aplomb. Possibly, he was ensuring his own job security.

In this case, he had been efficiently collecting the mail that had been slid through the slot and packing it away under his dog bed. Perhaps he'd picked up on her tension when she perused the bills. If only the debts could just be shoved under a cushion and forgotten. She thumbed through the half dozen envelopes politely demanding payment for services rendered. "Thanks, Noodles, but it's harder to make bills disappear than pencils."

He offered a lick to her wrist and she reciprocated with a chin scratch.

Underneath the bills was a postcard capturing a colorful hodgepodge of houses edging a cerulean sea. She flipped it over to read the message from her mother.

"Off to cruise the Greek Isles with Aunt Frida. The plumbing on the ship is in primo condition. Your father would have approved. Love and hugs, Mother."

Trinidad laughed out loud. Her father had earned a living in his early years apprenticing as a plumber on various cruise ships. It was how he'd met her mother Claudia. Opposites did indeed attract and held the two together until her father passed away. For all his days, her father had never lost his zeal for his craft, nor had her mother's passion for travel subsided. Even on their thirtieth anniversary cruise to France her mother had insisted on, her father had managed to meet the lead plumber and score himself a tour around the belly of the floating beast while his wife enjoyed a facial and massage. Their marriage was a study in contrasts, but the one thing they had in common was complete devotion to each other.

She sighed, wondering if she would ever experience such a thing. An image of Quinn flashed in her mind, but she promptly squashed it. There was no room in her life for anything but friendships. "Just you and me and a truckful of ice cream. Right, Noodles?"

The dog shook his ears.

On impulse, she pulled her cell phone from her pocket and dialed. Three rings, then four. Papa Luis did not answer, and neither did her brother Yolo. Last time she'd called, Papa had worked overtime to convince her to come back to Miami. He wanted to introduce her to Len the fishmonger. *"A real man who pays his taxes and changes his own oil. He smells a little like fish, but happily you like seafood, right? It is fortuitous."*

She had a feeling Papa would think any arrangement that resulted in her not living alone on the opposite coast would be fortuitous. The answering machine picked up. "Leave a message, unless you're the tax man," her grandpa said in heavily accented English. She waited for the beep.

"I...I just wanted to say I love you, Papa, and I miss you. I hope Yolo is taking good care of you while Mother is on her cruise." Maybe she should tell him about the murder and Juliette and the food truck and the combination of fear and elation and panic and pleasure that she'd felt since moving to Sprocket. Perhaps she could somehow explain that she was doing her best to play detective, when she wasn't scooping ice cream and pretending to be a paralegal. But these things would only make him worry, and that was the last thing she wanted to do. She knew her wrecked marriage had caused him plenty of consternation already, on the heels of losing his son. "See you soon," she added brightly before she disconnected.

"All right, feet," she commanded. "There's more ice cream to churn and supplies to be stocked."

Noodles offered another encouraging lick to her knee cap as she struggled to a standing position. "Why didn't I start this entrepreneurial stuff years ago?"

The time passed in a blur, and, when she finally stopped work, she was surprised to find that it was almost eight o'clock. As the street quieted and the vacationers headed back to their campsites by the lake, Trinidad felt suddenly restless in spite of her fatigue. Besides, she owed the dog a walk, and there appeared to be a refreshing breeze building.

"Should we take a stroll before we head home, Noodles, as if we hadn't a care in the world?"

Noodles sprang to attention and fell into step at her side. They crossed the street and passed Full of Beans, which was quiet. All the other businesses except for Pizza Heaven were already closed. Turning the corner onto Little Bit Road, Trinidad savored the breeze and the view. The sidewalk was overhung by mature trees interspersed with wooden benches and planters brimming with red, white, and purple petunias, twisted closed to await the morning sunshine. American flags poked from every planter.

A display in the Off the Rack secondhand clothing store caught her attention. "Clearance" was a word that attracted her with a magnetic pull—reasonable, since she'd sunk every meager penny into the Shimmy and Shake Shop. Again, she felt the thrill of fear. What if her grand plan failed?

Thoughts of bankruptcy prodded her.

"Then I'll get back up again like I did after Gabe," she muttered to herself. "One foot in front of the other, right, Noodles?"

He waggled his tail and peered with her through the glass window.

The secondhand shop was closed, but the display featured a mannequin dressed in red, white, and blue clothes, backpack slung over her shoulder and a used sleeping bag rolled up at her feet. A small sign proclaimed a FOURTH OF JULY HIT THE TRAIL SALE. *Clever*, she thought, her gaze wandering back to the clearance items: mostly winter hats, gloves, earmuffs, and snow boots. An idea popped into her head, a way to improve the Fourth of July experience for dear Noodles, and she made a mental note to return when the shop was open.

It was another few feet to the end of the block. Since Trinidad hated to leave things partly finished, she kept going. "We'll turn back at the curb, okay, Noodles?" She wondered if she was beginning to have too many conversations with her dog. All she needed was to add "nutty dog lady" to her title of "ex–Bigley wife" and whatever other monikers the townspeople had given her. Then again, Noodles was the truest friend she'd ever had, so maybe it was okay to chat with him as long as he didn't start talking back or giving her stock market tips.

They made it to the curb with only a few more stops for Noodles to sniff. She figured the extra exercise had earned her another late-night peanut butter and marshmallow fluff sandwich for sure. The last business on the block was a neat one-story building with the obligatory flag-festooned planter in front.

"Simon's Real Estate," she read. She'd found Candy Simon's lair. It was sleek and professional-looking, like the woman herself. Inside, a lamp glowed, but the place was obviously closed for the evening. There was a plastic cup of what looked like iced tea or chilled coffee on the desk with the Full of Beans logo stamped on it. The cup's sides were beaded with moisture. Something moved inside the shop, and Trinidad jumped back so quickly she stepped on Noodles's foot.

He let out a yelp.

"I'm sorry," she whispered to the dog. Two figures appeared inside the office, oblivious to Trinidad and Noodles. One was tall, bulky, male. Sonny Petrakis, she finally realized. The other was smaller, and the shine of neatly coiffed hair identified her as Candy Simon. She wore a sleeveless dress as if she was outfitted for a party.

Trinidad hadn't even straightened from comforting Noodles when Sonny seized Candy by the shoulders. Trinidad's breath caught at his intensity. His fingers pressed into her flesh.

Panic prickled her skin. *He's hurting her. Call the police.* She scrambled for her cell phone and dialed.

"Police. What is your emergency?"

She spoke in a hushed whisper. "There's a woman being attacked..."

"What is your name, ma'am?"

"Trinidad Jones. Candy Simon is being attacked at her office by..." Trinidad's voice trailed off as it dawned on her that something had changed. Candy's arms had snaked around the back of Sonny's neck, and what she'd thought was an attack had turned into a kiss. Her face went warm. "Oh, um, my mistake. It's not an attack."

"Miss Jones? Please explain. Is Miss Simon in danger? Are you?"

"Uh, no, um, actually Candy's, er, kissing the man I thought was attacking her."

There was a pause. "Are you certain?"

"Yes," she said with a sigh. "I'm certain." Though it had been a long while since she'd been a participant in such a thing, she still recognized a passionate smooch when she saw one. "I apologize for bothering you."

She disconnected, shoving the phone back in her pocket. The only course of action now was to make a covert escape as fast as humanly possible. She began to edge away before she could be spotted by Candy or Sonny, and the dog followed. "Good job, Noodles," she whispered. "Stealth mode." She was almost in the clear when she banged her shin into the cement planter and cried out.

Clapping her hand to her mouth, she knew it was too late. There was movement inside the shop as Sonny rushed to the window.

"Come on, Noodles." She galloped as fast as she could down the block, Noodles keeping pace right at her side. Behind her the shop door banged open.

"Who's there?" Sonny thundered. His footsteps scuffled along the sidewalk.

The right thing to do, the brave and ethical action, would have been to stop, turn around and explain what had happened with plenty of apologies sprinkled in. Instead, her nerves propelled her to hobble even faster until she and Noodles were practically sprinting. Lungs heaving, they flew around the corner.

Finally, when her limbs screamed at her, she stopped, back pressed to the stucco wall of what passed for the local post office. Had Sonny spotted her? Was he pursuing? Ears strained, she listened for the sound of feet pounding along the cement. At first her breathing was so loud she could hear nothing else. Forcing her lungs to cooperate, she listened some more. Nothing. Sonny, it seemed, had given up his pursuit.

Mortification juddered through her nerves. She'd probably made things 100 percent more dramatic than they had to be with her ridiculous sprint. What had she been thinking?

Noodles followed as they started up again, his tongue lolling from the unexpected exercise. "Well, that was embarrassing. I wonder what Chief Bigley will think when she gets wind of that call?"

Her cheeks were still warm when they made it back to the shop and loaded up into the Pinto. The muscles in the back of her thighs quivered as she hit the gas. Driving slowly, she mused about what she'd seen. Clearly Candy and Sonny had more of a connection than just a business arrangement. In small towns, everybody was supposed to know everything, yet it seemed to Trinidad that there were secrets around every corner. Someone should write a book...*The Secret Life of Sprocket.*

The coffee cup on Candy's desk popped into her head, the one from Full of Beans. One of them had been at Stan's recently, or the cold drink would not still be sweating moisture as the ice melted. Could it have been Candy or Sonny listening outside the door of Stan's office? Meg might not have remembered either of them lingering after their drink purchase.

Or maybe Trinidad was letting her imagination run amok.

When she got to the tiny house, she hurried out of the Pinto and dashed inside. Washing her hands, she stared out the quaint window. She noticed for the first time how lonely the road was that led to her place, the empty fields and the crowded patch of woods. Not a single soul around. A troop of bats swarmed across the sky on silent wings in search of their insect dinner. Her nerves prickled as she stared out into the night, the same feeling she might have if someone was watching her from behind the trees.

"Knock it off, Trin. You have no time for paranoia." She tried to pull herself together. She had a full schedule ahead with the open house and only days before the shop opened. In the meantime, Juliette was incarcerated, not eating properly, and likely close to despair.

The photos. They just had to reveal something that would help. If there had been a treasure in Lupin's unit, Juliette must have captured it on film.

In a matter of hours, Quinn would be retrieving the photos.

Would they break the case wide open or prove to be another dead end?

Bad choice of words, she thought, as she remembered what she'd found in that horrible iron kettle.

Very bad.

Chapter Twelve

OF COURSE, THE MORNING OF the Monday open house was a true sizzler with temperatures expected to crack the hundred mark. Trinidad chose to consider the bright side. There was no better weather to promote the finest ice cream than a scorcher of a summer day.

The food truck had been connected via a long electric cord to a plug behind the Shimmy and Shake Shop since the previous evening to ensure the chest freezer was properly cooled. The generator was ready to be fired up as soon as they reached their destination.

Carlos and Diego were doing their newscaster bit. "We're ready to go mobile this morning in Sprocket," Carlos announced into an ink pen while his brother pretended to film him. "Though everything appears to be calm and controlled here in this tranquil place, looks can be deceiving. What fresh horrors await in a town where there's a murderer on the loose? Only time will tell."

Trinidad almost dropped the box she was carrying. "Maybe we don't need to bring that up right now, huh, guys?"

Carlos did not miss a beat. "We will keep you posted, America. I'm Carlos Martin, Channel Ten News."

Diego zoomed in the lens. "And…we're out."

Quinn pushed through the back door of the shop. He was wearing a pair of brown denim jeans and a faded T-shirt that might have once been green but had come to roost somewhere far duller than its original hue. There was something that looked like a spaghetti stain around the belly button area. The obligatory unopened cigarette box was in his back pocket. One shoe was untied. Trinidad recalled how snappy-dresser Gabe would never be caught dead in a faded or stained anything. Somehow the disheveled look suited Quinn just fine.

"Everything's cold as a frosted frog, as my CO used to say," Quinn announced.

Diego put down the camera on the nearest pink table. "What's a frosted frog?"

Quinn chuckled. "I asked about that saying, too. According to Captain Clevers, some frogs actually hibernate by burrowing in the mud, and whatever is sticking out gets frozen."

Diego nodded. "We can add that to our news broadcast for some local color. I already got some footage of the monster truck ready for its inaugural voyage."

"Frozen frog butts will be a real crowd-pleaser." Carlos worked up a good stream of laughter until Trinidad stuck a box into his hands.

"Put this in the truck, okay?"

Quinn fished his car keys from his pocket. "I have to drop a load of nuts on my way out of town, but I'll be by the open house with those photos as soon as I can, and we can take a look when you're done."

She saluted him with an ice cream scoop. "Safe travels, Farmer Quinn."

He snapped off a smart salute of his own. "Ditto, Scooper Jones."

Next, she put Diego in charge of setting up a cozy cushion in the passenger seat of the food truck and installing Noodles with his water bowl and a container of biscuits. While she was once again reviewing her mental checklist, there was a tap on the door. Heart sinking, she shooed Carlos out to help his brother before she ushered in Chief Bigley.

"Hi, Chief."

"Hi, Miss Jones. I understand you called dispatch last night."

"I, er, misunderstood what I was seeing."

"When you were looking through the window of Candy Simon's closed real estate office?"

Trinidad smoothed her Shimmy and Shake T-shirt. "Well, yes, but it wasn't like I was stalking or anything. I know you won't believe this, but I was out walking my dog, that's all, and I thought Candy was being hurt. I didn't intend to spy on anyone."

She quirked a smile. "Actually, I do believe that."

"You do?"

"Yes. For two reasons. First off, it's too ridiculous a story to have been made up."

"Thanks, I think. What's the second reason?"

She hesitated. "My brother, ironically. He spoke highly of your integrity in a phone call one time."

She flat-out gaped. "He did?"

The chief continued. "He said someone left their credit card in a vending machine, and you researched their address and drove halfway across town to return it."

"But, I mean, well…" The floor felt like it had jerked a few inches to the left as the words tumbled out. "I…I'm surprised he mentioned it."

"Ironic he values integrity when he can lie like a rug?" Bigley sighed. "People can be many things, can't they?"

She swallowed. "I suppose they can."

"For the record, I don't like what my brother did, but I love him and I will support him no matter what. He's blood."

Gabe didn't deserve such a loyal sister. Still, she was moved by the chief's revelation. "I just wish he could have been honest with me and Juliette and Bonnie."

The silence expanded. Chief Bigley shifted a millimeter. "For what it's worth, I think maybe he saw in you ladies things he wished he had in himself."

"Not exactly enough to keep a marriage alive."

"No, I wouldn't think so, though I've never been married myself. But he loved you three. He wasn't lying about that part."

She didn't know what to say. She was relieved when the chief changed tact. "So you mistakenly assumed that Candy and Sonny were arguing—before they lip-locked, I mean."

"It sure looked that way."

"It's possible they were. Any idea what it would have been about?"

"No." She cocked her head. "Wait a minute. Why would you be interested in Sonny and Candy?"

Bigley didn't answer.

Trinidad ogled. "Are you are starting to think there's someone else involved in Kevin's death?"

She held up a palm. "Not necessarily. I like cases to be tied up as neatly as possible, and this one seems to be cut-and-dried. But, since we're a small town here, I'm doubly committed to making sure the police handle things professionally. I don't want anyone accusing us of being incompetent bumpkins."

"So, you're just dotting i's?"

"And crossing t's. It's bugged me from the moment you said you heard someone in Kevin's rear storage area. The ground was too dry to pick up prints, but some of the boxes were open, as if they'd been gone through. Kevin was a tidy guy from what I knew. When he provided the popcorn for the senior class prom, everything was ordered and meticulous. I was there to keep an eye out for any high school shenanigans. Kevin wore plastic gloves and an apron. All his popcorn was sorted into tubs, and he doled it out using a plastic scoop. Type A didn't really cover it. Which has me pondering: Why would a guy like that leave open boxes in his yard?"

Trinidad grinned. "So, you do think there's a possibility that Juliette is innocent?"

Bigley sighed. "Don't leap to any wild conclusions. I didn't say that. The preponderance of evidence is clearly against her. I'm just making sure I consider all the possibilities. Sonny and Kevin had disagreements in the past, so I'm following that trail. Do you have any information about a motive for Sonny?"

"He said Tanya used him to make Kevin jealous. She dumped Sonny. That could make a man see red."

"Yeah, I got that rumor from Virginia already."

"At the pizza shop?"

"Uh huh," the chief said with a smile. "Virginia's a talker."

That she was. "Sonny thought Edward Lupin had some sort of valuable item in his collection, something he misplaced."

"I've heard the rumors about Lupin, too. The whole town has. That's why Sonny bought the storage unit, but there's nothing shady about that. It was all aboveboard as far as I can tell."

Trinidad hesitated, weighing whether or not to share her suspicion. "I think Candy was letting Sonny look through Lupin's belongings when he didn't find what he was looking for in the storage unit. Most of the items went to the flea market, and Kevin Heartly made a purchase there the day before he was killed."

She nodded. "Hence the boxes behind the store."

"And I wondered, you know, since Sonny and Candy are close, if maybe they were selling some of Lupin's things without mentioning them to the family." She thought of the pocket watch Candy had been showing Donald.

"Hmmm. Could be, but I still don't see why that would be a motive for killing Kevin. Even if he knew they were siphoning off some valuables, it's petty crime at best. So that points me back to this supposed treasure that our town is obsessing over. I've asked Juliette what she saw in Lupin's unit, but she doesn't remember."

Trinidad figured it was time to come clean. She drew in a breath. "About that...actually, Quinn is on his way to—"

Bigley's phone buzzed. "Excuse me one minute."

Diego and Carlos returned, glances shifting from Trinidad to the chief. "Uh, we're all loaded up and ready to go."

"Great. I'll just be a minute."

The boys shuffled slowly to the back door, glancing again at the chief who disconnected the call.

"Has there been another murder?" Diego whispered, his eyes glittering with excitement. "Or maybe an attack or something?" He readied his video camera. "I can hop into my news reporter role at a moment's notice. I'm versatile that way."

"Sorry to disappoint you," Trinidad whispered back. "No further slayings that I know of."

Diego harrumphed.

"I've got to run," the chief said. "There's a brawl brewing up at Three Egg Lake. Some campers crashed a Jet Ski, and it's turned ugly. We'll finish our conversation later, Miss Jones." She strode out the door, and Trinidad locked it behind her.

"Too bad we can't go with the chief," Diego said. "It'd be awesome to witness a brawl at the lake."

The boys headed for the truck, commiserating over their missed opportunity. She watched the chief zoom away. She hadn't had a chance to tell her about the photos, but that could still be accomplished when Quinn returned with them. It was the other part of their conversation that floored her. For a moment, Trinidad stood paralyzed, the chief's words echoing back at her.

"But he loved you three. He wasn't lying about that part."

It hit her suddenly that the chief might have another motive for looking deeper into the case. Was she was trying to help the women her brother had betrayed? Maybe Trinidad had judged the chief wrongly after all.

People can be many things, can't they?

Well, why not?

With that startling thought, Trinidad marched to the food truck. It would be a long day, but, hopefully, a fruitful one. Perhaps, with a little luck, they could finally serve up some justice for Juliette and get her out of that jail and help the chief put away the real killer.

Get those photos, Quinn.

Fast.

The time had come for her to climb aboard the hulking food truck. After a few false starts, she guided the enormous thing to Lupin's home as best she could. It felt like trying to direct an elephant from the inside. At least it was a source of entertainment for the twins. The boys dissolved in laughter as she took some turns ridiculously wide and others so close that the tires jumped up onto the curb. By the final turn, she'd just about gotten the hang of the unwieldy behemoth. She felt a great sense of pride as she rolled the truck into Lupin's driveway.

Candy Simon did not seem to appreciate her driving prowess as she threw open Lupin's front door and hurried over.

How does she get such speed on those heels? Trinidad wondered as Candy hustled to the driveway. Her appearance was neat and professional with just a hint of provocativeness in her short tan skirt and V-neck lavender blouse. Now her nails were painted a demure shade of pink. Thinking of the last time she'd seen Candy through the window at her real estate office made Trinidad squirm. She sincerely hoped Candy hadn't gotten wind of her 911 call.

Candy charged toward the food truck and stopped dead, squinting up at the roof. “What is that thing on the top?”

“There are many theories on that, but actually—” Trinidad started.

“Never mind.” Candy pointed one long elegant finger at the street. “I don’t want that relic parked in the driveway. You have to move it.”

“All right,” Trinidad said in her calmest tone. *Keep thinking about the amazing antique ice cream machine,* she ordered herself, *and the promotional opportunity for the shop instead of the abrasive lady who is bossing you around as if you were a toddler.* She caught a whiff of fresh paint as she cranked the engine into reverse. The front of the old house had been given a face-lift with a coat of glossy ivory. There was no doubt who Candy had chosen for the work. Favors indeed.

With the help of Diego and Carlos, who shouted directions from the sidewalk, she was able to parallel park the monster vehicle.

“Further down,” Candy hollered. “Leave room for the potential buyers.”

Teeth gritted, she wiped the perspiration from her brow and eased the truck along a few more feet, grinding the rubber wheels against the curb. Candy watched the whole thing with a scowl on her face, which rapidly transformed into a gracious smile when several cars rolled slowly in view.

“The suckers are arriving,” Diego said in a stage whisper. As the Shimmy and Shake staff unwrapped the utensils and readied the window for orders, the cars pulled into the driveway, dislodging some visitors.

“That’s Stuart Blanding and his wife, Miriam,” Carlos said. “They’re not house hunters; they’re just being nosy. Everyone wants to see what Lupin’s house is like inside. I heard he hid away a coin collection and forgot where he stashed it.”

"Nah, not a coin collection, it was a deed to a gold mine," his brother put it.

Another car pulled up, and two more people got out. Candy greeted them at the door with an effusive welcome. An RV crowded in behind them. It seemed Candy's strategy was working.

Warren rattled up in the theater van, Cora in the passenger seat. She looked relaxed, less surly than in her theater surroundings. Trinidad thought she might have even caught the hint of a smile. Warren actually went around and opened the passenger side door for her. Gallantry from him? *More surprises,* Trinidad thought.

He caught sight of her and waved. It appeared as though he'd decided to head for their truck, but Cora redirected him towards the house by snagging his elbow.

No ice cream until the house is examined, she figured Cora was saying. Why would those two be interested in Lupin's? Curiosity, like Carlos had suggested? Surely they weren't in the market to buy the property when their back-to-back condos were in much better shape.

She was so focused on her thoughts, she didn't notice Vince Jr. waving at her.

She leaned on the window counter. "Hello, Vince. Did you come to see the house? I hear talk of something priceless once hidden in there."

He shook his head in disgust. "There's no treasure in there. It's been gone over by Candy with a microscope and everyone else she's had trailing through. Who would actually think there was a treasure lying around?" His tone was filled with the arrogant certainty that only a newly emerged adult could manage. "That's just dumb."

"How are things going at Store Some More?"

He brightened. "A couple of checks came in. I figured that might cheer up Juliette. That's actually why I came. I want to go see her, but I'm not on her visitor's list. Do you think you could get her to add me?"

His look was so plaintive that it struck at her heart. "I'll ask her, okay?"

"Okay. Let me know when I can go." He glanced over the hand-printed menu on the side of the truck, his gaze wistful.

"Do you want some ice cream?" Trinidad said. "You can be our first customer."

"Does it cost anything?"

Just an antique ice cream machine and a whole day's work, she thought. "Not a thing."

She parceled out a scoop, and Diego eased it into a waffle cone. Vince thanked them, and she thought she saw a bit of lightness creep into his posture as he tasted. It was why she loved everything about ice cream. The glorious creamy stuff was comfort in hard times and the perfect celebration treat. Balm to the soul, as Papa Luis would say. She remembered experimenting with him to create a mango and cream flavor to mimic his favorite sweet snack, a cookie topped with guava and cream cheese. Would Sprocketerians be interested in an unusual flavor combo? Key lime might be risky enough, she'd thought, for small-town Americana, but, lately, she was beginning to think she'd made all kinds of wrong assumptions about the people in this particular town.

When the first few visitors finished touring the house and strolled out, Candy handed them glossy brochures and pointed them to the food truck. "Enjoy an ice cream, courtesy of Simon Realty," she sang out. "You have my number if you have any questions about the property. Ring me anytime, day or night."

The flurry of activity started in earnest for the Shimmy and Shake team as the three of them snapped into action.

"What can we get you?" Carlos boomed from the order window. "We've got Vanilla Bean, Fresh-picked Strawberry, and Silken Chocolate."

Diego stood by with a scooper in each hand. "Tell them about the waffle cones," he whispered.

Carlos launched into an enthusiastic description of the made-from-scratch waffle cones. Trinidad grinned. These boys were naturals. Scooping madly, they dispensed a half dozen ice cream desserts before the next stream of visitors approached.

"Don't you have banana?" a man in shorts and a red, white, and blue shirt asked. Trinidad pegged him as a holiday camper.

"Not today," Trinidad hastened to explain, "but the Shimmy and Shake Shop opens on July Fourth on Main Street, and our banana custard will make your mouth water. Plus, we'll have key lime and maybe a surprise or two." She handed him a flyer along with his second-choice vanilla dessert.

"All right." He paused, craning his neck. "I don't get it, though. What's the fried egg on top of the truck got to do with ice cream?"

Trinidad started to explain until the line swelled behind him. "It's a long story. Come to the shop, and I'll tell you."

The scooping grew fast and furious as people began to arrive on foot as well, streaming up both sides of the narrow street and hoofing it to the open house. Noodles wagged his tail as folks meandered by the truck. The rising heat began to work in their favor. Who on the planet didn't want a cold ice cream treat on a sweltering day? She was glad the truck was cool enough to keep Noodles comfortable. Sweat bathed her temples, and the boys both had flushed cheeks.

"Three chocolates and a 'berry," Diego shouted. "What can I get the next in line?"

Trinidad knew she'd made the right choice hiring the Martin twins. Whoever said teenagers were slackers had never met these two. One of these days she'd have to thank their mother for raising two lifesavers.

Trinidad could not resist beaming as she surveyed the happy customers lined up at the van. None of them seemed remotely interested in buying Lupin's house, but they had plenty of enthusiasm for free ice cream. Noodles enjoyed shoving his head out the passenger window and greeting the guests. Could there be a more adorable mascot? A dozen more scoops left her breathless, her wrist aching from the repetitive motion. *Good training for Shimmy's opening day,* she thought. It reminded her she was going to need reinforcements to help run the store when the twins were unavailable, but she'd put off that problem until later. Quickly, she dispensed a strawberry dessert to a woman shielded from view by a wide-brimmed hat. When there was a lull in the line, she climbed out to stretch her legs and see if she could spot Quinn.

"I guess a lick won't hurt you," said a familiar voice from beneath the hat.

She twirled around to see Tanya Grant reaching through the passenger window to fondle Noodles's ears. Shadows under her eyes indicated she had not been sleeping well, but she was impeccably turned out, as always, in a crisp cotton jumpsuit and strappy sandals. She noticed Trinidad staring at her.

"Thought I'd try an ice cream, but your dog here stretched out for a lick while I was adjusting my hat."

"Oh. I am terribly sorry. Let me get you a new one."

"No. It's okay. I like dogs better than people most of the time. They never judge, you know?"

"I sure do. Are you...I mean, did you come to look at the property?" Dumb question, Trinidad. Why else would she be standing there?

She shrugged. "When Sonny and I were together, he used to go on and on about Edward Lupin and his collections. I figured I might as well come and see the place. Doesn't look like anything but a wreck to me."

"I agree, but it seems like lots of people were interested in whatever was in there. What did Sonny think it was?"

"Coins, stamps, gold bullion, the crown jewels… I don't know, and I don't care. I just figured, if there was any sign of it today, I'd buy the house on the spot and end any chance he had at finding it." Anger made her voice hard and flat.

"No love lost?"

"None. I used him to make Kevin jealous because Kev was dragging his feet, and I wanted to get married." She sighed. "I guess I got what I deserved. My father's private investigator caught Sonny selling a mirror he'd stolen from our home."

"Oh, wow. That's shocking."

One delicate eyebrow hitched up. "The fact that he was stealing or the notion that my father has my boyfriends investigated?"

"Both, I guess."

"Dad never could find any dirt on Kevin, though he surely did try." She tasted a tiny lick of ice cream. "I guess it still shocks me, too, that my love life is fodder for private investigators, but I should be used to both by now. Funny. Everybody wants money, but they don't realize that, when you have it, you never know if people love you for who you are or what's in your bank account. Dad espouses the concept of 'financial equality,' which means he wants a son-in-law as rich as he is."

"I'm sure Kevin loved you for the right reasons," Trinidad suggested gently.

"I thought so, but maybe I was wrong about that, too. I have the world's worst track record." Another tiny lick. "Perhaps time would have shown him to be an opportunist like all the others, but he died before I could find that out."

Trinidad searched for something to say. How unutterably sad to wonder, as Tanya did, if she was worthy of love without her shiny million-dollar wrapper.

Tanya toyed with the plastic spoon. "I've traveled Europe and been to the opera a million times and stayed in five-star hotels on a regular basis, and you know what my favorite memory is?

Eating greasy hot dogs and drinking store-brand soda, sitting on a tattered blanket with Kevin at Three Egg Lake." A tear traced a gleaming path down her cheek. She wiped it away. "I guess those days are gone forever now, huh?" With a sniff she dumped the unfinished ice cream into the trash container they'd set up.

"I'm sorry, Tanya. Very sorry."

"Me, too, but that doesn't bring him back. I understand why people say that now. Nothing is going to fill that empty spot, not even seeing Juliette go to prison for life."

Trinidad searched for something to say but came up dry.

Tanya lifted her chin. "I've planned a memorial for Kevin at the gazebo tomorrow, ten, before it gets too hot." She looked at Trinidad. "Come if you want."

"All right. I will."

"There will be a nice buffet, and Noodles is welcome too." She sniffed. "See? I'm really not as bad as I seem."

"You've been dealing with some strong emotions."

"Still am—some that will never go away. At least I know Juliette is going to pay for what she did. I'll make sure of it. It's something, anyway."

Before Trinidad could say another word, Tanya walked off, sliding into her Mercedes and driving smoothly away. Trinidad watched her go.

Tanya would no doubt use her considerable family resources to make sure Juliette lived out her days in prison. Only incontrovertible proof would change her view and that of the town.

She scanned the sidewalks for Quinn. Where was he? The muscles in her stomach cinched tight. She was about to text him when another half dozen people lined up for ice cream and she scrambled back to her duties.

Forty minutes later, Carlos finally set his scooper down into its water bath. "I'm gonna go in and use the bathroom."

"I don't think Miss Simon wants us mingling," Diego said.

The mischievous gleam was back in his twin's eye. "Miss Simon won't turn away a hard-working young boy in front of all the potential buyers. Besides," he said, "I want to sniff around and see if I can nab the deed to the gold mine."

"It was a coin collection," his brother insisted.

"I'll look for that, too. Maybe he hid it under the toilet tank. Nobody ever looks there. Too bad I can't bring the video cam, but I have my cell phone in case I find something."

She and Diego tidied up and doled out scoops to the next few patrons. She scanned over their heads searching for Quinn. It was almost 1:30, and she wondered what could be keeping him.

Diego returned, crestfallen. "No sign of any treasure, not in the bathroom or the kitchen anyway." He brightened. "I saw some dark-haired guy, though, in this sweet classic car. He drove right over the curb and parked his big old boat half up on the sidewalk. Miss Simon almost had a conniption until she figured out he might actually buy the place. The way he was filling his pocket from the candy bowl, he must be some kind of weirdo. That candy was gnarly. Tasted like it was from a World War II army ration or something." He put a finger to his lip. "Almost busted a tooth on one."

Mr. Mavis appeared next at the window.

"Hi, Mr. Mavis. How are your cousin's chickens?" Trinidad called out.

"Doing well, thanks to you and Quinn," he said. "And your dog. Sure do appreciate that."

"Are you here to see the house?"

He grinned. "Nah. Mostly just came over 'cause I heard there was free food. No business at the gas station right now since everyone's here."

"What can we get you?" Diego repeated the flavor options.

"Well, that's a lot to consider." Mr. Mavis scratched his chin. "The strawberry must be real good because summer is berry season. Local berries?"

"Yes, sir. I bought them at the farmers market right here in town," Trinidad said.

"Flavor should be pretty zippy."

"Oh, yes." The succulent berries had produced a rich, jewel-toned puree that made her mouth water while she was cooking it.

Mr. Mavis mused. "'Course, you can't go wrong with chocolate. And vanilla...is that the kind with the black specks in there?" He pointed to the vat. "Not sure I trust the specks."

"Those are bits of the vanilla pod."

"Vanilla comes from a pod?" His eyes went round. "You gotta be joshing me."

She smiled. "A pod," she assured him. "Actually, vanilla comes from an orchid. It's a tropical flower. My grandfather's been experimenting with growing some in his greenhouse in Miami. It has to be hand-pollinated because, in the wild, only certain bees and hummingbirds can get the job done. Explains why it's such an expensive spice. It's a tricky business. Very finicky."

"And I read that vanilla pods don't have any smell or taste until after they're cured," Diego put in.

"True," she said.

"Weird," Mr. Mavis said.

Trinidad smiled. "Also true."

"Huh. I'll have to tell the missus that. She's sort of a botanical whiz kid." He rocked back on his heels. Two more people joined the line behind him.

"What flavor would you like?" Diego said, trying to keep the Mavis train on the track.

"Huh. Well, that's pretty interesting about the vanilla, but I mean a good strawberry is hard to pass up. You know..."

"How about we put a half scoop of all three in a waffle cone for you?" Trinidad suggested.

"Which type of waffle cone?" Diego started.

"Let's go with the regular," Trinidad said quickly before

Mavis's train could leave the station again. When Mr. Mavis and the folks behind him were served, Trinidad finally remembered to check her phone. She found a text message from Quinn sent two hours prior:

> Truck had a flat. No spare. Had to stop in town for a replacement and then go do the nut delivery. On my way to pick up photos now. See you soon.

Relieved, she pictured him in his worn jeans and faded green T-shirt with his untied shoelace trailing behind him. There was something quiet and deep and sincere about Quinn Logan that made her want to smile. At that very moment, he was probably hustling back to Sprocket with the precious pack of photos in his hand. She'd make sure to save some vanilla for him and Doug to enjoy.

They were about halfway through their ice cream supplies, and the heat of the day was beginning to thin out the open house visitors.

"Hey, since it's slow now, can we go check out that hot rod car?" Carlos asked. "We never see sweet rides like that in Sprocket."

She laughed. "All right. Take a picture for me of this set of wheels in case it's gone when I climb out of here," Trinidad said.

"Sure thing, boss."

She was wiping down the counter and counting the remaining waffle cones when the boys returned.

"Awww, man," Diego said. "What a machine. It makes the Plymouth we want to buy look like a tin can."

"A squashed tin can," Carlos agreed.

"What kind of car is it?" Trinidad said. "Let me see."

Diego offered his cell phone screen.

Trinidad squinted at the photo.

A sky-blue vehicle with a convertible white top and sparkling whitewall tires.

Her heart thudded.

Diego's comments came back to her.

Some guy phoned for you; couldn't understand him.

He was filling his pockets from the candy bowl.

Carlos peered at the screen. "I think it's a Buick."

"No," she said slowly. "It's a 1954 Chevy Bel Air."

Diego whistled. "Wow, Miss Jones. I didn't know you were into cars."

"I'm not, but I know someone who is." Her breath caught as she left the two boys in charge of the truck and hustled down the steep steps. Without even bothering to remove her apron, she hurried toward the house.

Papa Luis. There could be no other person driving that car and matching the description. But it couldn't be. He lived 2,000 miles away on the opposite coast. What in the world was he doing in Sprocket?

Edging past a few straggling visitors, she made it to the front door just as Candy opened it and ushered out none other than her grandfather. Papa Luis was his usual tidy self, from the thick thatch of glossy dark hair, neat button-up shirt and trousers cinched around his stocky waist with a leather belt. His glasses glinted in the sunlight, and he blinked.

"Papa," she said at the very same moment he recognized her.

"My girl," he cried, throwing his arms around her and squeezing tight.

She was not sure whether to laugh or cry, but, for a moment, all she felt was the rush of love, wrapped in the embrace of the man dearest in the world to her. He smelled of that familiar pine soap, and his wide shoulders were the same sturdy set that had absorbed so many of her tears.

When he released her, he gestured to Candy, his brown eyes

sparkling with a mixture of intelligence and good humor. "This is my granddaughter, Trinidad."

Candy was rendered momentarily speechless, her gaze darting between them.

"I know," Candy said, confusion written on her smooth brow. "Trinidad and I have a partnership. She's scooping ice cream for me."

"Yes, I asked in town, where to find you," Papa said. "A fellow at the coffee shop told me my Trina would be here serving her treats. That's why I came."

Candy's eyes narrowed. "So, you're not here to see the house?"

He took Candy's hand and patted it. "I have seen it, but there isn't enough sun here. Living in the shade like that all the time?" He sniffed. "No good."

Candy rolled her eyes. "You've got to be kidding me."

Papa Luis did not seem to notice her dismay. He gave her a slight bow, pumped her hand and released it. "Thank you for your time, Miss Simon. I would suggest some cutting back of branches to let the sun in. Too much gloom. Bad for the soul." He took Trinidad by the arm, and they walked toward the sidewalk.

"What are you doing here, Papa?"

He lifted a careless shoulder. "Your mother is off on a luxurious cruise for a month, and Yolo is concocting some sort of business plan involving aquariums that keeps him busy. You never saw such fascination with fish filters in your life. My plants are happy for now, and I wanted to see this town where you've settled with my own eyes."

She goggled. "So, you drove here? All the way from Miami? With no GPS?"

"What's a GPS?"

"Never mind. How did you find your way?"

"With maps and a slew of kind strangers who helped me when I needed it. The world is full of helpers, just like I tell you. I got addresses so we can correspond."

No, there would be no strangers around Papa Luis. He'd saunter into any cafe in the world, sip strong coffee, and immediately launch into a lengthy conversation with the nearest patron. The image made her smile and gather him up for another hug. "I am so glad you arrived safely. And you called to tell me you were coming, didn't you? I'm sorry, but my teen employees could not understand you."

"Answering machines," he said. "Who can understand anyone on those things? Makes everyone sound like they are speaking from the bottom of a well."

Of course he would never believe it had anything to do with his accent. As far as he was concerned, he had no accent. He frowned as he took in the street. "It is much smaller than I pictured."

"It's nice, quiet. I am getting used to it."

"I thought you said it was near the water."

"There's a lake, Three Egg Lake. I haven't had time to see much of it, but you can fish there, I've heard."

He squeezed her arm and got down to the main point. "Fishing and quiet are fine, but it's so far away from your people."

Her people. She sighed. "I miss you and Mother and Yolo."

"And Len, the seafood man. He's disappointed that you didn't come visit so we can introduce you. You would like him, I think, and you would never lack for fresh scallops."

"Len is a great guy, no doubt, but I'm doing really well here," she said. "The shop is going to open on Thursday, and there's been a lot of interest already."

"But here it's..." He lifted a shoulder. "So close together. Small towns can be funny places." He turned a sober gaze on her. "I saw in the paper, when I was looking for you, there's been a murder, a young man killed in his store, close to yours."

She sucked in a breath. *Wait until he finds out that you discovered the body and you're trying to unearth the real killer.* "Yes, but that was a freak thing. Sprocket is a safe town."

They'd arrived at his shimmering Bel Air. Not a speck of dust anywhere on that vehicle. Two of the wheels were indeed perched on the sidewalk. Her heart leapt when she noticed Quinn's truck parked right behind. He'd finally made it, she thought with a sigh of relief. He was probably at the food truck searching for her.

Papa was frowning, his thick slash of brows drawn together into a single line. "If Sprocket is a safe town like you say…" He looked down at the curb. "Then how do you explain that?"

She followed Papa's pointed finger down to the street. Wedged between the truck and the curb was a limp bundle. She could not decipher what it was at first, until she caught a glimpse of fingers outstretched and still and an arm protruding from a familiar faded green T-shirt.

Chapter Thirteen

"QUINN!" TRINIDAD DROPPED TO HER knees and clutched at his wrist. Fingers trembling, she sought for a pulse. Nothing. Horror robbed her of breath.

"Oh, please don't let him be dead," she silently prayed. Repositioning her fingers, she tried again and felt the strong thud of the pulse in his wrist. The relief almost made her pass out.

"Oh, man," Carlos said as the boys arrived at full speed. "Is it another body? I should have brought the video cam."

"Uh-oh," Diego breathed. "It's Quinn."

Candy hurried up. "What now?" She paused. "What is Quinn doing there?"

"He's been hurt," Trinidad half sobbed. "Call an ambulance."

"We already did," Diego said. Carlos peered around his shoulder. "The chief and the ambulance are on their way. Maybe you should pull him onto the sidewalk."

Trinidad nodded, taking hold of his wrist.

"Hang on," Carlos interrupted. "I don't think you're supposed to move people when they're injured."

"Yeah, but if he's been shot, he could die if we don't stop the bleeding," his brother said.

Bleeding? Trinidad fought for breath. "We didn't hear any shots," she managed.

"Silencer?" Carlos suggested.

"Silencers don't completely deaden the noise, just muffle it," Diego said. "They're more appropriately called suppressors rather than silencers, so we probably would have heard something."

Carlos nodded. "Okay. What about a knife? Could have been stabbed."

Trinidad felt like screaming. "Stop helping. Both of you."

Carlos cocked his head. "I was just gonna say we should put him on his back in case his heart stops, and then we could do, like, CPR."

"It might work," Diego said, "but statistically nine of ten people who suffer cardiac arrest outside the home die anyway."

Stabbing. CPR. Survival. Trinidad's head spun, and she clamped her teeth together to keep from screaming at the twins. Her grandfather gripped her arm.

Carlos looked from Trinidad to his brother. "Uh…we should stop helping now."

With her grandfather's assistance, Trinidad grasped Quinn's arm, and they lifted him as gently as they could onto the sidewalk. She frantically scanned for blood but didn't see any signs of injury other than the fact that he wasn't conscious. As she monitored his pulse, he began to stir.

She put a quaking hand on his cheek. "Quinn? Can you hear me? What happened?"

One of his eyes fluttered open. "Owww."

Pure, sweet relief coursed through her body. He was alive and talking. One by one, her muscles seemed to shakily resume their functioning. She placed her palm on his chest and grimaced along with him. "Where does it hurt?"

His face tightened in pain. "The spot where someone clobbered me on the back of the head," he groaned. He pried his other eye open and tried to sit up.

"You should stay still," Papa Luis advised.

"Hello, sir," Quinn said, extending a palm from his prone position. "We haven't met."

"Luis," Papa said. "I am Trinidad's grandfather."

"Honored."

Trinidad would have laughed at the formal greeting, the handshake extended from Quinn on his back to her grandfather, if she wasn't so worried.

Quinn cleared his throat. "Not to alarm anyone, but I am going to sit up now."

"Bad idea," Carlos said. "We had a cousin who got a concussion from running into a doorknob, and he..."

Diego held up a finger. "We're not helping anymore, remember?"

Quinn sat up anyway. He braced himself with one shoulder against the driver's side door of his truck. His lips thinned in a grim line. "Owww," he said again.

Trinidad stayed on her knees by his side, checking to be sure she'd not missed any oozing blood or stab wounds. "Ambulance is on its way. Can you tell us what happened?"

Before he could get the story out, a siren echoed along the street. Chief Bigley jerked her squad car to a halt and leapt out. "Quinn, are you all right?"

He nodded, which made him wince. "Don't worry. I'm not on death's door. I have an extremely thick skull, just ask my high school English teacher."

She exhaled. "What happened?"

"I was getting out of my truck, and someone hit me on the back of the head with something."

"Probably that," Diego said, pointing to a hamburger-sized rock lying near the car. "Awww, man. A news crew would be all over this. There's some of Quinn's hair stuck to the rock."

Bigley looked closer. "And a trace of blood. Did they steal your wallet? Was it a possible carjacking?"

"No," he said, "I've got my wallet, and no one on earth would want my truck but…" His eyes widened, and he patted his front pocket and groaned, locking eyes with Trinidad. "They took the photos. I'm so sorry. They're gone."

Trinidad tried to keep the crushing disappointment from showing on her face. She pasted on a bright smile. "The important thing is that you're okay. You could have been killed."

"What photos?" the chief demanded as the ambulance screamed up.

The medics took over and assessed Quinn, edging away the bystanders. The chief grabbed Trinidad by the elbow and steered her a few feet from the action.

"What photos?" she repeated.

Trinidad took a fortifying breath. "Juliette took pictures of the contents of Lupin's storage unit. They were at the photo shop in Scotch Corners ready to be picked up. I started to tell you about it when you came to my shop but…"

Chief tensed. "But you didn't, and you didn't feel like sharing the info with me earlier, either, like say, giving me a phone call to inform me?"

"We were going to tell you if we found anything."

"You should have told me regardless. I'm the law."

She felt a flicker of anger. "I don't think you're exactly on Juliette's side. You sent her to jail."

The chief's eyes were cold. "The evidence sent her to jail, and you shutting me out might have just cost us information that could have cleared her. Did you think of that while you were playing detective?"

Trinidad felt like wailing aloud. She kept her lips tightly together to keep from making things worse.

The chief blew out a breath. "If you want to help Juliette, you need to trust me to do my job. If you're going to withhold information, then you look just as guilty as she does."

"I..."

"And what would you have done with the photos if they incriminated Juliette in some way? Destroyed them?"

"I... No, I wouldn't have, I mean..."

Bigley shook her head. "I should have known. Juliette didn't come clean about everything in my first interview with her, either. She conveniently forgot to mention her fight with Kevin and the threat she left on his cell phone. Looks like you're both pretty skilled with the sins of omission."

She lifted her chin. "I'm trying to protect my friend."

"And I'm trying to put away a killer," Bigley snapped.

"But you put the wrong person in jail."

Both women stared at each other.

Trinidad was still trying to think of what to say when the chief strode back to her car. Ambulance attendants loaded Quinn on a stretcher. She hurried over and gave his hand a squeeze.

"I'll be fine," he said. "The doctors will x-ray my pea brain to be sure it isn't cracked or something." Lines bracketed his mouth.

"I'm sorry this happened, Quinn. I feel so guilty. I should have gone with you to the photo shop."

"Not your fault. I can't believe I lost the photos right here in Sprocket." Defeat crept across his face. "I'm no good at the cloak and dagger stuff or most anything, for that matter, except growing nuts and fixing engines." He sighed.

"This is not your fault." She looked around at the bystanders trying not to outright stare as the chief talked to each one of them: Warren, Cora, Vince, Candy.

And what about the others who had been around only a moment or two before? Tanya, perhaps Sonny packing up his paints, all of the outwardly friendly Sprocketerians. Any of them would have had the opportunity to hit Quinn with the rock and make off with the pictures.

She forced a smile and pressed a quick kiss to his forehead.

"Don't worry about that right now. I will come to the hospital as soon as I pack up the truck."

"Actually, I know it's a lot to ask, but would you please go to the farm and check on Doug? Tell him I'll be home as soon as I can. He might be, er, upset so maybe play down the whole injury thing, okay? I mean, tell him the truth, I never lie to him, but...he may be fearful when he hears I got hurt. I'm sorry to ask, but..."

"Of course I will, and, if you have to be admitted overnight, I'll stay with him."

His blue eyes widened. "You would do that?"

"Yes, I would." She felt her cheeks begin to glow. "I'm just trying to live up to the townsfolk. Somebody told me that people in Sprocket are good sorts."

"So they are, except for the one who hit me with a rock." He blew out a relieved breath. "Thank you, Trinidad. I'm really sorry I lost the photos." His voice broke as if he might cry.

She squeezed his hand to reassure him. "Like I said, it's not your fault. Did you...I mean, did you happen to take a peek at them?"

His face crumpled. "All I did was glance to be sure they were photos of the storage unit. I figured it would be better if we went through them together."

"Do you remember anything in the photos? Anything at all?"

He closed his eyes for a moment. "Boxes, blankets, some stacked papers, some pots, an old fishbowl, it looked like." His eyes opened again. "Sorry, but nothing much else I can recall."

"It's okay. You didn't know you were going to be attacked for them. How could you? Did you tell anyone where you were headed?"

"No. No one." Quinn was loaded onto the ambulance. He waved a tired hand in farewell.

Trinidad waved back, fighting tears.

Papa Luis watched the police car and the ambulance roll away. "So, Sprocket is a nice safe town, huh?" He shook his head.

She wanted to answer, but her throat felt clogged with tears. Papa wrapped his arm around her shoulder and held on. "We will sort it out, whatever needs sorting."

She was grateful for the words, even if she had no idea how they would actually come to pass.

Somehow, they limped through the rest of the event. Candy locked up the house and got into her car without a word to the ice cream team. Trinidad took that as a dismissal. All that remained was to clean up the shrapnel and get back to break the news of Quinn's injury to Doug. She wondered how he would take it.

She parked Papa in a folding chair in the shade with some ice cream while she and the boys packed up. Noodles sat at his feet, mouthing a dog treat.

Carlos and Diego were electric with excitement. "Oh, man. This is insane. So, like, someone attacked Quinn to get their hands on some photos?" Carlos said.

Her mind felt like curdled milk. "Guys, how about we just clean up here and hold off on the detecting for a bit. I need to focus." Her hands trembled as she grabbed a roll of paper towels. Her mind kept replaying the horror: Quinn could have been killed, his skull cracked open.

Somehow, she managed to do the job. The twins helped her wash the utensils and wipe down the stainless steel counter until it shone.

Task finished, the questions remained. Who had known that Quinn was planning to pick up the photos in the first place? She hadn't told anyone, and neither had Quinn. She was sure Stan hadn't, either. The shadow outside Stan's office replayed in her mind. Whoever it was had overheard and decided they had to prevent anyone from seeing those pictures.

Why?

Obviously, it all went back to Edward Lupin and his phantom treasure.

She realized the boys were both standing there, waiting to be taken back home. Her gaze drifted to her grandfather.

"Tell you what, boys. How would you like to take a ride in a classic Chevy Bel Air?"

Her suggestion was met with enthusiastic whoops. Papa would love to show off his car, and it would give her time to check in on Doug.

Papa Luis greeted her idea with his usual geniality. "Of course. I'll demonstrate to them all the features of a truly fine automobile."

She kissed him. "I'll meet you back at the shop, okay? There's a great coffee place across the street where you can wait for me. Ask them to make you the strongest cup they can muster along with a banana square. You'll love them."

Noodles rejoined her in his co-pilot's position in Quinn's truck. As she drove away, she saw, in the rearview mirror, her grandfather greeting each boy with a formal handshake and a nod of his dark-crowned head.

Her thoughts still ricocheted like kernels in a popcorn machine. Some detail from the day poked at her, but she could not focus her thoughts to retrieve it. Visions of treasure, masked attackers, and poor Quinn rolled around her brain. And now, a friendly Cuban gentleman had joined the mental procession. Her frazzled nerves refused to settle.

Close to the farm, her cell phone rang, and she pulled over to answer it.

"I'm here at the hospital," Stan said. "Quinn called, and I came over immediately. He filled me in just before the chief rang. She was…displeased. My ears are still throbbing."

"I'm sorry."

"Nothing to apologize for, but I'm afraid we can't count on

much of a spirit of cooperation from her until she cools down. Quinn said to tell you he is done with the scan and expected to be released in a couple of hours. He asked about Doug."

"I'm on my way there now."

"I will tell him before I get going."

"My grandpa is in town, Stan. He might be showing up at your shop later."

"I will be honored to meet him." He paused. "Trinidad, someone is feeling threatened by our inquiries. Be careful. Very careful."

She felt a thrill of fear. "I will, Stan. You, too."

A few minutes later, she was entering the office at Logan's Nut Farm. Doug was standing behind the counter, tinkering with the tiny internal components of some sort of machine.

"Hi, Doug."

He gave a slight nod, eyes on Noodles who wagged his tail.

She told him, as gently as she could, that Quinn had had a minor accident, a bump to the head. "He's in the hospital, just for a short while longer."

The word hospital landed like a bomb. Doug backed away from the counter and began to rock back and forth, a pained keening coming from somewhere deep in his throat. She moved forward, hands out to comfort him, but that only increased his agitation.

Unsure, she backed away a few steps.

"It's going to be okay," she reassured. "He will be home soon, in a couple of hours, most likely." Her words did not soothe him, and her proximity seemed to further his agitation. He started to pound his thighs with his fists. She struggled to think what to try next. Noodles edged past her, hustled to Doug and rose up on his rear legs, his old front paws scrabbling gently at Doug's stomach.

"Noodles, don't..."

Doug's noises grew louder, and he tried to shove the dog away. "Down, Noodles," she said, reaching for his collar. Noodles ignored her. He kept pawing, ignoring Doug's attempts to push him.

She was just about to snag the dog when, suddenly, Doug dropped to his knees, and his arms went around Noodles. Trinidad froze. They stayed there, and Doug's moans grew softer and his body stilled. He buried his face in the thick fur of Noodles's back, and the dog licked his neck.

Breath held, she waited. The waves of Doug's agitation seemed to calm into gentler ripples. After several long moments, he rubbed his cheek on Noodles's graying head. The dog licked Doug under the chin and poked his nose into Doug's ear. She watched in awe. Some part of Noodles's training she hadn't even known about kicked in, and the dog had gotten between Doug and whatever fears were tormenting him. Doug's breathing slowed and his rocking stilled. They sat together on the floor until Doug went fully calm again, the agitation gone.

She stayed motionless, unwilling to break the tranquility. She was afraid to upset him again, afraid to ask him to come with her. Should she stay at the farm or try and get him to leave with her? After a while, she ventured a suggestion. "Doug, would you like to stay at the Shimmy and Shake Shop with me until Quinn comes? I could use some help with the machines."

For a while, he did not respond. The seconds ticked by. Without a word, he got up and left the office with Noodles trotting next to him. They both climbed into Quinn's front seat, waiting.

He seemed okay, in control, the storm of emotion passed. Noodles wagged his tail and lounged against Doug's leg. Doug kept his fingers twined in the dog's hair.

Starting the engine, Trinidad guided the truck off of the farm property, her own senses buzzing. She was not even sure what she had witnessed between Noodles and Doug, but she knew it was a powerful moment. The silent conversation between her dog and Quinn's brother had spoken louder than any human voice.

Heaving out a breath, she thanked God for Noodles, her angel in a fur coat.

Back at the store, she found her grandfather pulling up in his Chevy. "I stayed to chat with the Martins. Wonderful family." He beamed, offering his palm to Doug and introducing himself. Doug looked at his feet and ignored Papa's outstretched palm.

"He doesn't shake hands, Papa. This is Doug, Quinn's brother. He's going to stay here and help until Quinn comes." She avoided using the word "hospital."

Papa smiled broadly, and the three humans and one dog let themselves into the shop. She felt a surge of pride when she showed Papa the various machines and sparkling clean counters.

"A marvel of a place," he said, taking it all in. "When did you say we open?"

The "we" gave her a bit of a start. "On the Fourth of July."

"Excellent," he said. "I will be settled in by then. Refreshed and ready to report for duty. These machines are fancy, but the basics are the same."

"Um, Papa, how long were you planning to stay?" And *where*?

"I am at your disposal for the whole summer," he said grandly.

The whole summer?

"Your mother will be gone another three weeks, and then Frida will stay with her. Your mother will be in good hands, and I've hired Len, the fishmonger, to care for my greenhouse on the weekends. He's very generous with his time, you know. Very good man."

He moved around her, peering into the refrigerator and freezer before he checked the whimsical name tags for the ice cream tubs. Two still had yet to be filled. "You know what you need, Trina?" His brown eyes sparkled. "A taste of the Cuba. Our mango and cream, remember? That would be just the thing." He admired the antique ice cream machine she'd set up for display in the front window. "Fine workmanship. A treasure."

Doug examined the shake machine, his reflection mirrored in the immaculate stainless steel.

"I think we have a man with an eye for machinery here," Papa said.

"Me too."

Her grandfather had been an electrical engineer who had kept things humming in the rumbling Cuban sugar mills. Papa appreciated efficiency, clean design, and someone who exhibited lively curiosity akin to his own.

Papa yawned, glancing out the front window as a taxi rolled up. Quinn got out, and Trinidad met him at the door with a gentle hug. "Are you okay? You didn't have to get a cab. I would have come and gotten you."

"I've caused enough fuss already." Quinn pumped Papa Luis's hand as she introduced them. "Good to see you again, sir. This time while I'm upright."

"Please call me Luis." His look went sly. "I understand you were doing a favor for my granddaughter when you were knocked down."

"Yes, sir," Quinn said. Doug straightened from his perusal of the shake machine. Quinn moved to him. When he was a few feet away, he held out his hand, and Doug clasped Quinn's fingers tightly between his palms. Quinn covered their joined hands with his free one. It was oddly touching, the formal gesture, which held such deep feeling.

"I'm A-OK," Quinn said softly. "Are you?"

Doug nodded. His mouth twitched with some unspoken emotion before he let go.

"Thank you, thank you both for keeping Doug company." Quinn reached down to give Noodles an ear rub. "I'd better get us home."

"I'll drive you," Trinidad said. "You shouldn't be behind the wheel with a head injury."

"That's what the doctor said, too. I guess I should take you up on your offer. Stan said he and Meg would return my truck to the farm tonight."

"We'll take the Pinto, then." She turned to Papa with the question that had been bubbling inside her since she'd clapped eyes on him. He was still studying Quinn carefully.

"Papa, um, there's no hotel in town, but there are a few nice ones in Josef, about thirty minutes from here."

He waved her off. "Hotels are for travelers like your mother. I'm not so fancy. Your house will be fine."

"But, I, uh, it's small—tiny, in fact. I'm not sure..."

He smiled. "Not to worry at all, my girl. I require only a very compact space, a chair or sofa in a far corner. Point me the way. I will drive over and fix us something to eat right after I get some coffee at the shop across the street."

That seemed to be all there was to it. All she could think to do was give him directions to her miniscule house.

"I will see you there. Goodnight."

Quinn pulled the shop door closed. Trinidad's fingers fumbled with the keys before she got it locked up.

"Something tells me you didn't expect to have a houseguest," he said.

"No, I sure didn't. Two adults and a dog in a 200-square-foot tiny house with a store to open, Juliette in jail, and a killer clobbering you and swiping the photos. What else could possibly happen?"

She felt just the barest sliver of fear as she uttered the words. Stan's sober warning rose in her mind again.

"Someone is feeling threatened... be careful. Very careful."

If the attacker was desperate enough to risk clobbering Quinn at a crowded location in broad daylight...what would they do next?

Chapter Fourteen

PAPA ARRIVED AT THE LITTLE house a half hour after Trinidad returned, having lingered to get to know everyone at the coffee shop. He did his best to hide his surprise as he took in the features of the wee house from the loft bed to the miniscule kitchen counter. "Here," he said, settling his bag on what passed for a sofa. "The perfect bed for me."

"You are not sleeping on the sofa," she said firmly. "The big bed is in the loft."

"Where you will sleep," he replied resolutely. "I will not take my granddaughter's bed from her under pain of death. Besides, that ladder is much too steep for a man my age."

A man who recently drove two thousand miles and hauled bags of potting soil around his greenhouse with ease. "Papa…"

He was already headed to the kitchen. "I will fix us an omelette."

She sank into the chair and let him work.

"So, this man Quinn," Papa said as he whisked eggs. "He lives here in town?"

"Yes. He farms hazelnuts."

"Ah. A landowner. That is an advantage over Len but also a

deficit. Farming is not the life for you, Trinidad. Much too hard and never any rest."

She straightened. "Papa, don't get any ideas about matchmaking. Quinn is just a friend. When, and if, it comes time to find another husband, I'll do it myself."

He didn't reply, but the lift in his bushy eyebrow was enough. It said, "*Like Gabe*?"

Papa Luis had voiced his reservations about the exuberant Gabe. "I don't trust a man who likes to talk about himself instead of letting others boast about him," he'd said. "And he knows nothing about cars or plants or cooking or baseball. What is there left to talk about?" Gabe was one of the few humans on the planet that Papa Luis did not like. That should have blared a warning klaxon in her ears right there.

While Papa turned to his eggs, she flopped back on the cushion and tried to refocus on the case. On Juliette. She would go and talk to her again. Maybe something had jogged her memory, something she'd seen in the storage unit. She also had to ask her to add Vince to her caller list. How could she possibly break the news that they'd lost possession of the photos?

Papa interrupted her thoughts by sliding two plates full of eggy fluff on the table. Dragging herself to her feet, she sat across from him. The meal was delicious, and having him there, chattering about things he'd seen in his cross-country drive, fed her spirit. They talked, laughed, and reminisced until her body sagged. A shower and jammies, an extra blanket for Papa and a biscuit for Noodles was all she could manage before she hauled herself to the loft and slunk into bed.

Tomorrow would be filled with trouble, she had no doubt, but, at least for tonight, her heart felt content with Papa and Noodles cramming the corners of the tiny house.

Soon she was lulled to sleep by the mingled snores of dog and grandpa.

It seemed only moments had passed before her morning alarm blared. She'd already hit the snooze button three times. Her mind swam with jumbled thoughts and her muscles were sluggish. Papa Luis. Quinn. The strange doings at the open house.

All her muscles jolted to life. To top it all off, it was Tuesday, the scheduled memorial for Kevin and a meager two days before the Shimmy and Shake Shop would explode on the scene. Her pulse pounded. Scrambling into some clothes that might pass as halfway decent, she scurried down the ladder. It was still early, barely six a.m., but she'd intended to be up before sunrise.

Hastening down the ladder, she was heading towards the kitchen to start a pot of strong coffee for Papa when she noticed a neatly folded blanket resting on the sofa. A note written on a napkin lay on top.

I have gone to meet the locals.

The locals. She swallowed, remembering that it was likely some nefarious local that had bashed Quinn on the head and murdered Kevin. Many people in town were dubious of Trinidad and her connection to her jailed friend. She wondered what they'd make of the gregarious Papa Luis.

"What a day to oversleep," she groaned.

Noodles popped open one eye to indicate that the word "oversleep" was not in his vocabulary. Remembering his splendid performance with Doug the day before, she mixed a mouthful of tuna in with his senior kibble.

"You deserve some extra goodness," she told him.

Noodles wolfed it down in half the time it took her to eat her boiled egg and banana. There was a pile of candy left on the table, small rectangles that had lost some of their shine, miniscule scratches and chips marring their luster—the loot Papa had received at the open house.

She grinned. Papa and his sweet tooth. As a child, she used to equate his roomy pockets with some kind of magical vending machine that dispensed a sugary treat whenever her mother wasn't looking. Sugar was bad for the complexion and the waistline. How, she'd wondered as a child, could something so damaging make her taste buds stand up and do the tango? Not once had she had the same reaction to, say, an eggplant or lima bean. She scooped up the candy and set it on higher ground, away from the reach of her resourceful dog.

With a to-do list in her pocket and a fierce determination in her gut, she loaded Noodles into the Pinto and sped to the shop. Papa was not there, but she saw his Bel Air parked on the curb. Outside Full of Beans, she caught a glimpse of his dark hair as he sat and visited with whichever local he had happened upon. The oatmeal-turned-ice-cream truck had been returned to the shop courtesy of Mr. Mavis. The morning was glorious with brilliant golden sunshine, and she hoped Papa Luis would find a good supply of chatty townspeople to entertain him.

With Papa occupied and the twins not yet reported for duty, she had a precious few hours to start the custard base for what she'd intended to be another supply of vanilla, the perennial crowd-pleaser. Then she paused. Papa Luis's suggestion for a mango and cream mixture caught hold of her imagination. How would a Tropical Twist Freakshake go over in Sprocket? She envisioned the creation piled high with a wedge of pineapple, chopped macadamia nuts, and a gaudy paper umbrella above the glorious mango cream shake.

Caught up in the idea, she switched gears and found a can of coconut cream and some cane sugar along with the vanilla bean and vanilla extract and set it to simmer until the crystals dissolved. It would be creamy, and the extract would keep any ice crystals from forming. No eggs, no cow's milk, a perfect vegan offering. The other base would be a straight mango sorbet, and the two would pair better than Fred and Ginger. She immediately put in an order for the paper umbrellas and splurged on overnight shipping.

But how could she go about finding ripe mangoes? The small grocery store in town did not boast a large tropical fruit section, though she had spied a couple of pineapples there. Did she have time to go on a driving expedition to a bigger town to find them? Might it be a good errand on which to dispatch Papa? She was still mulling over her options when she realized it was approaching time for the memorial at the gazebo. Stripping off her apron and recapturing her hair into a neater ponytail, she let Noodles out into his favorite shady spot on the shop porch for his mid-morning snooze.

The gazebo was three blocks past the gas station, set in a green swatch of grass that fronted a burbling creek. Quinn had told her it was familiarly called Messabout Creek, a tributary of Three Egg Lake. At the moment, the water level was low. Tall trees straddled both the land and creek, their roots emerging from the soil of the creek bed to plunge gnarled toes down into the water. She wished she could do the same, since she was hot and sticky from boiling custards and her brisk half-jog to the gazebo.

The structure itself was a neat six-sided affair, painted blizzard-white and raised a few shallow steps off the grass. The shingled roof was decorated in red, white, and blue bunting for the upcoming holiday. How perfectly small-town America—very Sprocket. Vases of lush white roses and soft greenery adorned the gazebo steps.

For a moment her mind again flashed on the pink rosebush at Kevin's shop. Sad, to think of that gift that would never be given to Tanya, the woman he'd no doubt intended it for. Now she was presenting roses to him, after his death, a sad irony, a waste of a life.

A large photo of Kevin, smiling and handsome, perched on an easel. Since the gazebo did not leave space for much seating, rows of folding chairs had been arranged on the grass. A linen-covered table offered a buffet of vegetables, finger sandwiches, and cookies on platters over shallow bins of ice. A round table held sweating glass pitchers filled with lemonade.

Trinidad recognized Stan's sister's pecan tarts and realized that Full of Beans must have provided the sweets. That put her onto another train of thought. Stan had told her that the next step for Juliette was a pre-trial conference. Since she had pled not guilty, all that remained was to set a trial date. He'd already warned Juliette that there could be a delay, a long delay, six months or more, perhaps, before the case went to trial. Trinidad had nearly choked at that bit of news. Six months or more of Juliette locked up? And what happened if the trial didn't go her way? Would she be facing a lifetime in prison?

Trinidad sank down in a chair. A conversation to her left caught her attention.

"It's like the ex-wives are taking over the town or something. At least number two is locked up, just like her crooked husband."

The comment punched Trinidad like a fist to the gut. Who had said it? The casually dressed couple to her left? Mr. Mavis's wife who sat next to him a few rows in front of her? Virginia Dempsey, who fanned herself as she spoke to a woman who quickly looked away when she caught Trinidad eyeing her? She realized that there were many interested glances in her direction.

She'd been so busy with concern for Juliette, she'd forgotten that she herself was probably the subject of speculation by numerous people in town. Trinidad Jones...a Bigley ex-wife, defender of a woman condemned by the Sprocket court of opinion. Her throat ached with a combination of humiliation and outrage. This was the ugly side of Sprocket—gossip, judgment, people who would always paint her and Juliette and Bonnie with

Gabe's brush. Sprocket was too small, too smothering, just like Papa had hinted.

What had she done investing everything in this locale? Would she ever be at home here? She clenched her jaw and forced herself to breathe normally. *Calm down. What you need to do now is hold your chin up and not let them get to you.*

She was so lost in her thoughts that it took her a few moments to spot Papa Luis. He was standing by the buffet chatting animatedly with clergyman Phil Zapata, known to the town as Pastor Phil. She hastened over and received a bear hug from Papa and a handshake from Pastor Phil.

"Trina," Papa said, beaming. "Who do you suppose I met at the coffee shop this morning? The good pastor and I are like family now."

She was grateful that Papa Luis was oblivious to the ill will that some Sprocketerians felt at his granddaughter's presence.

The ex-wife... her crooked husband... Though her jaw was still tight, she forced a smile. "How wonderful."

Pastor Phil, though probably only in his early forties, did indeed look as though he was greeting a long-lost brother as he thumped Papa Luis on the back. His broad smile revealed a chipped front incisor. "I have been here for a year so far, and I have not met anyone in Sprocket who speaks Spanish fluently until now," he said. He arched a brow in mock disdain. "Though Luis and I have been arguing over which is the superior version, Cuban Spanish or Mexican Spanish."

"And we have agreed," Papa said with a laugh.

The two men spoke at exactly the same time.

"Mexican."

"Cuban."

They shared another good laugh.

Pastor Phil scanned the surroundings. "It will be a lovely service." He sighed. "So sad. This would have been the perfect spot for the wedding, not a memorial."

"A wedding?" Trinidad stared. "You mean between Tanya and Kevin?"

He flushed. "Well, yes. She mentioned it to me at the church last week. She thought…I mean…she was under the impression that he was going to ask her to marry him after he took care of a few things."

A few things like breaking up with Juliette?

Pastor Phil must have seen Trinidad's frown. "Perhaps I have misunderstood?"

"Oh, I'm sure you didn't." How could she explain that it appeared the wedding bells were ringing in Tanya's ears but not quite so loudly for Kevin?

Pastor Phil wiped his brow and checked his watch, a cheap Timex with a frayed strap. "Excuse me, but I need to chat with Tanya." His next comment was interrupted by movement under the buffet table.

"Scram, squirrels," he said. Two gray squirrels scurried from under the table back up into the tree, peering at the pastor with beady bright eyes, lush tails twitching. "They are the biggest pests. At our Sunday School Picnic, they actually snuck down and made off with a whole bag of chocolate kisses. Our children's ministry leader was beside herself." He squinted up at the critters chattering from the safety of their sturdy limb. "They have a ferocious sweet tooth and exhibit very little in the way of repentance."

"Sounds like me," Papa said.

Pastor Phil laughed. "Then you and I will get along like a house afire."

The squirrels hovered above them.

Trinidad squinted at the mischievous rodents. "I'll try to keep them away from the food." She figured it would give her something to do besides obsess about the judgmental townsfolk.

Pastor Phil gave her a thumbs-up. "Thank you. I think they've got an eye on the sugar cubes."

Trinidad had to admit the two critters did seem to be interested in the porcelain cup filled to the brim with sparkling cubes of sugar to accompany the carafe of coffee. She and Papa chose seats nearest the buffet, even though it set them off to the side of most of the group.

Trinidad didn't mind. It provided an opportunity to take advantage of the shade and distance herself from the guests. Determined to shake off her bad mood, she told Papa about her tropical Freakshake plans utilizing his mango and cream idea. "I need mangoes. Very ripe ones, since we're almost to the Fourth, but I don't know where to get them on short notice. Can you help?"

He jounced in the chair. "Of course. Absolutely. Don't worry at all. I will secure some mangoes, the very best fruit possible."

"Where?"

He arched an eyebrow. "If you ask the magician for a dove, do you care which sleeve he pulls it from?"

She had no answer for that. They watched the chairs begin to fill with the townspeople. Familiar faces, Warren, Cora, Virginia Dempsey, and Donald. Vince Jr. was there, several rows back, scowling at his phone. Candy and Sonny sat with heads together. Candy was wrapping something in a napkin. Stan's pecan squares. She must have arrived earlier and helped herself to some free treats.

Trinidad was surprised to see Quinn and Doug arrive and take seats in the back. She wiggled her fingers at them, and Quinn returned the gesture. He was moving gingerly, she thought, but he had even attempted to upgrade his look in honor of the occasion, wearing a plaid short-sleeved shirt, which she noticed was buttoned incorrectly. Doug's hair was plastered down in a dark helmet.

Tanya sat on the edge of the front row, gorgeous in a sleeveless black dress with a single strand of pearls and low pumps. Her eyes were hidden behind chunky sunglasses, but Trinidad could see her mouth was pinched tight with emotion. There was no sign of her father or any other family members accompanying her. Mr. Grant apparently did not feel Kevin's ceremony was worthy of his time and attention.

Pastor Phil cleared his throat, and the audience quieted. He began a speech, which highlighted Kevin's business acumen, his theatrical endeavors, and his enthusiasm for the annual Fourth of July festivities. There was no mention of his extended family, and the pastor danced around the issue of his relationship with Tanya. He had just launched into the more spiritual part of his talk, when the flick of a fluffy gray tail caught Trinidad's eye.

Both squirrels had crept out of the tree and onto the grass. As she watched, they darted in furtive starts and stops toward the buffet table. She craned to look around Papa's shoulder. The pastor introduced the local high school music teacher who began to sing a hymn to the accompanying music provided by an eighties-style boom box. The loud tune caused the audience to jump. "Be right back," she whispered to Papa. Clearing the chairs, she crept towards the squirrels.

"Shoo," she whispered. "Or I'll get my dog."

One of the rodents turned a beady eye on her. In a blur, the leaner squirrel leapt onto the table, snagged the cup of sugar cubes and hurtled off, sprinkling cubes in his wake. Trinidad gave chase. Instead of climbing the tree like his fatter counterpart, the thief dashed away from the park area and off along the sidewalk that led past the gas station and back towards town. "At least give back the cup," she huffed as she jogged after him. A few minutes later she wondered what exactly she'd meant to accomplish by chasing the squirrel. Silly woman. It wasn't as though she could confiscate the purloined sweets, and the cup would be found eventually. The pastor was right. Those squirrels had an insatiable sweet tooth.

Sweet teeth, rather, like Papa.

A bell pinged in her mind as an elusive thought finally took hold.

Sweets. Old sweets. Specifically the pile of stale treats Papa had left on the kitchen table. She remembered how Diego had described the moment at the open house.

"The way he was filling his pocket from the candy bowl, he must be some kind of weirdo. That candy was gnarly. Tasted like it was from a World War II army ration or something."

Gnarly. Old. Candy Simon was a cheapskate, a woman who could pinch a penny until it yodeled. What if she'd gotten those candies from a certain outdated penny candy machine?

Candy's comment came back to her when she'd spoken of Lupin and his collecting habits. "*Everything from a busted-up candy machine to sixty-five coffee grinders.*"

The same candy machine that was now spiffed up and parked at the Vintage Theater?

It must have been among the batch of unwanted items Sonny Petrakis had acquired in Edward Lupin's storage unit purchase.

Old, they'd likely determined, but not worth much.

Not worth much, but what if they'd been wrong about that?

She thought about the treasure-collector's books in Lupin's garage…with a whole chapter devoted to numismatics—coin collecting.

What better place to hide a rare coin than nestled among its less-worthy counterparts? What if…? But, surely, it was not possible.

A presence behind her made her whirl around and yelp.

Quinn yelped right back. Doug chewed his lower lip.

"Sorry I scared you," Quinn said. "We saw you chasing the squirrel, and we decided to supply a rear guard. Did you catch him?"

"No, but I just had the strangest idea. What do you know about coins?"

He screwed up his face. "If you have enough of them, you can pay for things."

"I mean the special kind. The rare kind."

"Those would be good to have," he said. "My uncle had a coin collection as a kid. I sure wish I had held onto those, but we needed the money to replant an acre of diseased trees a couple winters ago. Sold them to a collector for a couple thousand."

"Exactly. So, a penny, let's say, could be worth a lot more than one cent."

He lifted a shoulder. "It would have to be a pretty out-of-the ordinary penny to be worth a ton."

"Bronze Lincoln," Doug said.

Quinn looked at him. "What's that?"

"Bronze Lincoln." Doug fiddled with his phone and handed it to his brother.

Quinn squinted at the screen, shading it from the sun with his palm. "It's an article about rare coins. Says here the bronze Lincoln pennies were made in the 1940s. To preserve copper for the war effort, the U.S. Mint started making pennies with zinc-coated steel planchets instead of copper, but some copper planchets got caught in the presses and got struck in error and were released unnoticed." He gulped. "Do you want to know how much one of these things went for? You're not gonna believe it."

"$1.7 million," Doug said.

She stopped for a moment, struck dumb by the number. "Now that's a penny someone would kill for, don't you think?"

Quinn gulped. "Uh-huh. I'm pretty sure they would. So, you think that's what Lupin's treasure was?"

"I don't know, but Candy found an old penny candy machine in Lupin's belongings. I think she dumped out the candy and reused it at her open house before they sold the candy machine at the flea market."

"Man, that's cheap."

"Uh-huh."

She walked along the sidewalk back towards town, Quinn and Doug following. When they got close to the shop, Noodles stretched, unrolled himself from his cushion on the porch, and greeted them all with a tail wag. Doug scratched his ears.

"Okay, we're looking for a penny. But why are we walking through town? Do you think Kevin bought the candy machine? You think it's still in his shop?"

"No. I think if it had been there, you wouldn't have gotten bashed on the head. It's still missing, and I'm sure it's not at the Popcorn Palace."

"Okay. How about Warren's van? You mentioned that flyer that somehow made it out of his rear door. Could be he swiped the machine and stowed it in the van but somehow lost it again."

"It's not lost; it's at the theater."

"It is?" Quinn returned the phone to Doug. "And no one suspects what might be in it?"

She nodded. "That's my guess. Maybe they didn't open it up. I think that was what you believed was a fish bowl in Juliette's photos. I saw the machine in the theater lobby, so Cora must have bought it to refurbish. I thought I'd go take a peek while everyone is at the memorial."

He grinned. "Life sure has gotten exciting since I met you." His gaze was so focused, so kind. Warmth circled in her chest before nerves took over.

"A bit too exciting," she blurted. "How's your head?"

"Throbbing, but still functioning, at least as well as it did before, which isn't saying much. I wish I could think like you do. Incredible putting those candy clues together. You are really something."

She felt like a junior high school kid, awkward, shy, and completely thrilled by the compliment. "Oh, well, we haven't found any treasures yet," she managed. "It's only a far-fetched theory at this point."

They continued past her store, along the sidewalk, sweating in the sunlight. "Come here, sweetie." She reached down, and Noodles leapt into her arms. "It's too hot for your paws."

"Let me," Quinn insisted, but Doug reached in between them and gathered the dog to his chest.

"I guess you're buddies," Quinn said.

Doug nodded.

Trinidad went all melty inside at the growing bond between Doug and Noodles.

The theater was surrounded by a thick colony of overgrown trees, which dropped a carpet of needles onto the roof, but it also provided a blessedly cool spot to reconnoiter. Doug put Noodles down so he could nose about near the old wooden steps.

"Keep your eyes peeled for a squirrel with a cup of sugar cubes," she told him. "I'm not sure the door will be unlocked, but I thought I might be able to catch a peek at it through the side panes. I vaguely remember seeing it. Cora's a DIYer, so I don't think it's red anymore."

The windows on either side of the once-grand door were panes of beveled glass, partitioned with wrought iron veins. She peered through the glass, Quinn looking over the top of her head.

"I can't see it," she said. "It's tucked behind the curtain. Let's try the door."

Under the pressure of her hand, the warm metal knob turned, and the door swung open.

She gave Quinn a look. "Is this a good idea with a killer on the loose?"

"Probably not," he said.

"And we're going to do it anyway, aren't we?"

He chuckled. "I am happy to be Watson to your Sherlock."

Prickles danced again along her spine, but she lifted a casual shoulder. "You know what they say about pennies."

"What?" His brow wrinkled. "Hold on, I forgot. Give me a minute."

She smiled and pushed the door open. "In for a penny…"

He snapped his fingers. "That's the one…in for a pound." He frowned. "Actually, I've had enough pounding lately." He edged in front of her. "But, just in case, I'll go first."

Teeth clenched and fingers crossed, she followed him in.

Chapter Fifteen

COOL, MUSTY AIR BATHED HER face as they stepped into the gloomy interior. She didn't figure there was anything wrong with taking a look around since the door hadn't been locked. Nonetheless, she found herself whispering as if they were a pair of cat burglars.

"It should be right inside there." She reached out to push past a heavy drape that was cinched to the wall in the middle by a fancy tasseled rope. Before her fingertips found the fabric, there was a clang of metal and a crash from the darkness beyond. Her heart whammed in her chest.

Noodles careened through the front door and inside.

"No, Noodles," she whispered, but he'd plunged past before she could stop him.

"I'll call the police," she started to say, but Quinn elbowed her aside and darted ahead.

There was a shout, a man's voice.

Not Quinn's.

She raced in, searching for the switch that would activate the vintage pendant lights. Where was it? The theater was ink-dark, save for some dim illumination at the foot of the stage, but she didn't want to waste time fumbling to find her cell phone flashlight.

"Stop," Quinn yelled. He sprinted up the center aisle. Further ahead she could see a shadowed figure, large and heading quickly towards the stage, with Noodles right behind him. Whoever it was could not move as quickly as the dog or Quinn. In a moment, there was a grunt as Quinn and the stranger fell in a tangle of limbs.

Noodles barked at a deafening level. He was not a biter by nature, but the dog took his barking seriously. The switch. She had to find the switch.

Finally, her frantic patting paid off, and she slapped it on. The light temporarily dazzled her vision. Near her feet was the overturned penny candy machine. Blinking hard, she jumped over it and ran up the aisle to find Quinn kneeling on top of a prone figure. She finally made the identification.

"Warren," she said panting. "What are you doing here?"

"If this gorilla would get off my back, I'll tell you," he grunted, face pressed to the floor. "And call off the dog, wouldja?"

She succeeded in quieting Noodles and getting him to sit.

Quinn clambered to his feet, hands on his hips. "Go ahead and explain."

"I shouldn't have to explain anything." Warren got up and retrieved a screwdriver from under a seat where it had rolled after he'd dropped it. "I work at this place, volunteer anyway. This here is a second home to me."

Quinn pointed to the screwdriver. "And you had a sudden urge to fix something in the middle of the memorial?"

She couldn't tell exactly, but she thought he might have blushed. "I was...I mean...well..." He stopped. "There was a break-in. I was checking around to see if anything was taken."

Warren must have read the skeptical look on the faces staring back at him. "No, really. Come and see."

Warily, they followed him to a window on the far side of the lobby almost hidden from the road by a tangle of shrubs. "Look."

The window was indeed broken, a hole about the size of a fist indicated that there had been an intruder.

Warren shrugged. "See? I told you so. I saw the glass on the ground when I got here. The window was still fastened, so I must have scared someone off."

"That still doesn't explain why you're here with a screwdriver in hand," she said.

"Hey, it's a good thing I was here. Burglars and murders and all. That's why we've started locking the front door so whoever it was had to bust in." His eyes narrowed. "Figure I got more of an excuse to be here than you two."

Quinn stared at him. "You first. Take it one question at a time. How did you get in?"

"He borrowed the keys from me," a voice said. Cora stood behind them, arms crossed. "When Pastor Phil got about five minutes into his spiel, Mr. Handy Man Warren said he'd forgotten his phone in the bathroom. I thought that sounded like a bunch of hooey. A man can't lose his phone that often unless he's trying to."

Warren let out a breath from deep inside his chest. "Aww, shoot."

"Then you kiddos took off after the squirrels. More like a three-ring circus than a memorial. So, let's try the truth, shall we?" Cora said. "All of it. Right now. I missed out on a free buffet to follow you, and I'm hot and cranky, so quit stalling."

Warren swallowed audibly. "Okay. I came back to look for something."

Cora looked pained. "Please don't waste my time with the cell phone lie again. You wouldn't need a screwdriver to retrieve that from the men's room."

"No, it wasn't the phone," he admitted. "Anyway, when I was going to let myself in, I noticed the broken glass and heard someone running away. That part is completely true. Someone really was breaking in. Can you believe that? Busted out the window and everything."

"We saw the glass," Quinn confirmed. "But the window was still closed, so whoever it was didn't get in."

Cora rolled her eyes. "I had no idea the theater was so amazing that people would break and enter to get a seat."

Warren grinned broadly. "See? Isn't that something? We do good plays, what can I say?" His smile faded as his joke did not elicit any apparent softening from Cora.

"What were you looking for, Warren?" she demanded.

"You won't believe it, actually."

"No doubt it's something ludicrous, but try me anyway."

Trinidad stepped in. "I think he was trying to pry open the penny candy machine."

Cora gaped. "That old thing? Why? Are you that desperate for a sugar fix? There isn't even any candy in it yet. I bought the machine empty."

"No candy," Trinidad said, "but since the machine belonged to Edward Lupin before Sonny bought the contents of his storage unit, you think there's a valuable coin in it, don't you, Warren?" She saw him twitch and she knew she'd hit on the truth. He'd come to the same conclusion she had. What better time than the memorial to snoop around unnoticed?

He massaged a shoulder as if he'd strained a muscle. "To be honest, I'd be gobsmacked if there was anything but lint inside, but I heard everyone talking at the open house. Candy was playing it up like if someone bought the place they might find Lupin's treasure. I heard the Martin twins talking about coins. I couldn't get the thought of a priceless coin out of my mind. I remembered seeing the penny candy machine, and..."

"When?" Trinidad asked.

"Huh?"

"Where and when did you first see the machine?"

He pursed his lips. "Here, a few days ago. It appeared in the lobby like magic."

Cora snorted. "Magic is also known as hard work. I bought it at the flea market. I thought if I fixed it up, it would look good in the lobby, and maybe we could keep the kiddies entertained. But I haven't had a chance to fill it with candy yet."

Trinidad watched them carefully. "Nowhere else? You didn't see it before then?"

Warren shrugged. "How would I have seen it otherwise?"

"Behind the Popcorn Palace?" Quinn said.

Warren glared. "Whaddya mean? I didn't take anything from Kevin's, and I certainly didn't clobber him."

Cora shook her head. "Your theory is wrong, Trinidad. Kevin never had a chance to buy it. I happened to be at the flea market early, the first customer, in fact. Donald was unloading the unwanted stuff from the storage unit Sonny Petrakis bought. I saw it rolled in plastic. I purchased it on the spot before it was even unwrapped," Cora said.

Trinidad decided to take a risk and fixed Warren with a look. "Or you could have seen it when you were snooping around in Juliette's storage unit. That's where you lost your cell phone, isn't it? You were retrieving it the night my dog got loose."

He huffed out a breath, his tone a shade too glib. "Nah. I was just driving. I like to drive in out of the way places."

Another lie, Trinidad thought. Warren scanned the expressions on the faces of his interrogators. "Oh, all right. I admit I was poking around Store Some More on Sunday, the night before the auction. I figured maybe I could pick the lock or something and just take a peek is all, just to see if there really was something valuable. But, when I got there, someone was already on the property. I heard whoever it was walking around real quiet like, with a flashlight. Then Juliette showed up, and I scrammed because I didn't want to explain why I was there. I dropped my phone in the grass. It took me an age to find it with all the hubbub around here lately. Finally located it behind the birdbath. That's the truth. I never did see inside Lupin's unit, and I didn't know anything about the candy machine until I saw it in the lobby. Figured Cora bought it at the flea market and...well, you know the rest."

"At least you got that part correct," Cora said. "Like I said, I snagged the candy machine before it could go to market." Cora shrugged. "I'm into vintage. I paid twenty bucks for it," she added.

"I'll bet it'd be worth fifty if the glass wasn't cracked," Warren said automatically. His expression went sheepish. "I like to do online research."

Cora raked him with a look. "That's part of your problem, Warren. You like to do way too many things online. The red paint was flaking off everywhere, and he's right, there's a crack in the glass. Even with my spiffy new yellow paint job, it's probably not even worth the twenty I forked over."

"Unless there's something valuable inside," Warren said.

"So, you came here to see if there was a rare coin in the penny candy machine," Trinidad said.

He shrugged. "Why not?"

"Did you follow him here?" Cora said. "Are you a private eye now in addition to churning out ice cream?"

Now it was Trinidad's turn to look sheepish. "It started out with a squirrel chase, but yes, we came in search of the machine, too, actually," she admitted. "But we weren't going to open it up without your permission."

"Oh, sure. I believe that." Cora sniffed. "And what about you? If you had found this priceless coin?" She skewered Warren with a look. "Would you have told me about it so we could split the profits?"

Warren flashed her a toothy grin. "'Course I would."

"Yeah. I'm sure. Maybe, after you paid off your debts and ran away to some tropical hideaway, you'd send me a postcard." She grabbed the screwdriver from his hand. "Before I call the police to report the broken window and tell Bigley all about my parade of visitors, we might as well see if your harebrained idea is correct. I doubt there's anything in there. I would have heard it jingling around when I was painting."

She marched back up to the fallen penny candy machine, which was now a cheerful taxicab color. "I painted it myself and turned the glass so the crack doesn't show. If you damaged it any further, so help me..." Slipping the screwdriver into a tiny divot, she twisted a metal plate free. Rolling the entire machine, she stuck in the screwdriver and pried loose a couple of coins secreted in the interior. They tumbled out, twirled and spun on the aged wooden floor. "Well, I guess there were a few coins in there after all."

All of them crowded nearer to see.

Cora was closest, and she peered and poked at the collection until she straightened, holding up a silver coin. "Here's your treasure Warren. A genuine Canadian nickel. Don't spend it all in one place. Aside from that, looks like our windfall is twelve cents in change, none if it older than 1972."

Trinidad felt suddenly foolish...foolish and depressed. She'd not accomplished one thing with her great sleuthing skills except upsetting Cora and making an idiot of herself.

Warren's shoulders fell. "I should have known. The only kind of luck I have is the bad kind."

She scooped up the coins and handed them to Trinidad. "Here you go. Welcome to Sprocket. Land of the misguided treasure hunters. Buy some extra sprinkles for your shop, and don't sneak into my theater again."

"But, Cora..." Warren started.

"I'm going to call the police about the broken window, but

my advice to you, all of you, is quit making fools of yourselves looking for a treasure that doesn't exist. It's not worth wasting your life on."

Trinidad thought suddenly about Kevin, who was being memorialized while they lingered at the theater chasing phantom pennies. She was certain he must have unknowingly gotten his hands on something that was worth so much that he'd been killed for it. If it wasn't a precious coin, what could it be?

She dreaded what the chief would have to say when Cora told her about their theater adventure. They trudged back to the store, Doug carrying Noodles. By then the memorial service had ended, and folks were returning to their businesses. At the Shimmy and Shake Shop, Doug deposited Noodles gently on his cushion. Quinn offered to help Trinidad with her ice cream duties, but she declined. Instead she rounded up the two promised pints of ice cream and handed them over, resisting the urge to rebutton Quinn's shirt correctly in the process.

"Ice cream for Orville, and the brownies are for you two. Please tell Orville that his truck was a lifesaver."

Quinn laughed. "He'll be happy to hear it. I'll tell him. Are you sure you don't want to hang onto it for a while? Your grandpa and I could go up to Three Egg Lake with samples. Stir up some business."

"That is a fantastic idea, but it will have to wait. I've got a bunch of ice creams to churn, and then I'm going to see Juliette."

He nodded. "I wish we could have found something that might hint at another motive for Kevin's murder."

"Me too."

"I mean, what in the world could be so darn valuable and yet stay hidden in a small town like this?"

"I wish I knew."

All she had to show for today's sleuthing adventure was twelve cents and a whole lot of chagrin. Some detective.

Still burning with embarrassment over her sleuthing fail, she made the drive to the jail with fatigue gnawing at her all the way. Was the tiredness due to the hours standing in the food truck? Worry at finding Quinn injured? The sprint down the theater aisle? General wear and tear? She sighed, figuring it didn't matter anyway. At least coconut ice cream, silken chocolate, and a stack of waffle cones were added to the list of what was ready for the grand opening. Rows of glistening milkshake goblets lay awaiting their Freakshake transformations, and the shop was shining from pink tile floor to newly painted ceiling. If Papa managed to get his hands on the mangoes, she would prepare the base tomorrow morning, and it would be ready just in time to roll out the tropical delicacies. If nothing else went right for the foreseeable future, at least her beautiful shop was in order.

She'd left the twins chopping macadamia nuts and prepping the additional outdoor tables they'd added to the patio area. Two more days… The thought both thrilled and petrified her. The Shimmy and Shake Shop felt like a long-awaited child, a longed-for miracle. But along with the thrill came a good measure of guilt.

Look what your friend is going through, and you haven't found one solitary thing to help her prove her innocence. What's more, Trinidad had no idea what to try next or who to talk to. Sherlock Holmes, she was not.

She went through the jail security check and waited in the cheerless visitor room. She'd already fed one of the mundane coins Cora had given her plus a handful more into the vending machine to retrieve the only things left, a small bag of chips and a roll of Lifesavers. At least the ill-fated candy machine adventure had helped in some small way.

Juliette looked even thinner, downright gaunt, when she settled into the chair opposite Trinidad. Her hair was dull, her skin tone slightly grayish under the fluorescent lights. She didn't smile. Instead, she blinked hard. A tear escaped anyway, and she paused for a moment before she spoke. "Stan told me what happened to Quinn at the open house. Are you sure he's okay?"

"Very sure."

"It's just too crazy. I can't believe the photos are gone." She stuck her thumbnail in her mouth, but it was already bitten to the quick.

"The good thing is we know someone is worried about what might have been on those photos."

"But will it persuade Chief Bigley that I didn't kill Kevin?"

Trinidad tried to present the facts in a positive light. "I think we angered the chief by not sharing about the photos in the first place. I'm sorry about that. The good news is she's still investigating, so that's something to take hold of. Are you sure you can't remember anything else that was in that storage unit?"

She rubbed her forehead. "I've had hours and hours to think about nothing else. Honestly, all I can remember is junk. Cardboard boxes filled with old magazines, half-melted candles, a planter." She straightened. "Wait a minute. There was an old red candy machine, from the fifties, maybe, with a glass top and a slot for the coins."

"That one's a dead end, I'm afraid. It's at the theater, but there's nothing of value in it. What about Vince? Did he know what was in the storage unit?"

"I don't think so. He was always running to class or his other job."

"If Lupin had something in his unit, something priceless, wouldn't Sonny have identified it?" She was thinking about the treasure books he'd swiped from Lupin's garage. "Between him and Candy, I would think one of them might notice something of value."

"I don't know about Candy, but Sonny isn't the fastest car on the racetrack," Juliette said. "He stole something from Tanya's, Kevin once told me. Turned out to be a reproduction, and he couldn't get much for it. Almost got himself arrested by Mr. Grant, except Tanya threw a fit with her father to keep him from pressing charges. All that drama, and he didn't even know what to swipe that would be worth anything."

"But he avoided jail."

"Maybe a stint behind bars would do him good." She shuddered. "It gives you plenty of opportunity to think about your life choices."

"Could be it was something he didn't realize was valuable until after he sent it to the flea market. When he figured it out, he might have gone to Kevin's looking for it and killed him. Or maybe I'm completely off base and it was Warren."

"Warren Wheaton?"

"I heard he had gambling debts, and he's been skulking around looking for the treasure. He was at the open house, the Store Some More, and he was there when I found the…uh…Kevin. He admits he was sneaking around Store Some More but he says someone else was there, too, before you arrived and scared them off."

She frowned. "Hmmm. It sounds like he's a liar, and maybe he wouldn't turn up his nose at breaking and entering, but it's hard to picture him as a violent type."

"People do strange things when there's money involved. I just wish we could figure out what Lupin's treasure was in the first place. It might give us some direction."

"Vince Jr. might be able to help you if it's a precious painting or the like. Between you and me, he's a complete dweeb, but he knows a lot. If you get any ideas, you can run it by him. He…really wants to help me."

"Yes. As a matter of fact, he's anxious to come visit you. Can you put him on your list?"

She shook her head. "Um, I'd rather not. I'm really grateful to him and all for taking care of the shop, but…" She sighed. "I think he has feelings for me. He looks at me like I'm some sort of princess, and it drives me crazy. He's barely twenty-one, and I'm knocking on thirty." Her lip curled.

"Do you think it's possible that he got jealous of Kevin and killed him?"

She giggled. "I don't think he could kill anything. Not exactly a strong specimen. We were cleaning out a unit one time and a rat shot past us. He screamed louder than I did. Plus, he knew I'd broken up with Kevin, so I don't see what he would gain from murdering him."

"Maybe it had something to do with this mysterious valuable. He killed Kevin to get it."

"It's possible, but it's also just as likely there is nothing to be found." Her sigh seemed to come from deep down inside her. "I am too tired to think it through anymore. Anyone could have done it, but all the evidence points to me and only me." Despair washed over her face.

"We'll find something. We must be making somebody nervous if they stole the photos from Quinn."

She shook her head. "I don't want anybody else hurt, and you have a store to open. I know how much it means to you. That's where your focus should be."

There was a gravity underscoring her words. Trinidad went to snatch up her hand for a reassuring squeeze, but the guard shook his head.

"I'm fine. Don't worry about me," Juliette said.

"How can I not? You look so discouraged. We are going to get you out of this somehow. Try not to lose hope."

She shook her head. "It's hard not to, Trinidad. I know this town, at least a little bit. I am sure plenty of people have decided I got what I deserved."

Trinidad remembered the comments at the memorial. She tried for a bright smile. "Maybe a few, but not everybody thinks that. There are plenty of people who..."

She didn't seem to hear. "I told Stan I want to deed you my house."

"What?" Trinidad gaped. "There's no need for that. You're going to be out of here and back into your life, Juliette."

"I wish, but it's not looking good, is it?" Her mouth pinched white at the corners. "I have no one. My parents are gone, no husband, no kids. I want you to have my house."

"No, no, Juliette. Please, don't say things like that." Trinidad forced a smile. "We've still got all kinds of leads to follow."

"Like what?"

Called out on her fib, Trinidad fumbled for a reply. "Well, um..."

Juliette smiled. "I love you for trying, I really do. You're the best friend I think I've ever had along with Bonnie. No one else would stick their neck out for me like you've done, but I have to be practical. I might not ever be free again."

"No..."

She held up a trembling hand. "Bonnie has property and a home for Felice. You have only that ridiculous tiny rental house. My place would be bigger and better for you and Noodles."

Trinidad slapped her palm on the tabletop. "Juliette, I am not going to listen to this. You are going to get out of jail."

Desperation shone on her face. "I want to believe that." Her voice broke on the last word.

"Stan is whipping up a crackerjack defense for you, even as we speak."

She pressed her lips together and stood. "I'm going to ask Stan to work on the house and put my affairs in order, find out how to sell Store Some More. Please thank Vince for me. He's a good kid. I hope he gets out of school and moves on with his life at some point. Bonnie will be back from her trip next week, and you two should talk. Tell her everything, okay? Tell her I'm sorry I didn't get to say goodbye."

"Juliette..." Trinidad called, but Juliette was already being led away by the guard. The chips and Lifesavers still lay untouched on the table.

Chapter Sixteen

HOW WAS SHE GOING TO save Juliette? Trinidad was rapidly running out of time and ideas.

The drive back to the shop seemed endless, her nerves quivering. Her heart grieved for her friend, but she could think of nothing to do to help the case. The photos were gone, the candy machine a big, fat dead end. Every feeble sleuthing attempt had turned into a complete bust.

Noodles greeted her when she entered the shop.

Diego was wiping down the tables. He beamed excitement. "Hey, Miss Jones. I heard you broke into the theater. Did you find something?"

"I did not break in," she said firmly. "The door was open, and we didn't find anything." *Except a lying Warren and the remains of a real burglary attempt.*

His excitement ebbed. "Oh. Too bad. My friends are, like, *really* impressed that I work for a cat burglar."

She heaved out a breath. Now she was a cat burglar.

"What is this about a burglar?" Papa emerged from the back room with an apron tied around his waist and a net struggling to contain his thatch of hair.

"Hi, Papa. Nothing to worry about. What are you up to?"

He gestured proudly to the bowl of golden mango chunks. "I have been peeling, you see."

"Oh, Papa!" She hugged him, bowl and all, and pressed a kiss to his cheek. "Where in the world did you get these beautiful mangoes?"

He shrugged, going for modesty. "I have people, you know, in Miami, my good friend Farhan. He grows the most delectable mangoes. I phoned him, and..." He gestured with the paring knife. "Voilà!"

Carlos came in from the front porch with a crate of mangoes. "Here's another one, just delivered."

"Wow," Trinidad said. "That's a lot of mangoes."

Papa grinned. "Farhan is a generous man."

Trinidad directed Carlos to stack the crate in the corner for the time being. The scent of mango was so tantalizing her mouth began to water. Since Papa had already chopped the fruit, it was an easy matter to add simple syrup and a bit of lime juice and set the gorgeous golden mixture to churn.

Diego unboxed the tiny umbrellas, and Trinidad added the half dozen pineapples that would be perfectly wedged and sliced by Thursday.

The twins worked with their usual energy until their quitting time. They let themselves out the front door. Papa excused himself as well. "I am going to chat with Pastor Zapata over at the coffee shop. He's taking me to see Three Egg Lake, and then he has offered to make me an authentic meal of mole and roasted corn with tres leches cake for dessert. His wife's specialty." He gestured. "He said you are welcome to join in. Can you escape for a while?"

"No, you go ahead. I'll meet you at the house later." She glanced at Noodles who had been patiently waiting to leave the shop. "Papa, would you mind taking Noodles with you? He could really use a change of scenery, and Pastor Zapata is always real nice about people bringing their dogs to church. He's a dog lover, so I'm sure he wouldn't mind."

"I'd be happy to." He snapped a leash on Noodles who leapt up, tail wagging.

"Just keep an eye on your dinner, okay?" She handed Papa a plastic bag of kibble. "He believes he should have people food."

Papa eyed the kibble. "I think I might agree with him." His smile dimmed. "But, Trina, what is this about a burglary?"

"Oh, it's nothing to worry about, Papa."

"The same 'nothing' I should not be worrying about knowing that one of Hooligan's ex-wives was arrested for murder? I've heard all about this in the coffee shop, you know."

Hooligan was the name Papa had given Gabe since he vowed never again to utter the given name of the man who had betrayed his granddaughter. She hoped Gabe never happened to find himself crossing the street in front of Papa's Bel Air. She was not surprised that her grandfather had found out the sordid details of Juliette's plight, and she had a feeling she knew where the conversation was headed.

"Juliette is my friend. She didn't kill anyone. I'm trying to help her prove it."

His look darkened. "Trina, this is too much." He waved a hand. "This town, a murder, burglaries… You should come home to Miami with your family."

She kissed his cheek. "I am going to be just fine. I promise."

"But you're not a detective, my girl. Your passion is the kitchen. How is that going to help Juliette?" He lowered his voice. "Besides, the way she was treated by Hooligan…" He grimaced. "Might it have made her the kind who would kill?"

She took his hands and squeezed. "No, Papa. It didn't. No more than it made me a killer."

His earnest eyes searched hers. "You're sure about your friend? Very sure?"

"Positive."

He looked at her for another long moment, and then he nodded. "All right. If you are certain about her, then I am, too."

Heart brimming, she hugged him, then steered him toward the door.

"But Miami is still…"

She spoke over him. "Noodles is hankering for that outing. Keep the air conditioning on for him, okay? And, sometimes, he likes to open the fridge and serve up random jars of pickles, so look lively." She waved until he guided the Bel Air out of sight, then she went back inside to tidy up.

Before she got around to locking up again, Vince Jr. pushed in, a backpack on his shoulder and a crate of mangoes in his arms.

"This was on your porch," he said.

"Another one? I wonder how many Papa asked for." She took the mangoes and added it to the other crate. What she was going to do with Farhan's too generous supply of fruit?

"I heard you broke into the theater with Warren," Vince said.

"No, I didn't," she explained again. "I walked through the door, which Warren had unlocked prior to my arrival, but someone else was trying to break in."

His eyes went wide. "Wow. When it rains, it pours. Who?"

"I don't know. Apparently, Warren scared them off."

"Fingerprints?"

"That's for the chief to work out."

He nodded and then grinned. "You were looking for a rare coin in the candy machine, weren't you?"

She flushed. "Who told you that?"

"Like…everybody at the coffee shop."

The ruthlessly efficient gossip wheel. "There was no valuable coin to be found."

He snickered. "I'm not surprised. Just because it is an antique doesn't mean there was anything valuable underneath that old chipped red paint. People can be so naive. Did you find anything else?"

"No, but Juliette said I should ask you. You've been at the Store Some More and the theater. Have you noticed anything that might be worth a lot of money?"

"Juliette said to ask me?" He puffed up a bit. "I do know a lot about art history. I can't say I have too much expertise about coins, but I could find out."

"I'm not convinced the treasure is a coin. It might be something completely different."

He sniffed. "If there really is a treasure in the first place. Stuff like that doesn't happen in Sprocket. Nothing happens in Sprocket."

Except burglaries, murder, etc. "Just for the sake of argument, have you seen anything that might be valuable at the theater?"

"Well, I do advise Cora about her props and things. You know, to make sure they are correct with the time period and all. They buy all this junk from the flea market."

"Do you think any of it could be worth a bundle?"

He shook his head. "No. I would have spotted that."

"Did you get a chance to look in Edward Lupin's storage unit?"

"No. Never did. I wish I had, though. And I only got to the flea market after the remainders were picked over. I could have recognized a valuable piece in a heartbeat." He droned on. "My real expertise is painting, calligraphy, pottery, that kind of thing. Sure, though, I would be able to spot a rare coin, too, if it came to that."

Vanity, thy name is youth, Trinidad thought. "Did you ever see Warren poking around Store Some More?"

Vince pursed his lips. "I think he might have come by once to ask about storage, but I don't think he actually rented a unit. Hey, did you ask Juliette to put me on her visitor list? I want to go today. One of my classes was canceled, so I have some time off."

Trinidad sought a way to break the news gently. “Um, she’s really not up for visitors, Vince.”

His brows knitted. “She didn’t want to add me?”

“I’m sorry. Like I said, she’s very worried right now. Depressed, I would say.”

“Aww, man. I wish there was something I could do. Are you sure she won’t see me? I could talk to her about how good things are going at Store Some More. The office is clean, and I’ve been writing down all the phone messages and keeping the birdbath filled.”

“I will tell her next time I go. Maybe she’ll change her mind about visitors.”

“Right,” he said brightening. “Tell her I’ve been trying to think of how to get her out of this murder rap.”

“You and me both.”

She led him to the porch where he stopped and pointed. “Looks like you got another box of mangoes.”

With a sigh, Trinidad picked up the package to add it to the others.

When it rains, it pours, she agreed. The feeling was cemented a moment later when she saw the chief’s car roll up. Figuring she might as well head things off at the pass, she offered the chief a seat at one of the shady porch tables. “I’ll be right there, okay?”

The chief didn’t answer, merely sat down, fingers interlaced on the tabletop. Not an uber friendly posture. Time to apply some sugar to temper the bitter medicine she felt sure was coming. She served up a bowl of the canary yellow sorbet.

The chief raised an eyebrow. “Are you hoping to make me forget you busted into the theater?”

“I didn’t bust, and yes. Is it working?”

“No,” said the chief, allowing a smile, “but that looks refreshing enough to sweeten my mood.”

“The restorative power of ice cream, or sorbet, rather. It’s mango.”

"Exotic. Where'd you find mangoes around here?"

"I have a supplier, a very generous one. I've got key lime made also, but this one is right out of the machine."

Bigley dug into the satiny smooth dessert and rolled her eyes. "Fantastic."

"Thank you. Ripe fruit and the proper care and that's all you need."

The chief kept spooning until the sorbet was gone. "All right. I'm feeling better, but I am still more than annoyed to find you popping up in this investigation at every turn. You're like a human-sized whack-a-mole."

"I just want to clarify that I didn't break in. I..."

"I heard all that, but someone else was trying to break in. I assume it wasn't Warren, unless he was trying to throw suspicion off himself for stealing this fictional coin, if that was his intent. No prints. Whoever did it was careful."

"It might have been Warren. I'm not sure. I don't trust him." She'd already told the chief about finding the flyer blowing about outside Warren's van the day he was killed.

Bigley toyed with her spoon in thought. "I've been thinking. Warren could have taken something from Kevin's and slipped it in the van, moved it later, and no one would have been the wiser."

"Have you ever had trouble with him breaking the law before?"

She shook her head. "He's always on the edge of bankruptcy. Tanya said he's asked for his pay in advance in the past. Gambling."

"With Kevin Heartly."

The chief did not register surprise, which indicated she already knew. The flow of information definitely did not go both ways. "He's got debt, let's put it that way," the chief said.

"Well, somebody besides me thought about that old candy machine and tried to break in. Or maybe there is something else of value stashed away there."

"I went through the place personally, as did Officer Chang, not to mention Cora. There's nothing there except a cash drawer with less than thirty bucks in it. To be safe, she is going to have motion-detector lights installed around the theater."

"What about an alarm?"

"They don't have the money for that. I'll have my officers make more frequent rounds, but word has gotten out there was no priceless coin there. I think that's the end of the nefarious treasure hunters."

"None of this helps Juliette."

Her look sharpened. "It's not my job to help Juliette. I am looking for leads about the killer, and so far those leads all point back to her."

"She..."

Bigley held up a palm. "Let's not go down this road again. I know what you think. If you could give me something besides opinions and theories about phantom collectibles, that would be a different story. Otherwise, it's going to come down to what Stan can do for her in the way of defense."

"That could take months."

"The wheels of justice grind slowly. You should know that, right? Being a former stenographer before you got into the ice cream biz, and what with your new paralegal gig."

She fired a glance at the chief. Was she being needled? Ridiculed? "I didn't know you kept tabs on my former careers."

"Gabe and I are tight, you know. We still talk regularly, in spite of his current status. And, besides, cops generally look pretty closely at the person who is the first to find the body."

The first to find the body...

She swallowed hard as the chief got to her feet.

"Thanks for the sorbet," she said. "And stay out of trouble, huh?"

"Will you be keeping an eye on Warren? He has keys to the theater."

"Not anymore. Cora has stripped him of those."

"She doesn't trust him."

"If she did, they wouldn't have needed that divorce."

Trinidad gaped. Divorce? Warren and Cora had been married?

The chief smirked. "You didn't know that? And here I thought you were a detective in addition to your other duties."

Trinidad shook her head. "Obviously not a very good one."

"Don't beat yourself up. They don't talk about it publicly too much. Cora was smart to leave him, but she paid a heavy price." The chief raised an eyebrow. "Too bad she doesn't have a priceless penny at the theater. She could definitely use one."

Her thoughts churning as if they were in a blender, Trinidad grabbed the broom. Warren and Cora had been married, and he all but ruined her. Their relationship must be somewhat amicable in spite of all that. They both worked at the theater and lived practically next door to each other. It certainly was a juicy bit of information, but did it have anything to do with Kevin's murder? Should she add Cora to the suspect list, too?

As she did a final sweep of the store, her stomach growled. When she could no longer resist her rising appetite, she put a mango in each pocket for a midnight snack, locked up, and let herself out only to find yet another box of Farhan's fruit on the front porch. At this point, it hardly surprised her. Picking up the carton, she lugged it to her Pinto, since she was running out of space in the Shimmy and Shake Shop. There was a lovely scent of garlic and herbs in the air, mingled with the scent of ripe fruit.

Pizza. The fragrance made her mouth water. On impulse, she scooped up a handful of mangoes and hurried to Pizza Heaven. There were only a few tables set up inside with tiny battery powered candles flickering. It did not do much to enhance the Formica-topped tables and dark, paneled space. One wall was entirely papered with photos that had begun to yellow and curl at the edges.

Vince Jr. and his mother greeted her from the counter.

"Large combo for Candy Simon, deliver to her office," Virginia said to her son. "Don't forget the extra napkins or I'll get a phone call again." She slid the box into a red insulated container.

A large pizza, Trinidad thought. She must be entertaining again. Trinidad's cheeks burned considering her previous ill-fated 911 call.

Vince nodded to her. "Hey, Miss Jones. Try the spinach and artichoke. It's the best." He sauntered out with the delivery.

Virginia smiled. Her long hair was braided into a coil and pinned on the back of her head. "It is a crowd favorite. How's the shop coming along?"

"Slow and steady." She plopped a handful of mangoes onto the counter. "Thought I'd share the wealth."

"Well, isn't that nice. Can I get a pizza started for you and maybe I can sit for a minute and thank you properly? Spinach and artichoke?"

"Sounds great."

While she rang up the sale, Virginia admired the mangoes with as much enthusiasm as if she'd been given something more than a bunch of very ripe tropical fruit. When the pizza order was submitted and payment taken, she vanished into the kitchen. A few minutes later, she reappeared, perching on the chair with such energy that Trinidad envied her.

"Thank you so much for the mangoes. Vince Sr. doesn't go in for much in the way of fruit except for the occasional banana, but I will enjoy them. Vance would, too, if he wasn't knee-deep in med school." She beamed. "I still can't believe we're going to have a doctor in the house, so to speak."

"That's wonderful."

"It wasn't always an easy road. Vance got into some rough patches in high school. But he's rallied, and now we couldn't be prouder. He's the only one in his high school class who went into medicine. Do you have children, Trinidad?" She colored. "Oh, well, I mean, I know you and Gabe split up."

"It's okay. No children. Only a sweet old dog."

"Much easier than children."

"So I've been told. I guess you've lived in Sprocket a long time, then?"

"Since we were married forty-two years ago. My father bought this place as a wedding gift to us. He painted the pizza slice on the front himself."

Trinidad figured she had hit the jackpot in the chatty, long-time Sprocketerian pizza maker. "Was the theater here when you moved in?"

"That old eyesore? Yes, indeed, but Cora didn't come on as manager until about ten years ago." She lowered her voice. "She was married to Warren at the time, did you know that?"

"I only heard that recently, that something went wrong between them."

"Money, that's what. He can't hold onto it because he's a gambler. Spent all of his money and then started in on hers. Cora gave him the boot."

"But they're still friends."

"Yes. He always said, when he hit the jackpot, he'd win her back, but Cora's a tough lady. She's not about to hand over the checkbook a second time."

"Fool me once," Trinidad said, thinking about how she'd be hard-pressed to trust another man after Gabe. Juliette had, and look where she had landed. Trinidad refocused on Virginia.

"I've been thinking about Warren recently," Virginia said. "He did some work for us, planted a floral display in the front area outside our entrance doors."

"I didn't notice."

"That's because everything's dead. Not his fault, though. Watering is Vince Jr.'s job, and he can't be bothered to remember." A hairy arm slid another pizza onto the receiving counter.

"That pizza's for Warren," Virginia said. "If we ever run out of pineapple and sausage, he'll starve to death."

While Virginia boxed up Trinidad's pizza and the one for Warren, Trinidad perused the photos on the wall. One curled specimen caught her attention. It was a picture of Edward Lupin, a video camera on his shoulder. She peered closer. Could it be the same camera the twins had purchased from the flea market? He was aiming it at a small stained glass window.

"Where was this taken?" Trinidad asked.

Virginia squinted. "The side of our restaurant." She pointed to a small window set high up in the dark wall. "There used to be a pretty stained glass panel there, which Lupin got into his head was some kind of artifact. He was always taking video of anything and everything, and that included our stained glass. Vince Jr. finally climbed up on a ladder and took photos to prove it had been made in New York in the 1970s. It broke during an earthquake last spring. At least it got a few folks in the restaurant who were curious about what Lupin was videotaping. That poor man was always believing he was right on the cusp of a major discovery. Sad, really. He was crestfallen when Vince showed him the window wasn't worth all the fuss."

She said something else, but Trinidad's mind was elsewhere. Lupin was always videotaping with his old clunky camera. Videotaping. She remembered the bag of VHS tapes at the flea market the twins had described.

"Nothing too exciting. Old history stuff and home videos, looked like."

The "what ifs" made her breath catch. What if Lupin had videotaped his supposed treasure, or even the contents of his storage unit? She checked her watch, almost five.

"What time does the flea market close?"

Virginia cocked her head, and Trinidad realized the question had been abrupt.

"I just remembered something I have to get today for the store," she explained.

"Closes at five, I think."

Trinidad took her pizza. She pressed on the door just as Vince Jr. pulled it open. She stumbled but caught herself.

"I forgot the napkins," he said sheepishly.

Virginia sighed and grabbed a stack.

"If you're headed back home, can you give me a lift to Candy's, Miss Jones?" Vince said. "Faster than taking my bike, and I can walk back to the store."

"Sorry, not headed that way. Thank you for the pizza," Trinidad said.

"And thank you for the mangoes," Virginia called. "Better run if you're going to get to the flea market on time."

Chapter Seventeen

SHE DROVE FASTER THAN SHE should have down Main and onto the quieter Fruitvale Road, which took her away from town. Just as she sighted the old airstrip, her cell phone rang. Pulling to the shoulder, she thumbed it on.

"Hey, Trinidad."

Her pulse ticked up at Quinn's cheerful baritone. She pictured his strong chin and the twinkle in his blue eyes. "We wanted to invite you to dinner. Mostly it's…you know…a social thing to, you know, uh, thank you for taking care of Doug."

A dinner invitation? She realized she was clutching the phone a little too tightly. "No need to thank me. Doug's a friend…just like you are." Did that sound weird? Might it have come out wrong?

Quinn didn't seem to notice. "I've been told I add way too much spice to my cooking, but I will try to tone it down for you."

For her? She was trying to think of what to say when he continued.

"And I've been digging up some info on Kevin I thought you might want to know. Maybe Stan would join us. What do you say?"

Stan, too? Was it a business meeting or a date? No, surely

not a date. She was not ready for that, not anywhere close. But Stan might be there. "I…um…that's so sweet, but I just bought a pizza."

"Oh, sure," he said, the disappointment clear in his voice.

She'd disappointed him, and, what's more, she realized she would have very much liked to enjoy a meal with Quinn and his brother and Stan. Gabe's betrayal had stripped her of confidence, but she wouldn't allow the roots of the past take hold in the present. She cleared her throat. "But would you all like to join me for pizza? It's way too much for me, and Papa is out for the evening. I may have some info of my own, but I have to stop by the flea market first. Meet me at the tiny house?" She bit her lip, but he didn't hesitate.

"Super," he said, the warmth back in his voice. "I'll bring a salad and something for Doug. He doesn't eat messy foods. I'll give Stan a call, too. Meet you at your place in an hour?"

"Deal."

Her spirit swelled. Not a date, just a meal with her Sprocket friends. What better way to end the day? Hopping out, she found the flea market gate closed and padlocked. "Oh, man."

"Gotta come back tomorrow."

She whirled to see Sonny Petrakis standing there, hands in the pockets of his painter's overalls. For the first time, she noticed how tall he was, how muscled his forearms.

"Oh, well, I'll do that. Thanks."

He moved between her and her car. Her heart beat faster. "Excuse me. I need to go now."

"You're always in such a hurry. That's not how we do things in Sprocket."

Her nerves quivered. Somehow, she tipped her chin up and looked him full in the face. "Get out of my way, Sonny."

"Just a quick question first. Why were you spying on us at Candy's office the other day? I saw you out there. Not too sly."

"I wasn't spying. I was walking my dog."

"You called the cops."

"I thought… I misunderstood. It looked like you were hurting her."

"That was none of your business."

Trinidad fingered the phone in her pocket. "It was if she was being hurt."

"I wasn't hurting her." His eyes were hard, flat stones. "I love her. We are going to get engaged soon."

"My mistake. Congratulations to you both." She tried to edge around him, but he did not move.

"Did you find out anything about those photos that got taken from Quinn? A picture of some valuables or something?"

"How did you know about the photos?"

"You can't keep anything a secret in this town. So?"

"Why are you asking?"

His mouth twitched. "Because I bought that storage unit. Whatever was in it, if there was something worth money, it's mine."

"Not if you released the items to the flea market and someone else purchased it. You signed a contract, didn't you? Once you handed the items over, they aren't yours anymore."

He glowered. "Is that why you're here snooping around now? Do you know something about Lupin's treasure?"

She backed up a step. "Not a thing. As far as I know, there isn't any."

He leaned in, bending closer. "I don't care what any form says. Remember, if you find anything in Lupin's stuff, it belongs to me."

Not in the eyes of the law, she thought.

She scooted around him. "I'll remember that."

He watched as she climbed into the Pinto and locked the doors. He got into his truck and drove away. She tried to quiet her thundering heartbeat. It wasn't exactly a threat, was it? Certainly, he'd meant to intimidate her and had succeeded. There was no way she was going to do any more skulking around by herself. Swallowing hard, she started to switch on the ignition when she saw Donald behind the chain-link fence, sauntering across the tarmac. He clutched a paper grocery bag and sipped from a can of grape soda. She got back out of the car.

"Donald," she called.

He jerked towards her and smiled, approaching the gate. "You scared me, Miss Jones."

"Call me Trinidad, please. I need to ask you a question."

"Okay. Shoot."

"Did Edward Lupin have any VHS tapes that wound up for sale at the flea market?"

"Tapes?" He glugged his soda and considered. "Yeah, as a matter of fact, he did. There were some sent over by Candy from his house, I think. The twins bought his old video camera to horse around with, but they didn't want any of the tapes. Neither did anyone else, as far as I can remember. Most folks have switched over to streaming services and DVDs and whatnot. Old VHS tapes are going the way of the woolly mammoth. Think I still got 'em in the back."

She kept her tone calm. "Would you mind if I bought them? My grandpa is visiting, and we have this old VHS player in the unit I'm renting. Hard to find tapes to go in it, these days." It was mostly true. Her grandfather had been known to sit through hours' worth of skippy, VHS John Wayne movies that took up an entire shelf in their Miami home.

"I'm supposed to be closed, but I guess I could ring you up real quick." He unlocked the gate and opened it enough for her to pass through. She shot a glance through the chain link, into the glare of the sun edging behind the mountains. Was Sonny still out there? Watching? Quickly, she slid inside. As long as she was with

Donald, she didn't have to worry. She missed Noodles's comforting presence.

Donald led her to his booth, covered with blue tarp. Pushing it aside, he rummaged around until he came up with a paper bag. "Here it is."

She peered inside. There were a dozen or so video tapes. Some were commercially made covering historical topics, "China Through the Ages and Colonial Woodworking." Several were labeled only "one" and "two." There was another with a pink stripe running down the label in permanent marker.

Donald grimaced. "Think your grandpa would be interested in any of those?"

"You never know," she said. "How much for all of them?"

"Fifty cents each, cash only. Six bucks."

She patted her pockets and came up with only four dollars and twenty-five cents. "Do you like mangoes? I could throw in two." She withdrew them from her pockets.

He laughed. "All right. Two mangoes and add a free ice cream when you open your shop and we'll call it done."

She handed over the fruit. "Come in anytime. We open Thursday." It gave her a thrill to say it.

He pocketed the money, but seemed to be making no moves to leave. He sipped his soda.

She shifted the bag in her arms. "Um, I am sorry to ask, but would you mind walking me to my car?"

He stopped drinking his soda and looked at her. "Well, sure, but why? Are you thinking someone is going to mug you for your VHS tapes?" he teased.

"You just never know, do you?"

His smile waned as he considered. Perhaps he, too, was pondering the recent murder and break-in at the theater. Not to mention the attack on Quinn.

"No," he said, downing the rest of his soda. "I guess you don't."

Trinidad couldn't believe she'd actually gotten her hands on the video tapes. Still, she reminded herself as she drove, they might be nothing at all, a bunch of hooey like her brilliant candy machine theory. Nerves prickling, she kept checking her rear-view mirror for any signs that Sonny had followed her. Once, she thought she saw a flicker of movement on the shadowy road behind her, but no one materialized. Still, she kept the doors locked and her foot hard on the gas. Papa's Bel Air was not in the driveway when she arrived, so she practically sprinted up the steps with her bag of tapes and pizza and into the tiny house, bolting the front door behind her.

She caught a glimpse of her reflection in the wall mirror, hair flying everywhere, face blotched, jaw tight. *Paranoia does not suit you.* It would be another twenty minutes until Quinn, Doug, and Stan were set to arrive. She put aside the history tapes for the moment and selected number one of the hand-labeled cassettes. Feeding it into the VCR, she sat on the kitchen chair and waited. The video was grainy, taken at some sort of outdoor area crowded with picnic tables full of merchandise. Perhaps a swap meet or another flea market? Lupin was not a skilled videographer, and there was a moment of him peering into the lens of his camera, another of his boots, and several of the grass and sky before he focused in on the items on the table. Old games, pottery, a statue of a rider on horseback. It seemed he was struggling with the focus when a rotund man stepped into the field of view. There was no sound to accompany the video, but the man appeared to be waving Lupin off.

She read his lips clearly. "No taping." Then there was more conversation from the peeved looking man until the film went dark. She continued perusing the tape all the way to the end, but there was nothing else. Had the footage contained anything significant? She had no idea.

The second tape looked a bit battered. Trinidad was not at

all sure it was playable, so she skipped to the one with the pink magic marker stripe. Just as she reached to slide it into the VCR, the front door rattled. She froze, clutching the tape in a death grip. Quinn would have knocked. Maybe it was Papa Luis, but she'd given him a key. Might he have forgotten it?

She'd made up her mind to creep to the kitchen and peek out from behind the curtain when the rattling stopped. She stood there, muscles rigid, holding onto the tape with fingers gone ice cold. Perhaps it had been Papa and, next, she would hear the key inserted in the lock. But it was silent, so silent she could hear the drip of the kitchen faucet.

"You're okay," she told herself. "Whoever it was can't get in. You're safe..." The thought died before it fully formed as she recalled she'd left the sliding door open a bit for Noodles. She'd turned and lurched towards the door just when she heard it roll open.

Panic swamped her. Sweat erupted on her forehead. Was it Sonny come to threaten her further? Should she run out the front door? But the intruder would hear and catch her before she could make it to the Pinto.

Feet slipping in her haste, she ran to the bathroom, slammed the door and locked it. Her panting was so frantic she was sure it could be heard clearly. Didn't matter, anyway. In such a tiny house, there was only one place she could be hiding. She dropped the tape with a clatter and fumbled for her cell. The phone shook badly as she dialed 911.

The bathroom knob rattled. She screamed. "I called the police. Get out of my house."

There was a mighty kick on the door that shuddered the whole panel. This time she clapped her hand over her mouth, the scream locked deep down. Her ears rang with the sound of her pounding blood. The door was flimsy, the lock even more so. She was trapped.

The terror tapped into something she had not expected. Sudden rage percolated through every pore. No one had the right to scare her in her tiny house. No one had the right to reduce her to helplessness.

And then she was screaming and hollering in a volume she hadn't known she could achieve.

"You will not hurt me, whoever you are. If you get through this door, I will kick and scream and bite and karate chop until there is nothing left of you but a pile of parts. You got me, buster?" She finished it off with a kick on the door from the inside, just to show him she meant business.

Heart pounding, she listened. Nothing but a faraway noise. She did not at first recognize the sound of the siren wailing.

The police.

There was the thump of booted feet trampling into her kitchen and to the bathroom.

"Police," a voice shouted. "Miss Jones, it's Officer Chang. Are you okay?"

She flung the door open and tumbled out so fast she almost knocked off the officer's glasses. She flung her arms around him. "I'm so glad to see you."

"Er, yes ma'am." Chang helped her into a chair.

Bigley ran in through the back door. "Gone. Saw someone just vanishing into the trees. Too far away to make an ID. Might have been carrying something. Looked like he or she was wearing gloves and a ski mask. No sign of a vehicle."

Trinidad struggled to get air in and out. She was okay. She had defended herself enough to survive. "It might have been Sonny. He…he scared me at the flea market." She panted out the story.

Bigley frowned. "We'll check that out."

"I want to see her," Quinn's voice carried from outside. "Is she hurt? What happened?"

"Let him in," Bigley said. When Quinn charged through the

front door, she pointed to the chair next to Trinidad. "Sit there until we see if we can get prints. Stay out of the way."

Quinn sat with a thud and grabbed Trinidad's hands. She took comfort in his calloused touch, his fingernails stained from hard work and nut oils.

"Are you okay?" he said. "We got here just as the cops rolled up. Your skin is like ice." He chafed her hands between both of his.

"I'm okay," she said through chattering teeth. "S…someone broke in, but I locked myself in the bathroom. The…intruder kicked at the door, but it held." The words did not seem real to her own ears. "The tapes…" she cried suddenly. It was no surprise to find the bag gone.

She reported it immediately to the chief. Bigley nodded and went back to her radio. Officer Chang trotted to his car to retrieve a fingerprint kit. Trinidad didn't hold out much hope. She knew from her days in court that a home can contain thousands of prints that might never be sorted out, even if the stranger hadn't been wearing gloves.

After Chang dutifully did his best at retrieving prints and thoroughly photographed the place, Bigley released the house. Doug and Stan were allowed to join them. Doug clutched a bowl of salad and a plastic wrapped de-crusted cheese sandwich. Stan carried a bottle of lemonade and a plate of lemon squares. They both paused uncertainly in the doorway.

"Please come in," she said.

Officer Chang looked longingly at the pizza.

If there was one thing Trinidad could not abide, it was seeing people hungry. "Everyone, sit down, please," she said. "Since you're all here, we might as well divvy up this pizza, even though it's probably stone-cold by now."

The officer looked hopefully at the chief.

"Oh, all right." Bigley and Chang sat in chairs, and they all crowded together.

Trinidad opened the pizza box. Was it weird to be sharing a pizza on the heels of being stalked by an intruder? Probably, but everything was weird in this nutty town. At least there would be conversation to fill up the corners of the tiny house until Papa and Noodles returned. The thought of being alone made her flesh crawl.

"I'll get some plates," she said.

Quinn stopped Trinidad from heading to the kitchen. "Stay right there. You're not doing a thing after what you just went through."

She sighed in gratitude since her knees were still shaking. Everyone loaded up with a slice of pizza and salad, except the chief who stuck with lemonade and Doug who nibbled his cheese sandwich. Trinidad had no appetite, but she sipped some lemonade. The zingy tartness revived her a little.

She related the whole story again from her pizza purchase to her conversation with Sonny before Donald let her in and sold her the tapes.

Bigley looked grim. "I already dispatched someone to have a conversation with Mr. Petrakis."

Quinn was thoughtful. "By my count, the list of people who knew you went to the flea market is seven." He counted off on his fingers. "Me and Doug, Stan, Virginia, Vince Jr., Sonny, and Donald."

"And anyone else who might have been told by any of those people," Stan said darkly. "Or seen her driving that direction and decided to follow and see what she was up to."

"Like Warren. He was due to pick up a pizza from Pizza Heaven when I left."

"And Sonny might have told Candy, etc., etc.," Officer Chang put in. His eyes flicked to Trinidad's uneaten slice. She passed her plate to him. "Thanks," he said. "I missed lunch."

Stan sliced into his pizza with a plastic fork and knife. Trinidad watched the process in fascination. After he chewed and swallowed, he carefully wiped his mouth. "And, again, we are without any evidence. The tapes are gone, like the photos."

Tapes. Trinidad stood up so quickly she almost knocked over the table. It could not be possible. Could it?

Ignoring the cries of alarm from the group, she bolted.

Chapter Eighteen

"TRINIDAD," QUINN SAID, CALLING AFTER her. "What's wrong?"

Shaking her head, she ran to the bathroom, emerging a second later.

"Are you sick?" Quinn said. "What can I do?"

She jiggled the tape at him with a grin. "Not sick. I just remembered I had this in my hand when I locked myself in the bathroom. It slipped behind the trash can after I dropped it."

He pumped a fist in the air. "Score one for the good guys."

Bigley took the tape. "Let's hope there's something on it."

They edged their chairs around as the chief slid it into the VCR. It lurched to life with a shot of Lupin's laced boots and a quick view of his hairy nostrils as he readied the camera to record. A metal-sided structure came into view.

Quinn gasped. "That's the Store Some More."

The camera continued to pan over the clutter. "It's unit three, that was Lupin's," Bigley said.

"Date on the bottom says it was recorded in March," Chang said. "He must have made a video when he rented the unit. Smart thing to do, actually."

They watched in tense silence as he hauled open the metal

door, which squealed in protest. His movement caused the camera frame to judder unsteadily. Ten seconds later, the door was fully open, and an overhead light bulb flicked on.

Trinidad realized she was holding her breath as the camera panned over the clutter. Everyone watching had angled forward on the edge of their seats. Slowly, Lupin went from one side to the other until a car engine noise crept into the background. Lupin immediately stepped out of his unit and slammed the door. The video ceased. They watched to the end, but he did not resume taping, at least not on that cassette.

"He didn't want anyone else to see. We finally have a video account of what was inside," Stan said. "I will need a copy of this to study."

Bigley nodded. "We'll get it to you." She ejected the video from the player.

"I want to watch it again," Trinidad protested. "In slow motion."

"We'll analyze it frame by frame, I promise," Bigley said. "And we will get a copy to Stan as well, just like I said. You can go over that with him."

"But..."

Bigley frowned. "Sorry. That's all you get for now. It's more than I should have allowed. We'll be in touch." She darted a look at Chang who was helping himself to a treat Stan had brought. "If you've had enough to take the edge off your hunger...?"

He flushed. "Sorry. I got four boys, and I'm lucky if there's a rind of cheese left for me by dinner time," he explained. With the chief out of range, Trinidad quickly wrapped a lemon square in a napkin and handed it to the hungry officer. He whispered a thank-you and trotted out of the tiny house. In a moment, they had driven away.

"I am tremendously sorry this happened," Stan said. "But it does show that someone is still either searching for the treasure or perhaps trying to cover their tracks."

"You said you found out something about Kevin," Trinidad reminded Quinn.

He looked chagrined. "My mama always told me never to gossip, but this is straight out of the rumor factory."

Stan took a small bite of lemon square. "At this point, any trifle might help."

Quinn shrugged. "Rumor at the memorial before I left to follow Trinidad was that Tanya was pressuring Kevin big-time for a marriage proposal, but he wasn't on board."

"Who did you hear that from?" Stan asked.

"Mrs. Mavis said she heard from her friend who works at a hotel over in Scotch Corners that Tanya was looking at possible venues for her wedding."

"Pastor Phil shared the same sort of feeling," she said. "Did Kevin know she was going so far as to plan the ceremony?"

"Yep. Turns out our nosy local Warren heard the same thing from Mrs. Mavis. She said Warren blabbed it to Kevin at poker night, but Kevin said he had no intention of getting married for a good long while, even if she booked Buckingham Palace for the nuptials."

"That must have been an uncomfortable situation," Trinidad said.

"Uh-huh. Apparently, she and Kevin had a bit of a tiff about it, and he was trying to smooth things over with a present, but he didn't tell Warren what it was."

"There was a rosebush on his porch. I think he meant to give it to her, but he was murdered before he could. It's there still, half-dead of the heat. The day of the murder, he was giving her a ride on his motorcycle. They seemed cool towards each other. Perhaps he'd told her he wasn't ready for marriage."

"And maybe she came back later to convince him and things got out of hand and she clobbered him."

"No prints, though," Quinn said.

Trinidad frowned. "Could be she grabbed up a towel or something."

"That speaks more to premeditation," Stan said.

Quinn rubbed his forehead. "I guess you're right. So where does that leave us?"

The clatter of dog toenails announced that Noodles and Papa Luis had returned. Noodles bounded in and nosed Trinidad in the thigh. She stroked his ears and kissed the top of his head.

Papa arched an eyebrow as he took in the gathering, his arms filled with grocery bags.

"Are you ready to become the house chef?" Trinidad said, hoping Papa would not realize something terrifying had just occurred.

"It's for the cookout."

"What cookout?"

"The Fourth of July cookout."

She blinked. "Whose?"

"Ours, of course."

"Ours?" She watched him slide a pork roast into the cramped refrigerator and lay a package of dry beans and a bulging sack of rice onto the counter. "Oh, Papa. Are you…I mean…are you planning to have a party? Here?"

"Sure," he said. "Where else?"

No surprise. She should have anticipated it. Papa needed no excuse to organize a party. Once he'd had a "Monday party" just because he could think of no other reason to gather. The Fourth of July would not disappear into obscurity without a soiree as big as Papa could make it. "But it's too small here," she said.

"Oh, pooh. Always room for friends. We can sit outside. Make a bonfire and watch the fireworks." He beamed at Quinn, Doug, and Stan. "You'll all come, of course?"

All heads nodded. "But we might need to leave before the fireworks," Quinn said uneasily.

Doug looked at Noodles.

"And Noodles certainly isn't a fan, either." Trinidad stroked his graying muzzle.

"Maybe we all will be having so much fun you won't even notice the fireworks." Papa continued to unload the food.

Quinn's expression was doubtful.

"Papa, how many other people did you invite?"

"Everyone," he said simply.

She passed a hand across her eyes. "Oh, dear."

"I think I'd better bake more lemon squares," Stan said with a smile.

"And I'll bring over some folding chairs," Quinn added. "Do you need hot dogs or buns?"

Papa looked mortified. "Not hot dogs. Pork roast, beans and rice, tostones. No one can live on hot dogs." Papa yawned and stretched before settling at the table. "So," he said. "I passed a police car on the way here. What did I miss?"

"You're not going to believe it," Trinidad said.

"Hold on, then," Papa said. "I will fix myself some coffee and settle in for the report."

She knew how he would respond when she got to the end. He'd insist she move home to Miami.

Her body rippled in goose bumps as she recalled the vicious kick to the door, the rattling handle, the desperation of the intruder to attempt a break-in before dark.

If anything else happened, she just might start to come around to Papa's way of thinking. Miami was beginning to sound like paradise.

Wednesday morning arrived, and Trinidad couldn't believe how the time had flown. A mere six weeks before she'd landed in this outwardly sleepy hamlet. The next phase of her life would start in earnest the following day when her shake shop launched into the world. She was alternately thrilled and petrified. It was definitely a better way to occupy her mind than replaying what had happened at the tiny house the previous night. If the door had failed… If she hadn't been able to call the police… With a concerted effort, she pushed the anxiety away and got back to work.

By midmorning, during her return from her second trip to the grocery, this time to replace the bag of sugar she'd spilled all over the floor, she saw Cora walking up the steps to the Vintage Theater, peering at something under the eaves.

Trinidad stopped. Nosiness, she'd learned, was a key quality in sniffing out the facts people would like to keep buried. It worked for Miss Marple and Jessica Fletcher, after all. Of course, those two characters never went anywhere without being followed by a trail of carnage. Trinidad plastered on a smile. Cora eyed her approach.

"This is your fault," Cora said.

Trinidad faltered. "Uh, what is?"

"That I've had to change the locks and put up these motion detector lights." Cora rolled her eyes. "Everyone in town thinks there's the Irish crown jewels hidden in my theater." Her voice was thick with sarcasm.

"I wasn't the only one who bought into the candy machine theory."

"But Warren is a nut. I would have thought better of you."

She wasn't sure whether to be offended or amused. "Kevin was killed for something he got at the flea market. You regularly purchase items from the flea market, right? You and Warren?"

"Yes," she conceded. "I like to do crafts. It's a cheap way to get supplies for my hobby. Warren's problem is he can't stand having money in his pocket. If there's something with a price tag in front of him, he has to buy it. I should know. He was my husband, once upon a time."

Trinidad pulled in a breath. "I didn't know you and Warren were married."

"That's a surprise to you? I would have thought the gossips would have filled you in the moment you hit town." Her expression turned sly. "We heard all about you and the other two exes before you even arrived. The Bigley babes. You could start a club."

Trinidad knew her face must be a fiery shade of strawberry, but she kept her voice level. Fletcher and Marple must have had to deal with a bit of mortification from time to time as well. "Well, yes, it did surprise me. I mean, most exes don't stay so closely connected."

Cora sighed. "We were married for ten years, divorced for nearly that long now. Warren was different back then. I thought he had more of a spine. That's important. I need to have someone strong enough to stand up to me, and I thought he was that way, at first." Trinidad saw what looked like honest grief soften Cora's sharp features. "He's addicted to gambling, and he can't beat it—or he won't." She shook her head. "The annoying thing is he's a good man, a wonderful man, except for that ugly part of him."

The chief's words about Gabe came back to her. *People can be many things.*

"That ugly part..." Cora sighed. "It's a monster that he has to feed by any means necessary, so he'll lie and cheat if he has to." She shook her head. "It's not a good feeling to be in that kind of a relationship, you know, with someone you can't trust."

She did. Intimately. But living so close together? How could Cora stand it? The woman was made of tough stuff indeed. "I do know how you feel."

Cora slid a look at her. "Yeah, I guess you would, being a Bigley babe."

"An ex–Bigley babe. I'm sorry."

"Me too." She chewed her lip. "Warren's gotten himself involved with some dangerous men in the past, men who insist he repay his debts. I worry what will happen one day when he can't."

"Did Kevin loan him money to pay them?"

Her eyes narrowed. "I don't know, but Warren wouldn't have hurt Kevin, if that's what you're thinking."

Not even to feed the monster? She debated whether to press, but time was growing short for Juliette. "The day I found Kevin, there was a flyer from Warren's van caught under my tires, but he said he hadn't opened the back doors."

Frown lines grooved her forehead, and she toyed with her beaded necklace. "Are you saying he was lying about it?"

"Not necessarily. Someone else might have opened the doors, hidden inside, maybe, or stashed something there. Did you look in the van after Warren returned to the theater that afternoon?"

"Yes, eventually. It was a colossal mess, as usual, and I threw a fit, demanded he clean it out. He moved the boxes of flyers into the storage room along with other stuff. I helped for a few minutes, but I had to take a phone call, so I didn't see it all. Warren dumps everything he can't find a place for in that storage room, so it's a mess."

"What other stuff came from the van to the storage room? Do you recall?"

She shrugged. "Cleaning supplies, bags of old props, miscellaneous office supplies. Really, I'm not sure what he brought in that day, and neither is he. Like I said, the storage room is a catastrophe."

Here goes nothing, she thought. "Can I get a look in there?"

Something between concern and curiosity crossed her face. "No, I don't think there's anything worth spit in that room, and I'd rather let this inane treasure business die of its own accord."

"But, Cora," she said softly, "do you think Warren will ever stop searching for Lupin's valuables?"

The seconds ticked by until she shook her head. "No."

"One look. Fifteen minutes."

"I don't see how it will put an end to the rumors."

"If we find something it will. Let me look. Please." She hesitated. "Kevin was killed for something that might be in your storage room right now."

"Not likely. We are in and out of there all the time. I'm telling you, there's nothing."

"Maybe you just didn't recognize it."

Cora huffed out a breath. "Okay. Let's get it over with."

Trinidad swallowed. "And just to keep myself out of further trouble, I'm going to call Chief Bigley to supervise."

Cora waved a hand. "Whatever, just tell her not to make a big spectacle of herself. I don't want every harebrained thrill seeker in Sprocket showing up thinking we've found Montezuma's Treasure or something."

The chief arrived in a jogging suit and athletic shoes ten minutes after Trinidad called. "You've messed up my run again, Trinidad," she said as Cora ushered her through the door into the theater lobby.

"Sorry, but I figured you didn't want me poking around on my own."

"Truth," the chief said.

"Have you discovered anything on the tape?" she said quietly so Cora wouldn't overhear.

"I've got Officer Oliver going through it frame by frame. He should have a report any time now. Before I came here, I dropped a copy with Stan, so you can look to your heart's content."

"A copy of what?" Cora asked before she waved off the question. "Never mind, I don't really care." She led the way down a narrow hall to a door on the end.

"Has it been unlocked all this time?" Chief Bigley asked.

"Yes." Cora was indignant. "What is someone going to steal? A mop? A bottle of floor cleaner?" She flipped a switch, and a weak bulb buzzed to life. The cramped room had a metal shelving unit on one wall. Each shelf was stuffed to the brim with old flyers, plastic containers labeled "wigs," "shoes," "etc.," and a tangle of what looked to be silk flowers.

The other side of the room housed a beat-up desk piled high with papers, a crooked fake palm tree, and all manner of odds and ends. Cardboard boxes were jammed under the desk.

The chief grimaced. "This is gonna take a while." She shot a look at Trinidad. "And I'm going to do it myself so it's methodical and by the book, just in case. Both of you will have to wait elsewhere."

"But…" Trinidad said, deflated.

"Miss Jones, you're turning into a pretty committed sleuth, but this is still a police investigation." She paused. "And, besides, I think you have a shop to open tomorrow, don't you?" The chief left no room for negotiation.

Trinidad closed her mouth. "Yes, I do. Will you promise to let me know if you find anything?"

But she had already turned her back on both of them.

"I'm going to spend the weekend with my sister," Cora said. "It's my last chance to get away before we open *Our Founding Fathers*. I'll be in the mountains. If you make the find of the century, leave a message on my cell phone because, unlike the rest of the natural-born world, I don't keep it on when I'm driving." She stalked away, returning a moment later with a duffel bag. "Happy hunting."

Chapter Nineteen

AFTER SHE LEFT, TRINIDAD TRUDGED to the lobby. She tried to fend off the wave of discouragement at being shut out of the search. There was still a video that might provide more clues, and the chief was right; the hours until the Shimmy and Shake Shop opened were melting away like ice cream on a sultry summer day.

Pushing out the front door of the theater, she plowed smack into Tanya Grant. She stumbled backwards, toppling a white plaster container with ABSOLUTELY NO CELL PHONES stenciled in an angry font on the side. Trinidad lugged it back into position.

"Ouch," Tanya said, rubbing her nose where Trinidad's head had made contact.

"Sorry." Trinidad tried to pull the door closed behind her, but Tanya's dropped purse was in the way. As she bent to retrieve it, Officer Chang hustled up the front walkway with a box of rubber gloves. He held the door while Tanya retrieved her purse and nimbly stepped around her, putting himself squarely in the doorway.

She tried to pass him.

"Apologies, Ms. Grant. You can't go in there right now."

She blinked. "I have to pick up a script." She pushed the door, but Chang held it fast.

"Ma'am, there is police business going on inside. I will have to ask you to leave."

"Police business?" Her eyes narrowed. "What do you mean?"

"I am not at liberty to say."

Tanya's expression went haughty. "If this has anything to do with that stupid treasure or Kevin's murder, I have a right to know. My father funds this theater."

Chang's forehead shone with sweat, but he did not relinquish his hold on the door. "Come back later, ma'am."

"I'm going to complain to the chief."

"Yes, ma'am," he said. "At the station, there's a stack of forms you can fill out about how we've annoyed you."

Tanya stared at him. "Are you being sassy with me?"

"No, ma'am. Just informative. There's a box of number two pencils on the counter next to the forms."

Trinidad hid her smile. Passive aggressive sassiness. She'd have to try it some time. "Thanks, Officer."

He nodded and closed the door, locking it from the inside.

Trinidad tried to hurry away, but Tanya caught up with her. "You know what's going on in there, don't you?"

"Hmm?"

"What they're doing?"

"Ah, well, it's a police thing. I was just…I mean, talking something over with Cora."

"I heard about the burglary during Kevin's memorial. This has something to do with his death."

"Honestly, we've just got to wait to hear from the chief, Tanya. That's all I can say."

She pressed her lips together, and Trinidad was ready for an outburst. But, instead, she blinked hard, and her lower lip quivered. "He was going to be my husband, you know. We were planning to leave this town and everything in it and start over somewhere else, no matter what Daddy had to say about it."

"You mentioned that your father wasn't a fan of Kevin's," she said gently.

"My father isn't a fan of *me*. Mom died when I was thirteen, and Dad, well, let's just say he doesn't have much instinct for parenting. He's never liked anyone I dated, especially not Kevin. It was a good litmus test, you know?"

"How so?"

"Kevin knew my dad would cut me off if we got married, and he loved me anyway. It wasn't just about my money."

So, Tanya and Kevin would really turn their back on the Grant fortune? And Kevin would leave behind Popcorn Palace and his home? Was she in denial about Kevin's reluctance to marry her or merely lying to save face?

"I'm sorry, Tanya. I know you loved him very much."

Tanya's expression hardened. "I will find out what's going on with or without your help." She waited a beat, but Trinidad knew she had to keep the chief's search on the down low.

After a moment more, Tanya muttered something under her breath before she stalked to her car, slamming the door so hard the window vibrated. Trinidad watched as she drove away. Tanya might raise such a ruckus that, soon, everyone would know something big was happening at the old theater.

Cora and the chief would be furious, but that was not her problem for the moment. She found her compatriots already gathered at the Shimmy and Shake Shop, Papa Luis having let Quinn, Stan, and Doug inside.

She slid in next to Quinn who sat at a posh pink table, peering at Stan's computer and comparing it to a printed page. Doug sat next to Noodles, kneading his ears until the dog's eyes rolled in bliss.

Papa insisted on handing around bowls of mango sorbet. "There were a few more crates delivered today, so we have plenty."

"How many did you tell Farhan we needed?"

He shrugged. "A few. He has an accent, you know. Hard to understand him sometimes."

Trinidad smiled. Papa always insisted that he himself had no accent whatsoever. She accepted the bowl. "Thank you."

He stood behind Quinn. "What are we looking for?"

"That's the problem. We don't know," Stan said. Eyes straining, they squinted at the video and tried to match it to the list dutifully typed up by Officer Oliver.

"There's a baseball bat," Quinn said, pointing with his spoon. "Could that be worth a mint?"

"Baseball is the greatest sport in the world," Papa said. "But that list the officer typed up says this bat was made in 1975. No one good went to the world series that year, only the Red Sox and the Reds. I wouldn't pay a nickel for that bat."

Even a Sox or Reds fan would be hard-pressed to pay a million for a game bat, she figured.

They ticked on through the list. "How about the clock?" She scanned an item halfway down the column. "It says on the list the model is undetermined. Are there priceless clocks?"

Stan nodded. "I believe so."

Papa agreed. "I saw one at a museum once. Your mother insisted I go with her. Some sort of treasures from China exhibit. They had a rare clock. It had music and automata."

"Was it valuable?"

He shrugged. "Worth four million, as I recall. I wanted to see inside, but no one would open it up for me."

Papa Luis, like her own father, always wanted to see the innards of machines to understand how they worked. In his days an electrical engineer in the sugar mills and copper mines, he was always pondering the "how" of things. An engineer's mind, through and through.

"This clock isn't worth much, I'm afraid," Stan said, zooming the screen. "See the battery compartment in the back? You can just make it out. Too modern to be valuable."

They scanned another half hour of footage. After a fifteen-minute stretch break, they watched the whole thing again. Going on hour two, they still had found nothing of note. What was a broom worth? A scarred kitchen chair? A crate of wooden bowling pins?

Trinidad massaged the kink forming in her neck. "This is getting us nowhere."

"Wait, rewind a moment," Papa said.

Trinidad's pulse jumped.

"There, I'll bet that's it," Papa said triumphantly.

They crowded close. "What?" Quinn said. "That ceramic pot?" The wide-mouthed squat piece was blue on the bottom and yellow on the top. In the center was a round area with two fish painted on what looked like choppy waves.

"Mm-hmm," he said, spooning up more ice cream. "I saw something like that at the museum also. Some expensive thing from Emperor Qianlong's dynasty, as I recall."

The pot was lying on its side, but they could not gauge height. Maybe eighteen inches or more?

"What was it worth, Papa, the one you saw in the museum? Do you remember?"

"More than I would ever pay for a pot."

Quinn looked at Doug. "Hey, brother. Can you do a search on your phone?"

In under a minute, Doug handed over his cell. Quinn held the tiny screen next to Lupin's video. They stared. Quinn broke the silence with a long low whistle. "Sure looks like the same type of pattern to me, the coloring and the fish."

"And how much is that pot worth, the one in Doug's picture?" she asked.

He scrolled down and swallowed hard. "Seventy million dollars," he said.

Seventy. Million. Dollars. It was so quiet in the shop she could hear the soft whir of the ice cream mixer.

"That's a lot," Doug said.

"It sure is." Quinn's face was pale, and he gulped. "Almost too much to be believed. Seventy million dollars for a pot."

Her theory came into focus, sharp and clear. "Tanya Grant loves roses. Her yard is full of them. Kevin had a Pink Princess rosebush on his porch when he was killed. Princess was Tanya's stage role in one of the theater productions they did together. I think..." Trinidad squeaked before she got her vocal cords back online. "Kevin bought something at the garage sale to plant the rosebush in for Tanya. He thought it was just a plain old pot."

"But someone figured out it wasn't," Stan said.

She nodded slowly. "So they killed Kevin at the Popcorn Palace, but, when they were stealing the pot from the boxes out back, I interrupted them. My scream caused Warren to rush into the shop. The killer ran from the back and stowed the pot in Warren's van. That's how the flyer came to be floating around. It flew out when the killer opened the van's rear doors to hide the pot so they wouldn't be seen with it."

"It wouldn't do to be caught lugging a pot out of Kevin's yard," Stan said. "Impossible to explain."

Trinidad connected the dots. "Warren drove the van to the theater where Cora demanded he clean it out. The pot probably got unloaded into the storage room, though Cora doesn't remember exactly what was in there, and neither does Warren, or so he claims."

Trinidad fumbled for her phone and dialed Chief Bigley. She answered on the third ring.

"We've been going over the video," Trinidad said breathlessly, "and we think Lupin had a rare piece of Chinese Qianlong pottery."

"Describe it for me and text me a photo," she snapped.

Trinidad texted a screenshot of the blurry pot from the video and the image of the Qianlong on Doug's cell.

She heard the chief blow out a breath. "Then we have a problem," she said. "Because Chang and I have gone through the storage room inch by inch, and there wasn't anything like that to be found."

"Maybe you missed it."

"I don't see how we could have. I'll call Cora now that we have an object. She might remember a pot like that, and maybe it's in another part of the theater. I don't think she'll pick up her cell until she arrives at her destination, though. In the meantime, Chang and I will go through the whole theater after we're clear of our Fourth of July duties. I'll bring some others on to assist and interview Warren again and call in an officer on overtime to keep the scene secure."

"Do you think the pot might have already been removed from the theater?" she asked.

"Plausible, but perhaps the killer is unaware of that fact. They broke into the theater, remember? And why was an intruder after the tapes at the tiny house? Had to be to cover their tracks or prevent anyone else from finding the pot. I have a feeling the murderer hasn't yet been able to retrieve it, or maybe your theory is wrong and it was never there in the first place."

The murderer...Trinidad swallowed. As exciting as it was to consider a priceless treasure, it had cost a man his life, his girlfriend her future, and Kevin's parents their son.

And what if she was wrong? What if the pot was just a cheap garden-variety type or a reproduction? No one had been inside Warren's van. Perhaps it all added up to another fat zero.

She was relieved that the next part of the investigation would be handled solely by the police. Positive thinking was the order of the day. The pieces were falling into place. They'd find the Qianlong, or Cora would surely remember where it might have gotten to. It was a matter of time now before Juliette would be released from prison.

Chief Bigley's somber tone poked through Trinidad's day-dreaming.

"Don't expect miracles, Trinidad. As soon as we get the fireworks display area and the parade details sorted out, I'll go through it again with whomever I can round up, but I'm telling you I would have noticed a pot like that. It's pretty distinctive."

"Do you know much about Chinese pottery?"

There was a long pause. "All right. Fair point. My entire experience with pottery is the clay ash tray I made at reform school summer camp. At least we know what it looks like now, so I'll have a better shot at finding it."

"Good luck."

"Thank you." She paused. "And thanks for the help."

Trinidad disconnected with a gusty sigh and reported what she'd heard from the chief.

Quinn shook his head. "But if it's not in the theater, then where could it be?"

"That's what the killer is trying to find out," Stan said, closing up his computer. "At least we have the 'what,' now. I will start working on some angles to pressure the chief about releasing Juliette. I'm not sure we have enough to poke holes in her case, but it's something, anyway." He paused at the door. "Will I see you all at the town concert this evening?"

"Doug and I are handing out lemonade," Quinn said. "As a matter of fact, we'd better head over there now." He looked hopefully at Trinidad. "Are you coming, too? You both, I mean," he said, gesturing to her grandfather. "And Noodles."

A sweet invitation. She could not resist. "Yes, absolutely. We'll be along in a while."

They departed, and Papa drummed thick fingers on the table, apparently lost in thought.

"What?" she asked.

"He's a nice boy, good to his brother, but Len the seafood man..."

She held up her palm. "Papa, now is not the time to worry about my love life."

He shrugged as a delivery man popped his head in the shop. "Got some more mangoes for you."

"Excellent," Papa said, hustling over to accept the fruit. Trinidad bit back a comment. Now was not the time to worry about an overabundance of fruit, either. With a smidge of luck, the chief would find the pot and lift prints from it—anything that might free her friend.

Finally, she could focus on her mission, to make sure the Shimmy and Shake Shop was ready for the grand opening.

Let it rain mangoes, for all she cared.

Rolling up her sleeves, she set to work.

"It's not there," Bigley said over the phone two hours later.

She gripped her cell. "It has to be."

"I am telling you there is nothing remotely resembling a priceless Chinese pot at the Vintage Theater. Closest we came was an ugly plaster urn and a set of stacking Rubbermaid containers with the lids missing." Her frustration crackled through the phone connection.

"Did you call Cora?"

"I left messages, but she isn't answering. It's spotty coverage where she's going, so it might not have gone through. I showed Warren a picture, and he claims never to have noticed it in the van or the theater. Says it could have been tucked in some of the boxes he unloaded, but there's no telling for sure. And, before you ask, I sent an officer to the flea market to scour the property just in case, and there's no sign of it there, either."

The priceless pottery, if there was such a thing, was more elusive than the proverbial haystack needle. Not in the storage unit? Not in Kevin's yard? Nor the van, nor the theater, nor at the flea market. Poor Edward Lupin wasn't even sure where he'd put it. Perhaps he did not really understand its value in the first place. It seemed like nobody did. Almost nobody.

Like her priceless penny-in-the-candy-machine theory, it had turned out to be nothing. She had to be the worst sleuth on the planet. All she'd dug up was a worthless coin in a vintage candy machine.

Candy machine.

Something from her memory clamored for attention.

She pictured the old sturdy relic that Cora had stripped and repainted. Red paint to yellow. She recalled a snippet of conversation.

"...underneath that old chipped red paint..."

Hang on.

An idea began to churn through Trinidad's mind. It was too incredible, but it allowed all the loose ends to settle into a tidy knot. But what if she was wrong? This would be more than just egg on her face. If she followed up on her idea, she would be accusing a longtime Sprocketerian of murder. Reputations, hers most of all, hung in the balance.

She sat at her lovely pink table, thinking, alone with only the whir of the mixing machine. Should she, or shouldn't she? Right or wrong? Risk it all or stay quiet? She did not like risk. She was not brave. Was she? The old Trinidad was not one to step up and be counted, but the new woman she'd become? Was she willing to risk everything for the sake of Juliette?

She spent several more minutes enveloped in the comfort of her shop. She knew what she had to do. Jittery and cold, she called the chief.

"I think I know who killed Kevin."

The chief sighed. "There's nothing to contradict the proof that it's the person already in jail for the crime. Yes, all this treasure business is interesting, and obviously there's a criminal at work, but as far as murder goes… I'm sorry, but it's still your friend on the hook."

"Please. Just listen to me. I know we've not gotten along very well, and things are…awkward between us, but I'm asking you to hear me out. Ten minutes. That's it."

The chief heaved out a tortured sigh. "All right. You have ten minutes. Start talking."

Trinidad shared her suspicions with the chief in painstaking detail. Her speculation had to sound bizarre, outrageous even. Her words were met with silence. Trinidad's pulse rocketed with each tick of the ice cream treat clock. Finally, the chief cleared her throat.

"As much as I don't like to admit this, I think your theory may hold water."

Trinidad smothered a victory shout.

"But we need proof."

She scooted to the edge of her chair. "I have an idea. It seems to me that the easiest way to draw the killer out is to offer them something so sweet they can't resist."

"Hmmm. It's a long shot."

"Yes."

"But you're willing to risk it? For Juliette?"

"Yes."

"You're a good friend."

"I am trying to be. So, Chief Bigley, are you in the mood to set a sticky trap?"

"Do you agree to let me handle things and not try to go all 'Scooby-Doo Mystery Machine' amateur sleuth on me?"

"Yes, ma'am."

"Then I'm in with both feet," she said.

Chapter Twenty

EVERYONE IN SPROCKET HAD TURNED out for the concert in the town square. It was a long-standing tradition, she was told, increasing in popularity with tourists over the last few years. What had started out as a neighborhood performance was now a full-on event with folks filling the seats for patriotic tunes from the high school band. It was also the perfect scenario to set her plan to catch a killer in motion. The gazebo, which had so recently been the setting for a memorial, was now decked out with flags and red, white, and blue balloons. People brought picnic blankets or their own camping chairs. A kiddie area offered bubbles and a pinwheel-making station. Several people had brought their dogs along. Noodles sported a festive star-spangled kerchief around his neck as he greeted humans and canines alike. At least he was relaxed. Trinidad felt like there were a half dozen elephants trampling through her innards in search of a way out. She offered polite hellos and small talk, but all the while her pulse was stampeding.

Quinn waved a cup at her in greeting before he began to mix up another giant vat of lemonade. The table next to him was festooned with every kind of cookie imaginable. She was not surprised to see that Papa had contributed an enormous bowl of chunked mango to the sweets. He was moving among the chairs, shaking hands and introducing himself as if he were running for office. The band warmed up as they prepared to offer up John Philip Sousa's finest marches to kick off the weekend festivities.

She wished she could sit back and enjoy her first celebration in her new town, but the job ahead left her coated in cold sweat.

Carlos and Diego hustled over, cookies in hand. "We've been telling all the tourists about the break-in at your house and stuff. Figured it would be good for business if people thought there was somebody still searching for Lupin's treasure."

"Well," she said, raising her voice one notch, "As a matter of fact, I think I know where that treasure is. The chief has an officer posted there until seven, but as soon as he leaves, I'm going to see if I'm right."

"Really?" Carlos's eyes popped. "Can we come?"

"No, but I'll let you know right away if I find it. Are you ready for our big day tomorrow?"

They both nodded. Diego's cheek bulged with a mouthful of chocolate chip cookie. "Oh yeah. We'll be there at nine a.m. sharp. Are you still gonna work if you find something priceless? I wouldn't. I'd go to a ball game and buy a motorcycle and a completely off-the-hook sports car."

She laughed. "Even if I find it, it wouldn't be mine to keep. I'm satisfied having the world's best ice cream shop."

They ambled off towards their friends, whom she figured would hear all the news in a matter of minutes. Harnessing the Sprocket gossip wheel could be tricky, and she hoped it would pay off. Step one, complete.

She walked around handing out flyers for the Shimmy and Shake Shop, especially targeting the campers who had arrived from Three Egg Lake in scores to attend. They would hopefully buy an ice cream the next day when they came to town to stock up for their Fourth of July grill out by the lake. She stopped next to Papa and Pastor Phil.

"I am ready to report for duty at the shop as soon as I finish dessert," Papa said. She eyed his napkin, stacked with uneaten cookies. He was no doubt so busy chatting that it might take a good long while for him to finish.

She squeezed his shoulder. "You take your time, Papa, and enjoy. You'll be on your feet all day tomorrow scooping ice cream, so rest up while you can."

Pastor Phil saluted her with a half-eaten brownie. She meandered on.

Warren sat in a row of chairs with Vince Jr. and his mother. At the other end, Tanya picked at a macaroon, and Sonny and Candy chatted, heads close together. Mr. Mavis marched in dizzying circles dispensing plastic cups of iced lemonade that Quinn and Doug filled.

It was as good a time as any to put step two into action. She strolled over to Quinn.

She waited a beat and made sure her whisper was just loud enough, with an edge of contained excitement. "I can't tell you the details, but I know where it is."

"You do?" Quinn said, a little too loudly. "Lupin's treasure?"

She waited a beat and then answered in an appropriate volume for those who might be listening. "Yes. It was hidden in plain sight this whole time. I'm going over there at seven after I close the shop and the cops leave. I'll call you as soon as I find it."

Scooby-Doo would be impressed. The second piece of bait had been delivered.

Warren hustled over to the cookie table. He patted his stomach and grinned. "I figure it's a sin to pass up free baked goods, right? The first one whet my appetite."

"We've got containers of them, so you can refill all you want." Quinn gestured to the table.

"Thanks very much." He paused. "So, uh, how's it going with your store and all?"

Trinidad smiled. "Just fine. We're ready to open tomorrow."

"Yeah?"

"Uh-huh. Just a few more things to finish up tonight."

Warren selected a snickerdoodle and took a bite. "Great. I will be the first in line tomorrow for a Funkshake."

"A Freakshake, and I'll make sure it's extra generous."

He shoved in another bite and about-faced to return to his seat.

Quinn gave her a sly wink. "Mission accomplished?" he whispered.

"We'll find out," she whispered back. "As soon as the chief calls."

"Meet you at the Shimmy as soon as we finish with our lemonade duties." He wiped a hand across his apron.

"Bet you never figured when I showed up at your nut farm that you'd be involved in a thing like this."

He winked. "In for a penny, you know..."

He handed an empty cup to Doug who filled it and gave the drink to Trinidad. Then he slipped a dog biscuit out of his pocket and offered it to Noodles.

The dog accepted the prize with a vigorous swish of his tail instead of his usual slurpy thank you lick. He seemed to know that Doug was not comfortable with that kind of gesture. *Smart dog, Noodles.*

She headed to the shop with Noodles, sipping her lemonade on the way. Excitement buzzed in her veins. She passed the food truck, where she'd left it parked on the curb, ready to be returned to Orville. One more thing to check off the list. There only remained a few more details to finish up before the grand opening. Visitors had been strolling by all day, peeking into the window and reading the flavor descriptions on the flyer she'd posted. She'd had to stop herself from personally rushing out to greet every one of them.

This was it. Her dream would finally be realized on a bright and glorious Fourth of July morning. Maybe the plan she'd cooked up might just catch a killer and Juliette could resume her life in Sprocket, too, if Chief Bigley made an arrest at the theater, completing the third step in their plan. All the wagging tongues would be silenced. It would be an Independence Day for both of them.

Breathing the satisfying sugary smells in deeply, she got to work thawing the brownie stars and slicing wedges of pineapple for the Tropical Twist Freakshakes and decorating the shortbread cookies to top the key lime extravaganzas.

With meticulous care, she polished the glass windows, admiring the way the Shimmy and Shake Shop lettering sparkled in the waning summer sun. After all the self-doubt, the heartache of Gabe's betrayal, her angst over moving to Sprocket, her anguish at seeing Juliette jailed for murder, it felt like things might actually work out. Her shop filled her with pride she hadn't felt before, a sense of satisfaction that had been sorely lacking. She fingered the immaculate white aprons hanging from the silver hooks, ready for her, the twins, and one for Papa Luis. How perfect that he had arrived to share in the moment.

"I think we're actually going to make it," she said to Noodles.

He sniffed, then cocked his head, alert to a sound she could not hear. She figured it was the clanging and banging of the band scooting chairs together for their concert. Out the front window, she saw the colorful blankets folks had laid out along the sidewalks earlier that morning to reserve the prime parade viewing spots.

"It's okay, baby. Just some holiday prepping going on out there."

Noodles barked.

"It's going to be over soon," she consoled. "And I've got a plan for how to get you through the fireworks, don't you worry."

The dog jumped to his feet, ears pricked. He barked again.

Had he heard someone shooting off a firecracker? Was he going to freak out again?

He was standing, the scruff on his neck pricked up.

"What is it, boy?" She heard it now. A revving, churning noise like the sound of an oncoming train. She hurried to the window.

"Noodles," she screamed, grabbing the dog and leaping behind the counter. They hit the floor just as the food truck smashed through the front corner of the store. Glass shards flew in all directions. Chunks of plaster and wood rained down on the counter. The noise sounded like a bomb blast. Noodles yelped and whined and Trinidad did, too. "Help," she screamed, but the din drowned out her cry. The tiles under her knees shook as the food truck plowed further into the shop, burrowing toward the counter where they sheltered.

She clutched the dog tighter. She was not sure if the trembling was her or him or the onslaught of the truck. Another scream built in her throat. The ice cream clock shot off the wall and smashed to the floor. A piece of plaster struck her shoulder. The counter broke from its foundation and tipped over, caging them underneath. They were going to be crushed as the truck ground forward.

"Help," she screamed to no one, cradling Noodles to try and somehow shield him from what was coming. Head buried in his fur, she held him close. "I'm so sorry, baby," she whispered.

When she thought she could not stand the din a millisecond longer, the terrible cacophony began to die away into a soft tinkle of falling glass.

Seconds ticked by, her ears ringing from the crash. Hardly able to breathe, she tried to take stock. She was curled in a ball with a quaking Noodles pressed against her ribs. Somehow the counter was still above them, wedged there. Slowly, she crawled from under the broken slab of Formica that had protected them, Noodles still clutched in her arms.

"It's okay," she murmured. He was still whining, but she did not see any wounds on him. Plaster powder covered them both, and he blinked, his lashes dusted white.

In disbelief, she looked at the food truck, which had stopped inches from the counter that had undoubtedly saved their lives. The engine was still revving, no driver behind the wheel. The keys, which she had left tucked under the visor, were in the ignition. Through the flopped-open door, she could see where the accelerator had been wedged down by a stick jammed into position, causing the truck to jump the curb and torpedo her store.

Time seemed to grind to a halt as she realized the truth. She knew exactly who had caused the disaster. The same person who had murdered Kevin Heartly for doing nothing more than buying a pot from the flea market. Her plan to trap a killer had certainly provoked a desperate act—only she'd not anticipated this. No, never would she have imagined it would have come to this.

Papa Luis rushed in.

"Trina," he yelled, his voice tortured.

"I'm okay," she said. He began to crunch over the debris, kicking slabs of plaster out of his way.

Mr. Mavis appeared next and turned off the food truck's engine. "What in the Sam Hill has happened here? Are you hurt?"

Somehow, she summoned a spot of calm as Papa reached her. "Papa, please take Noodles. I don't want him cut on the glass." She placed the shivering dog into her grandfather's arms. Sirens wailed. Quinn showed up at a run, pushing aside fragments of the ruined front wall to get to her.

Stan was there, too, calmly keeping the onlookers away from the broken glass once he'd seen her up and talking. "Please stay back, everyone. Rescuers are on the way."

Quinn reached out and clasped her around the waist. He swooped her up and began to climb back through the mess. She wanted to protest. *I don't need help. I am not hurt.* In reality, she was not sure her legs would hold her up any longer. He carried her out of the store, and she took stock as they progressed.

Her senses were on overload as she absorbed the details. Her beautiful windows were shattered, the front wall buckled in, her charming pink tables were wrecked, the pristine floor a scarred mess. In the middle of it all, the food truck sat on its side like a giant metal marauder, one wheel still spinning.

"My shop," she choked out as he eased her onto the curb. "My beautiful shop is ruined."

Quinn knelt alongside and squeezed her hand. "It's not so bad."

"It's beyond bad," she wailed. "Everything is wrecked."

"I know it looks that way, but we can fix it. All it needs is some repair, a whole lot of elbow grease, and a new coat of paint." But she could hear the forced cheer in his tone. He knew the truth, too. "It's fixable," he insisted. "The important thing is you and Noodles are okay."

At that moment, the fiberglass sculpture of the bowl of oatmeal slid off the top of the truck and pancaked the lone table that had survived. A puff of plaster powder poofed into the air and dissipated.

Quinn pulled her to his chest as she began to sob.

An hour later, the strains of a Sousa march warbled through the night air. Trinidad did not blame the community for continuing on in spite of the mangling of her shop. This was a small complication to them, but to her it was everything.

She moved through the rubble in a daze. She had not listened to the police officer order her to stay back, and he apparently hadn't had the heart to arrest her for disobeying. Noodles was safely secured outside with Papa who'd moved the intact chairs to a safe corner of the porch. Carlos and Diego carried all the salvageable supplies to the back room before she sent them home with thanks. Quinn and Doug swept up piles of glass from the sidewalk until Officer Chang cordoned the whole area off in yellow tape to keep the onlookers away while he photographed and radioed the chief.

Trinidad accepted another embrace from her grandfather but refused a seat. She was not certain she would be able to get up again. She could hardly bear to look at her ruined shop, her dream destroyed. Tears flowed down her face as Papa handed her a pristine handkerchief from his pocket.

"I am so sorry, Trina. And to think someone did this on purpose."

She sniffled.

"This town..." He waved a hand. "It isn't right for you. Come home, to Miami. We'll open a shop together, if that is what you want."

Home. She'd thought this place might be her home, but everything had come crashing down in a matter of moments. The shock and despair rose in waves through her body. Maybe Papa was right. This place, these people, weren't going to be her home. What did she have left here? A ruined shop, which she'd sunk every penny into? A rented house so small you could make a sandwich while taking a shower? Some friends, yes, but more enemies in the people she'd offended the short six weeks she'd been in town.

She cried onto Papa's shoulder until Officer Chang interrupted with a tactful clearing of the throat.

"We'll take a look at the prints," Chang said. "I've photographed, and the chief will come before we get Mr. Mavis to call his cousin to haul the truck out." He grimaced. "That big old honking thing is almost unscathed except for the oatmeal bowl, but your shop..." He sighed. "You aren't going to be opening up tomorrow."

"Or anytime soon," she added with a wobble in her voice.

"Awww. It's crummy. I'm real sorry."

Trinidad stopped him with a shake of her head. "Thank you, but there's no need for you to stay now that you've taped it off and Officer Oliver is here. I know you have to get to the theater. Is there any word from the chief?"

"Not yet, ma'am, but I am on my way. Oliver will keep your shop secure." He about-faced and hurried off. She surveyed the wreckage again from the outside. Maybe it hadn't been as bad as she first thought. That notion lasted as long as it took her to blink. The Shimmy and Shake Shop, without a doubt, was a total disaster.

This secondhand shop, with her secondhand dog by her side... It was supposed to have been her chance at a do-over. Every teeny detail represented a decision she'd made, a risk she'd accepted. Gone, in the space of a moment.

Quinn watched her in silence. "It can all be fixed," he said again.

But did she want that? Did she have the energy and funds and, most of all, the will?

She felt only defeat at first until a tiny edge of anger began to carve its way through. Someone had intentionally ruined her new life. And she knew exactly who had done it. The anger cemented itself into a rigid mass in her belly. There would be justice this time, for her and for Juliette.

With every ounce of energy remaining in her body, she stood. "Papa, I will meet you back at the house. Can you take Noodles home and keep an eye on him?"

Papa frowned. "Yes, but where will you be?"

"There's something I need to do." One last thing. She looked to Quinn. "What time is it?"

"Nearly seven." His quirked eyebrow said it all. "Do you want to...?"

"Yes," she said. "I am going to the theater. The person who ruined my shop and sent Juliette to jail is going to be caught tonight, and I want to see it, if it's the last thing I do in this town."

And it would be, she decided just then. She would deal with the insurance company, pack her things, roll up her dream, and return to Miami.

Quinn took off the heavy work gloves. Doug looked from his brother to Trinidad. "We're right by your side," Quinn said. "Let's go to the theater and see if the trap worked."

Throat still thick with grief, she ducked under the yellow tape, refusing to look back.

Chapter Twenty-One

QUINN AND DOUG AND TRINIDAD walked to the theater. The music from the concert accompanied them.

"I'm so sorry," Quinn said. "I can't believe this happened. All for some crummy pot."

She felt her eyes well up again, and she moved a step away as they took up position in the deep shade of the massive elm tree. *Focus now on Juliette.* Chief Bigley and Chang must be inside, though their vehicles were out of sight. They would have called if the culprit had already shown.

Were you wrong about this, too, Trinidad? About everything?

As the music of the exuberant drumline swelled and echoed from the faraway gazebo, a light snapped on inside the theater.

Her breath caught. It was time.

"Police," she heard Bigley shout.

"Hands where we can see them," Chang added.

"They must have got him," Quinn whispered, gripping her elbow. She clutched his strong fingers in her own.

Sixty long seconds later, the front door shot open. Trinidad jumped. The chief beckoned them. "After what happened to your shop, Trinidad, you have the right to be in on this. Come."

The three of them hurried through the lobby. Trinidad's legs wobbled, but she forced herself onward. The stage lights were on, and Vince Jr. stood blinking as Officer Chang grasped his shoulder. Vince took in the gathered group. His face was stark, pale as tapioca.

Quinn gasped. "Him?"

Vince's Adam's apple bobbed up and down as he shook his head with emphasis. "I don't know what's going on here. I just came here to pick up something I left."

"A Qianlong vase, maybe?" Trinidad said.

Vince's mouth snapped shut. He looked from her to the chief before his gaze settled on the floor of the old theater.

"You..." She could hardly get the words out. "You ruined my store."

She thought he wasn't going to answer at first. Then he exhaled, long and slow. "I didn't mean to. I heard you at the picnic. I wanted to keep you out of here for a few hours. That's all."

He was almost cringing, moisture in his eyes when he finally looked up. She might have felt sorry for him under different circumstances. Fury outweighed any pity at the moment.

Quinn was still gaping. "Vince...you killed Kevin?" He looked at Trinidad, eyes wide with astonishment. "How in the heck did you figure that out?"

In spite of her spent emotions, his bare admiration made her blush. He was so boyishly handsome, standing there, not smooth or glib, like Gabe. So very different. She pulled in a shaky breath. "He said he'd never been in Lupin's storage space, but he described the candy machine as being red. Cora bought it before it was fully unpacked and she promptly painted it yellow. The only way he could have seen it red was when he was in the storage unit. Once I knew he was a liar, everything else made sense. He bragged about being an art expert, probably the only one who would have known the pottery's worth, mixed up in the junk that Sonny bought."

The weak light aged Vince, added shadow and lines to his young face. "I saw it the first time in one of the boxes when we prepared to auction Lupin's stuff. Can you believe the guy was so out of it he didn't even know what he had?" Vince closed his eyes, pained. "If only I'd have figured out a way to get it before Sonny bought it, none of this would have happened."

"How can you justify what you've done?" Trinidad's voice caught. "I thought you loved Juliette, but you let her go to jail."

He groaned. "That wasn't my fault. Everything went wrong. I plotted for days about how to swipe the key from the office and get into the unit myself before the auction, but I couldn't manage it. She almost caught me snooping and changed all the locks. Then Sonny bought the contents, that jerk, parading around like a big shot. Of course he wouldn't know a valuable piece if it bit him. He scavenged everything he thought was worth a buck, and the pot wound up at the flea market. I didn't get there fast enough to beat Kevin. None of this was supposed to happen. I was going to take it from the storage unit and say I bought it at a garage sale or something. I could have helped Juliette with the money. She'd see me differently, so would my folks." He began to rock back and forth, hands shoved into his pockets.

"Oh, they'll see you differently all right," Quinn said darkly. "Everyone in this town will know you're a liar and a murderer in a matter of hours. You killed a man."

The whites of his eyes shone with fear. "I..." His voice pinched off in a squeak. "Kevin saw me going through his boxes. I had gloves on because I didn't want to touch a Qianlong with my bare hands. Do you know how much money it's worth?"

"Not more than a man's life," Bigley said. "Or a woman's freedom."

"Oh, please." Vince yanked his hands from his pockets and stabbed a forefinger at them. "Don't be so sanctimonious. Any one of you would have done the same thing to snag a fortune like that."

His comment was met with stony silence.

He shifted. “I told you I didn’t mean to kill Kevin. I’m not some cold-blooded murderer. I wanted to wait until nighttime, but I heard Kevin at the pizza place talking on the phone to someone about his plans to give Tanya a potted rose. That idiot. He was actually going to stick some crummy plant in a priceless Qianlong. I couldn’t wait any longer, so I tied a bandanna over my face and wore a hat and gloves, just in case. Good thing, too, because he saw me out the window, poking through his boxes. I charged into the shop and hit him before he could call the police. He sort of half-folded over the rim of the pot, so I helped him in the rest of the way. Figured he wouldn’t be found for a while. I was sneaking around the back of the store when I heard Trinidad coming inside. I panicked.”

“And stuck it inside the van. You must have been surprised when Warren drove off and unloaded it into the storage room,” Bigley said.

His eyes rolled. “I looked in his van the moment I had the chance, and I couldn’t find it. I’ve been going crazy trying to figure out what happened to it.”

“And to keep others from connecting the dots,” Quinn said. “You clobbered me.”

“I was at the coffee shop, and I heard the plans to get Juliette’s photos. I didn’t even know she’d taken those. I couldn’t risk you seeing the Qianlong in the photographs.”

“And you went after the video tapes at my house, too.”

“Yeah, but man. You went nuclear with all that screaming. You’re tougher than you look. I ran for the woods.”

Trinidad recalled her motive list...greed, love gone wrong, power. Sonny and Candy may have been motivated by greed into taking a few items from Lupin’s belongings, but that was as far as it went. In the love category, Tanya was indeed the “jealous woman,” but she really was devoted to Kevin. So, was this pathetic killer acting solely out of greed? She didn't think so, not entirely, anyway.

"Oh Vince," she said. "You thought you'd finally be the big man, didn't you?"

He jerked as if she'd slapped him. "I just wanted people to notice me."

She sighed. *Be careful what you wish for.*

Quinn shook his head. "And all for a pot. I still can't believe that."

"Not a pot, a vase, a Qianlong vase," Vince said, swiveling a look at the chief. "So where is it?"

She folded her arms. "I have no idea."

"It must be here. It has to be. I tried to break in earlier, but Warren was messing around. It's not at the flea market, not at Kevin's, and not at Lupin's house." He was sweating now, breathing hard through his nose. "So where is it?" There was an edge of hysteria in his voice.

Bigley's cell phone rang, and she stepped away to answer.

Trinidad stared at the young man who'd become a murderer. Part of her could not believe that she had actually done it, ferreted out a killer. Ice cream scooper, paralegal, sleuth. At least she'd got one thing right, but it did not lift the weight in her heart.

"Well," Bigley said, clicking off her phone. She whispered something to Officer Chang who disappeared. "I finally heard back from Cora. She's a real independent lady, not to mention a creative type." Chang returned a moment later with the white plaster pot Trinidad had knocked over when she'd run into Tanya. Vince read the ABSOLUTELY NO CELL PHONES stenciled on the side. His face went slack with horror. "Oh no. She didn't."

"Yes, she did," Bigley said. "Cora plastered and spray painted your Qianlong and stuck it in the lobby to collect cell phones. She had no idea it was priceless."

Vince shuddered as if he would faint. "No," he moaned.

"Maybe we can save it. Maybe it can be restored." He lurched forward. Bigley caught him quickly, but the movement startled Officer Chang who jerked, the pot slipping out of his grip.

The vessel hit the floor and smashed into a half dozen pieces, revealing a lustrous, satiny finish. Inside was a lone cell phone that someone had forgotten to retrieve.

"Would you look at that?" Bigley said. "I guess Cora's craft project really did work. There's one lonely cell phone in there."

Vince took on the pallor of a perfectly churned vanilla ice cream before he collapsed into a heap on the floor.

Trinidad's heart wasn't really into the Fourth of July cookout at the tiny house the next day, but it would have been an unforgivable sin against her heritage to rescind an invitation. After her shop was left in ruins and Vince Jr. arrested, she'd slunk away, ignoring phone calls and texts. She'd not even been able to sift through the wreckage of her store, since the police still hadn't finished their tasks. Though she'd tried to hide from the world, her spirit would not allow her to stand by and let Papa host the party solo.

Giving in, she'd helped Papa with the dinner preparations. He didn't prod her to talk, as she prepared the plantains for frying. She didn't ask him where he'd gotten the tropical bananas, grateful simply to have him there, a quiet and steady balm to her frazzled nerves. The kitchen chores did not quite keep her mind off the ruined Shimmy and Shake Shop.

But Juliette will go free, she reminded herself. The thought did not completely erase the sadness, but it was all she had to cling to. The day passed in a blur of chores and more voicemails that she did not return.

At almost seven o'clock, she was dead tired and wanted nothing more than a snuggle with Noodles and the comfort of her bed, but it was time to plaster on a smile and greet the guests. How she would navigate the inevitable prying questions, she had no idea. All the drama was probably just more proof that Trinidad, a Bigley babe, did not belong in their quiet town.

Quinn caught her in the kitchen. "I've been trying to call."

She forced a smile. "We've been up to our ears in party planning around here."

He nodded, but she knew she hadn't fooled him.

The aroma of garlic and roasted pork filled the air as Papa and Quinn put platters of meat and a massive bowl of black beans and rice on the tables Quinn had brought. Plates piled high with fried tostones completed the offering as well as the obligatory bowls of sliced mango. Stan brought containers of sweets, and the arriving townspeople did as well, hauling their own lawn chairs and arranging them around the bonfire Papa had constructed inside a ring of stones.

Sprocketerians filled the tiny yard and spilled over onto the surrounding expanse of grass. It should have been a glorious evening, an event heralding her assimilation into Sprocket. Instead, she could hardly keep from sobbing.

Diego and Carlos arrived, whispering between themselves. When they saw her, they straightened. "We're gonna help, Miss Jones. Mom is, too. She said she's gonna come to the shop and clean up the moment we can get in there."

"Thank you," Trinidad said. She didn't think it was a good time to tell them she'd decided not to reopen. Let them enjoy the festivities without having to worry about losing their jobs. They wasted no time zeroing in on the food and began to load up their plates.

Warren was shaking his head in astonishment as he talked animatedly with Cora. "I can't believe Vince Jr. would do such a thing. I thought he was kinda a wimp, to be honest. Who would guess he was a bona fide killer?" He put a hand to his heart. "And I can't believe you ruined a bazillion-dollar vase, either."

Cora shrugged. "C'est la vie."

Warren began to laugh so hard he almost dropped his dinner. "Only you would react that way, Cora…only you."

Chief Bigley showed up carrying a container of peanuts. "I don't cook," she explained, and then, in a louder voice, added, "Just so you know, Juliette's release is being processed right now. She'll be free in a couple of hours."

A few of the nearby guests let out a cheer, and there was a ripple of applause.

The chief had made it public. She had been wrong. Juliette was not a killer. Trinidad heaved a sigh. "Thank you."

"Ditto. I am not too proud to say I don't think I would have put the pieces together without your help." She hesitated. "And I'm truly sorry about your shop. So is everyone in town. I know it doesn't seem like it, but this really is a nice place to live, murderers and secrets notwithstanding."

Very nice sentiment, but it did not ease Trinidad's ache. She nodded anyway. The guests settled into lively conversations interspersed with lavish praise for the food. Papa Luis went for modesty, but Trinidad could see he was pleased.

Pastor Phil waved a fork with a tostone speared on it. "Almost as good as mine," he said.

Papa laughed and sat beside him. Friends. How had Papa Luis managed to make them so quickly?

A flicker of movement caught her eye. Tanya stood by herself, just outside the circle of firelight. Trinidad went to her.

"I didn't know you were here. I'm glad you came."

Tanya shrugged. "Your grandfather invited everyone in town. I don't think he realized you and I haven't always gotten along."

"No, he wouldn't. Can I get you a plate of food?"

"No, thanks. I'm not very hungry." She toyed with a balled-up napkin. "Thank you for figuring out it was Vince. I was so sure Juliette had killed him. I mean...Vince didn't even know Kevin that well."

"Vince was desperate to be important, to be a big shot, and his greed overrode everything else. I feel sorry for his parents."

"I don't. They raised a killer who took Kevin away from me. Ruined your shop, too." Her tone was acid.

She wondered how the Dempseys would handle the knowledge that their son was a murderer. He'd destroyed their lives as well as his own, and Kevin's and Tanya's... The ripples from his decision had turned into tidal waves.

"Lots of people were hurt. You most of all. I'm just glad the truth came out."

"That's a small comfort. Nothing is going to bring him back." Her face was bleak.

Trinidad took her hand and squeezed. "Please come to the fire. Sit and have a bite to eat."

"Thanks, but no. I don't belong here." She turned to go.

"Tanya, wait."

She swiped at the tears staining her cheek. "What?"

"Come with me."

Tanya followed her around to the backyard of the tiny house. Noodles sidled up and greeted her with a lick. She smiled and returned his greeting with a chin rub. "I think I need a dog," she said.

"The best friend you'll ever have, but you have to keep a sharp eye on your snacks." Trinidad led Tanya to a bucket in which a desiccated rosebush was sitting. The leaves were dried and mostly gone, but a few clung stubbornly to the thorny branches. Papa had suggested soaking it might inject some life back in the sorry plant.

Trinidad felt suddenly uncertain. "I, um, I think Kevin bought this for you. It's a..."

"Pink Princess," she whispered. "I know the variety."

"It was really dry by the time the police released the crime scene. I couldn't stand to see it there dying every time I drove by, so Chief Bigley said I could take it." Trinidad paused. "It was meant for you."

Tanya hid her face in her hands and cried. Trinidad wrapped an arm around her shoulders. She held on until Tanya's sobs subsided and she blew her nose with a pink tissue.

"Thank you," Tanya said. "I will never forget this."

"Let's load it in your car."

Though Trinidad tried one more time to convince Tanya to stay, she left after giving Trinidad a tight hug, her rosebush nestled in its bucket behind her driver's seat. For a moment, Trinidad wished she could drive away, too, leave the cheerful chatter and wildfire gossip behind her. Instead, she heaved in a breath and returned to the party.

Officer Chang stood wolfing down his second plate of food as the chief sipped a glass of root beer. "So, Miss Jones, what are your plans now that you've solved your first case?" Bigley said. "Going back to scooping or setting up shop as a sleuth? What's your heart telling you?"

Her heart still lay among the splinters of her sweet Shimmy and Shake Shop. She was searching for something to say when a horn sounded, a familiar *ahooga* splitting the air. She stared in disbelief as the food truck rumbled up, Mr. Mavis behind the wheel and tapping on the horn to clear the way. It had been cleaned up and looked good as new, minus the fiberglass bowl of oatmeal and not counting the dent in the front fender. The side sported lettering that still smelled of fresh paint. THE SHIMMY AND SHAKE SHOP. Her mouth fell open as Quinn sidled close.

"It's a mobile unit, until you get your shop fixed up. Orville insisted. We fixed it as best we could so you can fire it up tomorrow, for opening day. Your ice cream survived, right? So you've got product to sell."

"Well, yes, but..."

"Everyone's on board to help you fix the shop, too. Mr. Mavis's cousin's nephew has a construction business, and he'll do the work cheap. The twins took the ice cream clock home, and their mom is doing some tricky gluing, but she thinks she can save it. Doug and I will help as much as we can until you're back on your feet again. Sonny volunteered to paint the place gratis, if you're not picky about the shade of pink."

She gaped. "Sonny would do that?"

"Yep. Apparently, he's not holding a grudge about being a possible murder suspect." Shyly, Quinn took hold of her shoulders and turned her to face him. His fingers caressed her arms, sending little pinpricks of warmth dancing through her body. "Like I said, there are lots of good people here in town." He pressed a kiss to her cheek, his lips soft. "Give Sprocket one more chance, okay? Please?" he whispered.

Now her eyes filled for a different reason. Mr. Mavis climbed down, gave her a nod, and headed for a plate of food. She stared at the shined-up truck, struck dumb. Papa finally dragged over a folding chair nearer the bonfire. "Sit, Trina," he said, "sit here with your friends."

She saw in his smile that he understood she was not going back to Miami.

He hugged her and whispered in her ear, "Too bad for Len the fishmonger."

She laughed. The Shimmy and Shake Shop would be reborn in all its pink and sugary glory. Gratefully, she took the food Papa had lovingly prepared and settled down among the crowd of chattering Sprocketerians. Quinn and Doug sat next to her, the firelight making their faces glow.

It was a long, lingering meal, as was every family gathering she'd ever experienced. As the sky darkened, people turned their attention to the dessert table, shoring up for the fireworks display. Quinn shifted on his folding chair.

"I think maybe Doug and I should go," he said. "I would rather stay here, truly I would, but I don't want to embarrass myself by screaming like a toddler when the fireworks go off."

"Wait just a minute. I had an idea. Hold on." She fetched the bag she'd gotten from the thrift store. First, she put a set of ear-muffs on Noodles. He cocked his head quizzically but accepted her zany idea.

She handed another set to Quinn, one to Doug, and, so they wouldn't feel odd, held up a fuzzy pink set for herself. "What do you think?"

Quinn's face split into a wide grin as he snapped on the plaid earmuffs. "Brilliant," he said. "What would I do without you?"

Cheeks warm and heart full, she covered her own ears and settled back to enjoy the festive light show. The sky over Sprocket glittered with showers of golden sparks.

After the fireworks show ended, the visitors scattered, some helping to clean up and others heading to their cars. Trinidad retrieved paper plates, stopping to admire the behemoth truck that she would pilot in the morning. A soft opening to her shop, so to speak.

Papa yawned and stretched. "Morning will come early, Trin," he said.

"I'm ready for it," she said, giving him a hug.

A Note from the Author

Dear Reader,

I hope you have enjoyed this first installment of the Shake Shop Mysteries as much as I have enjoyed writing it. I have already fallen in love with the little town of Upper Sprocket and the tantalizing adventures that await. The story features Papa Luis, inspired by my own grandfather, an engineer in the sugar mills and copper mines in Cuba before the Revolution. He was a brilliant man, passionately curious, who would gleefully retell the same jokes about Grant's tomb every time we saw him. But, perhaps, my fictional Papa Luis is more like my father who grew up in Cuba and absorbed all the generosity and friendliness the island had to offer and greets everyone with warmth and geniality. I hope you get a taste of their love and devotion right along with Trinidad. She's going to need all the help she can get to solve all the mysteries awaiting her!

If you'd like to know more about me or my books, you can message me through my website at danamentink.com. There is also a physical address there if you are a fan of snail mail!

With love and hugs, Dana

Get the scoop on the next Shake Shop Mystery from Dana Mentink!

Chapter One

TRINIDAD JONES HAD NEVER BEFORE realized how much her dog, Noodles, appreciated yodeling. Some primal instinct prompted her elderly Labrador/failed service dog rescue to chime in with abandon when the bearded visitor took the stage. Not a stage, actually, but the stump of a Douglas fir that sat just to the side of the charming train car bed and breakfast. A couple dozen visitors sat grouped around on card chairs, tapping fingers and toes along with the music. Was it actually music? Trinidad was not convinced.

Music or not, Alpenfest was bringing people to Eastern Oregon in droves, and if it meant a yodelfest, that was fine by her. The tiny town of Upper Sprocket was finally poised to rake in a share of the much-needed tourist money with the recent addition of the pedal-powered railway. Now Bonnie's quaint bed and breakfast would be a draw as well. Trinidad intended to scoop up her own portion with the Shimmy and Shake Shop, home of the massive Freakshake creations that would become famous if she had anything to say about it.

Upper Sprocket could not compete with neighboring Josef for the number of amenities to offer Alpenfest tourists, but when the hotels were booked up, the overflow yodelers had come to stay in Sprocket, and Bonnie had barely finished preparations in time to offer them rooms. The group had decided a small outdoor concert would be the perfect warm-up for the Alpenfest yodeling contest set to begin the following day. Storm clouds were gathering in the sky, and Trinidad hoped the rain would hold off for another hour or two.

She noticed the mayor of Upper Sprocket, Ramona Hardwick, sporting a smile that looked suspiciously like a grimace as she gazed at the yodeler. How did the mayor manage to appear so youthful when she had to be knocking at sixty? Trinidad would love to try some of Ramona's skin cream on her own thirty-six-year-old face. The Miami sunshine had not been kind to Trinidad when she lived there with Papa Luis and her parents before moving to her new Oregon home.

Ramona looked disapprovingly in the direction of Trinidad's dog and put a finger to her lips. Her hand looked every bit of sixty, which made Trinidad feel better and worse about herself.

Trinidad again shushed Noodles. He made a valiant effort, but whines and howls kept spurting out of his lips like a tea kettle venting steam. Every inch of him quivered to join in the yodelfest.

"He's a natural," Quinn said. "You gotta get him signed up with the troop."

Quinn's green eyes were framed by adorable little crow's feet. Why did everything that handsome hazelnut farmer said warm something deep down in her belly? One would think after her disastrous marriage to a liar and felon, she would be more calloused. Still, she found herself tucking her frizzy dark curls behind her ears and remembering her mother's admonition to stand up straight. Silly. Trinidad was a generously pear-shaped woman with a sweet tooth and little regard for fashion. No amount of straightening or tucking was going to make her any more glamorous.

She let the rain scented wind blow the thought away as she took in the view. Glorious. It still stunned her to think that all of Gabe Bigley's former wives were now collected in this one tiny spot on the globe: number one, Bonnie; number two, Juliette; and now, Trinidad herself, running her very own ice cream shop. She clutched her stack of flyers tight, calculating how many milkshakes the average yodeler might consume during the two weeks of Alpenfest.

It was hard to keep her mind on business with such scenery pulling at her attention. This piece of land that Gabe had deeded Bonnie was exquisite, the perfect place for a quaint train car bed and breakfast. Bonnie's Sprocket Station exuded charm year-round, but it shone like a jewel in autumn. Tall trees and a thicket of succulent blueberries created a lush backdrop to the four brightly painted railroad cars that now served as rooms.

Bonnie's beautiful piece of land might have made her envious were it not for the fact that Gabe had deeded Trinidad a storefront, which had given her a new lease on life. That storefront was now the Shimmy and Shake Shop, her own piece of paradise.

"Don't miss anyone," Trinidad said to Quinn, handing him more flyers to disperse to the spectators in between yodeling numbers. The inn's dining hall was still partially unfinished and there was the slightest scent of fresh paint underlying the pine, but at least the first paying customers had arrived. Those new guests would surely meander into town to partake in artisan ice cream during their stay, wouldn't they?

Her insides quivered with the combination of terror and titillation. The bare-bones truth was the Shimmy and Shake Shop needed an infusion of income desperately, since her store had to be rebuilt after a criminal tried to destroy it...and her. So much for the quiet small-town life. Murder, mayhem, and milkshakes. Who'da thunk it?

Quinn frowned. "Uh oh. We've got competition."

A short, red-bearded, barrel of a man, Forge Emberly, was thrusting his flyers into the hands of anyone in the vicinity of the impromptu yodelfest.

"Come experience the rails on the Forge Railriders pedal-powered adventure," he said. "It's a four-hour excursion following the rail tracks as they pass through timbered canyons and some of the loveliest farmland you'll ever see. Definitely worth the price. If you come back this summer, we'll have a second route that will take you right along the river with views of the Wallowa Mountains," he said as he pressed flyers into hands.

That last comment brought Mayor Hardwick to her elegantly booted feet. She cinched her knitted sweater against the late September chill and marched over, stopping inches away from Forge. Her blond hair flashed in the sunlight that was peeking through the gathering storm clouds. "You will stop touting that second route right now," she muttered through clenched teeth. "There is no way the council and I will approve that project. I cannot stomach cutting those old growth trees just to suit your sight lines."

Forge's eyebrows formed into a grizzled row. "Maybe you won't be the mayor in November anyway."

She went pallid, lips unhealthily red against the white. "You're not going to win the mayor seat. People know you're just in it to take care of yourself."

He laughed. "Me? Talk about a hypocrite. Think people can't see through your 'Betty the Beaver' scam?"

Trinidad was a relatively new arrival in Sprocket, but even she had heard the accusations. Mayor Hardwick was hanging onto her seat by the skin of her proverbial teeth. Rumor had it that the mayor "suggested" to organizations negotiating deals with the city that they purchase supplies of her children's book, *Betty the Beaver Brushes Her Teeth*. The local dentist bought 3,000 copies and suddenly found the sidewalks repoured outside his office. The hospital board, upon which Hardwick resided, ordered 50,000 copies while applying to the town for expansion of their facility.

Now Hardwick's pallor turned to cranberry. She poked a finger into his barrel chest. "There is nothing illegal about any of my actions. You're not going to get that second rail route approved."

Forge shrugged. "Already got Quinn here to agree to sell me the two acres I needed as a cut through. I'll get the approval for the rest in time."

Trinidad gaped at Quinn.

Quinn's gaze was firmly fixed on his boots. Why would he, this man who was passionate about his privacy, his land, and his environmental principles, have agreed to such a thing?

Hardwick looked to Quinn. "Is this true?"

Quinn raised his head but didn't quite meet the Mayor's eyes. "Yes."

A one-word reply? No explanation? Trinidad wanted to pepper him with questions, but Forge started in again.

"I am going to unseat you for mayor in November because you're crooked." Forge raised his voice. "And everyone in town knows it."

At that moment, the mayor lunged forward and with one determined palm, knocked Forge Emberly onto his solid derriere. His flyers floated to the ground like lazy fall leaves in the quickening breeze.

Noodles broke off from his yowling to eye the action with concern.

"You saw it," Forge cried from his position on the ground. Was he speaking to the crowd or Trinidad? "You saw her assault me. Did someone get that on video?"

Someone did.

Bonnie approached, towering over them. At six foot eight, Bonnie, the former professional basketball player towered over pretty much everyone, and with a six-year-old child perched on her shoulders and a cell phone in her hand, she loomed even larger. Bonnie's white-blond hair was pulled into a ponytail, which her daughter, Felice, held in one small hand, but plenty of it frizzed around her face, the same pale color as her skin.

Felice waved at Trinidad. Trinidad's heart always skipped a beat when she saw the child of her ex, Gabe. Of the three wives, Bonnie, Juliette, and Trinidad, Bonnie was the only one with a child. Trinidad's friendship with Bonnie was still in its infancy, yet she felt a strong connection, like she had to Juliette. It was that odd "sisterhood of exes" thing, she figured.

"I was recording the yodeling," Bonnie said as Felice twirled her ponytail like a propeller.

Quinn was already helping Forge to his feet.

"I'll need that video," Forge said.

Bonnie smiled. She always smiled. "No."

Forge frowned. "I'll call Chief Bigley, and she'll force you to turn it over."

Bonnie's smile didn't diminish. "Sorry, but the video will be deleted before she gets here."

"You better not do that."

Bonnie still smiled. "It's my land, Mr. Emberly. I want people to love being here. This isn't a place for politics or arguments. I don't want that around my girl." She held onto Felice's little shin with one hand and toggled it playfully. Felice's hair was caught up in a knit cap with a massive pink pom-pom on the top. Her luminous blue eyes were wide, taking it all in.

"Pollyanna," Forge spat.

Still the smile. "Not the worst I've been called. So let's just listen to the yodeling, okay? This isn't a place for name calling either."

"You should be helping me," Forge said. "A second railway will be good for your business."

Bonnie shrugged. "Some things are more important than

winning in business." She turned her back on the two bickering people and gestured for the yodeling to recommence. "I'm sorry," she called out. "Let's hear that again, okay? Verse two? There's a storm coming, and I don't want us to get rained out."

Now two yodelers took their places next to the one on the stump and began a complicated yodel jousting. Noodles wagged his tail and joined once again in hysterical accompaniment. Forge resumed his friendly flyer delivery demeanor and continued on with his duties. No sign of Mayor Hardwick who had slipped away in the confrontation.

The collected crowd, an even mix of locals and visitors, did not seem too concerned about what had happened. Most were still seated in the provided chairs and occupied themselves with friendly chatter and sips of the free hot cider Bonnie had provided. The yodelers were equally calm as they finished one song and plunged into another. They looked straight out of a postcard in their poufy red skirts and gold-laced black vests. She was disappointed the men wore long pants with their snappy vests instead of lederhosen.

The chief yodeler cued them up for another song. Trinidad wanted to have a private moment with Quinn, but he was already passing out Shimmy and Shake flyers during the pause, a smidge too focused in her mind. When the yodeling was done and the flyers all distributed, she couldn't spot him at all. She looked at Bonnie, who was now chatting with her newly hired cook, Gretchen Torpine.

"Where did Quinn go?" she asked.

"Didn't notice," Gretchen said, adjusting the clip that caught her mane of white hair.

Bonnie hoisted Felice down. "Felice and I picked and packaged the blueberries. They're all boxed up for Papa Luis. He said he's coming by later."

Papa Luis, her dear grandpa newly transplanted from Miami,

to the rescue. He'd made a bit of a business for himself, schlepping people and property around in his gorgeous 1951 Chevy Bel Air. For Bonnie, she knew, he'd do it for nothing. Trinidad didn't know yet what she would concoct with the blueberries growing wild behind the train cars, but the succulent jewels were too precious to be passed up. Gretchen could only use so many for the blueberry scones she was going to bake for the guests. "I'll have Papa pick them up when he delivers your first official overnighters."

Bonnie turned pink with pleasure. "I keep pinching myself. This is going to be the most wonderful place for people to visit. They can let go of their troubles and just...be."

Trinidad found Bonnie's sanguine nature a puzzle. After all, this was a woman who'd earned the nickname Bruiser as a power forward for the Oregon Pistons. She'd broken plenty of noses in her heyday.

Quinn's strange behavior and the altercation between Ramona and Forge left no room in her psyche for her to ponder Bonnie's peculiarities. The flyers were gone, there were shakes to be invented, and a pair of eager teen boys were running the shop. The boys were incredible, but she dare not leave them too long.

Time to get back to business. When she could finally tear Noodles away from his yodeling fanfest, she packed up her Pinto and returned to the shop.

Back aching and hands tired from scooping, Trinidad finally locked the door of the Shimmy and Shake just before sunset. Noodles settled himself in the passenger seat. When they reached Main Street, the first sprinkles of rain appeared on the windshield and he activated the wiper with his left paw.

"Thank you, Noodles." She had adopted Noodles after her divorce from Gabe, unable to resist the old Labrador who had been surrendered so his family could acquire a newer model. She could relate since Gabe had started up with Juliette while married to Trinidad. *Ugh, stop it Trinidad. Don't go there again,* she ordered herself.

Noodles had so many hidden talents, being a service dog flunk-out in his younger days. He revealed them at the most surprising moments. The driving assistance was a fairly new development. She stroked his satiny ears as they drove out of town.

"Love you, sweetie," she said.

He answered with a lick to her wrist.

They headed toward her rented home. Along the way, she passed the tree-studded hollow of land that separated her place from Bonnie's property. Raindrops fell in earnest as she drove along. After a long, sizzling summer, it was a treat to activate the car heater. She hoped she would feel as cheerful when the winter snows hit. She'd lived in Oregon with Gabe during their marriage, but Portland apartment-living was not the same as the wild winters of Eastern Oregon.

The storm swept in as Trinidad arrived with Noodles at the tiny house they shared. Tiny was the appropriate word for a structure not quite 700 square feet. When her grandfather abruptly arrived from Miami two months earlier, bunking on the sofa, the house had gotten even tinier. But Papa's perpetual good cheer, uniquely Cuban outlook on life, and his near genius brain had swept away some of the grief she'd experienced over Gabe's departure and the ruination of her store.

Like a phoenix, the Shimmy was rising again, in large part thanks to the efforts of Papa Luis and Quinn. Thinking about Quinn reminded her of the bombshell. Quinn had actually agreed to clear some of his property at Forge Emberly's urging. Forge was certainly a wheeler and dealer in town, the loudest voice at town council meetings and a go-getter. There had never been any rumors that he was untrustworthy, but his blunt, aggressive demeanor did not seem to be the kind of personality to win over quiet, gentle Quinn. She still could not wrap her mind around their unexpected agreement. Was Quinn desperate for money when Forge had offered a deal? She knew hazelnut farming was not a massive moneymaker, and Quinn was the sole provider for his younger brother, Doug, who had special needs.

She and Noodles scurried into the tiny house through a curtain of steady rain. She set about warming up a pot of stew Papa had made in his newest efforts at batch cooking. The fragrance of garlic and black beans made her mouth water. Headlights from Papa Luis's Bel Air shone as he rolled up the drive.

"You stay here, Noo," she said. The dog wagged his tail from his spot on the squashed beanbag he used as a cushion. He was getting old, she thought with a stab. Silver washed his muzzle, and his back legs were stiff. Impulsively, she draped him with an old blanket to keep off the chill that would inevitably reach him when the front door opened.

Papa pushed inside as he always did in a cloud of enthusiasm. "Those train cars—so amazing, don't you think?" he said, his Cuban accent thick as ever. "Bonnie has done such a fine job, excellent judgment in such an endeavor, which unfortunately did not kick in when she chose the Hooligan."

Papa would only refer to Gabe as the Hooligan. She was happy Papa had become close with Bonnie, but then, he had never met a stranger, making friends with everyone from the pastor to the postman since he arrived in Sprocket. Did she feel it again? That wee pinprick of jealousy that her beloved Papa had grown an affection for Bonnie? And the other ex-wife, Juliette, for that matter? Wasn't Papa's love supposed to be exclusively hers? Wasn't *something*?

She shook the uncharitable thoughts aside as she kissed him. "Raining hard?"

"A real palmetto pounder." He shivered. "And so cold here. This rain is not the same water that falls on Miami."

She laughed. "Wait until the snow comes."

He groaned. "I will have to fortify. That stew smells good, if I do say so. Let me bring in the blueberry box before we eat."

"Why don't you wait until the storm passes?"

He gave her that look. The one that meant, *You can't possibly suggest I leave that untidy box in my impeccable and precious machine known to others as a car?*

"Need help?"

He waved an airy hand. "Of course not. You spoon up the stew. And make me a cafe, will you? Such cold."

She began work on the strong coffee, which Papa could somehow swill even into the wee hours of the night. Of course, the man only required four hours of sleep. Another blast of chill air sent Noodles burrowing deeper into the blanket until he noticed that Papa had re-entered but left the door ajar.

The dog crept out and nosed the door closed and sat looking at Papa, puzzled.

Now Trinidad looked closer, too.

Papa stood with an indescribable expression on his face, his thick thatch of black hair speckled with raindrops.

"Trina?"

"Yes?"

"There is something...unexpected in my trunk."

"Like what?"

"Perhaps you should come and see."

Something in the tone made her hurry to grab her raincoat and follow him out. The porch light illuminated the shining sides of the pristine Buick. Papa had closed the trunk but not all the way. He opened it again, and they looked inside.

Next to the blueberry box was a rug.

Under the rug was a bundle.

To the side of the bundle, something white protruded.

The white thing had five fingers and a palm.

Before she could get out a sound, Papa took the tire iron and poked vigorously at the hand and then the bundle. It didn't move. He reached in and gently applied two fingers to the wrist.

"What...what is it?" Trinidad asked stupidly.

Papa shook his head and withdrew his fingers. "A dead person."

"Dead? How dead?"

"Thoroughly."

Her stomach clenched. "Who?"

Papa reached in again to sweep away the blanket when a rumble of thunder roared across the sky followed by a spray of lighting.

"I..." she said, just as the electricity failed and the porch light extinguished.

Trinidad's common sense kicked in. "Don't touch anything, Papa. We have to get inside and call the police and an ambulance in case...I mean...to help."

He nodded, closing the trunk lid with his elbow but not fully. "We should stay inside with the coffee," he said practically, leading her by the elbow back to the porch where Noodles awaited.

She stumbled as if in a dream.

But this wasn't a dream.

It was a real dead body...in Papa's trunk.

Trinidad's Easy Key Lime Ice Cream

1 (12-oz.) can evaporated milk
1 (14-oz.) can sweetened condensed milk
2 cups whole milk
⅔ cup heavy cream
1 cup granulated sugar
1 (3-oz.) package lime-flavored gelatin
2 egg yolks, beaten
1 cup lime juice
6 whole graham crackers, broken into big pieces

In a saucepan over low heat, combine the evaporated milk, sweetened condensed milk, whole milk, and heavy cream, whisking often. Once the mixture is almost hot to the touch, whisk in the sugar and gelatin mix, stirring until the sugar and gelatin are completely dissolved. Add a little of the hot sugar mixture to the beaten egg yolks to warm them, then add the yolks to the milk mixture. Raise the heat to medium and cook for five minutes, stirring constantly. Remove from the heat. Stir in the lime juice. Let the mixture come to room temperature.

Pour the mixture into an ice cream maker and churn according to the manufacturer's directions. Once the ice cream has started to thicken, open the canister and add the broken graham crackers. They will break into smaller pieces as you churn for about five minutes more. Transfer to a freezer container, and freeze until solid for six to eight hours. Serves 8–10.

Acknowledgments

First and foremost, to the readers who have taken a chance on my little cozy. Thank you for coming along with me to Sprocket!

To my Uncle Barry, who has Cuba in his heart, and my amazing parents, who shared their stories with me.

Sisters, you know who you are! It's not easy having an eccentric writer-type sibling who can't remember the month or day, but you all keep me on track.

Papa Bear, you're my everything.

Bear cubs, one day we will write a book with quicksand in it, I promise!

Jessica Alvarez and BookEnds Literary Agency, you put the "super" in superagents!

About the Author

Dana Mentink is a national and *Publishers Weekly* bestselling author. She has written more than forty mystery and suspense novels for various publishers and is the recipient of the HOLT Medallion and Romantic Times Reviewers' Choice Award. A Northern California native, Dana is married to Papa Bear and mother of two young-adult bear cubs, affectionately nicknamed Yogi and Boo Boo.